A · NOVEL

Reel Love

ADDIE WOOLRIDGE

Delacorte
Romance

Delacorte Romance
An imprint of Random House Children's Books
A division of Penguin Random House LLC
1745 Broadway, New York, NY 10019
penguinrandomhouse.com
GetUnderlined.com

Editor: Bria Ragin
Cover Designer: Angela Carlino
Interior Designer: Cathy Bobak
Production Editor: Colleen Fellingham
Managing Editor: Tamar Schwartz
Production Manager: Tracy Heydweiller

Library of Congress Cataloging-in-Publication Data is available upon request.
ISBN 978-0-593-89931-1 (trade pbk.) — ISBN 978-0-593-89932-8 (ebook)

The text of this book is set in 11-point Warnock Pro.

Manufactured in the United States of America
1st Printing

The authorized representative in the EU for product safety and compliance is Penguin
Random House Ireland, Morrison Chambers, 32 Nassau Street, Dublin D02 YH68, Ireland,
https://eu-contact.penguin.ie.

To the grandparents who get us

TrendCon

LAS VEGAS

Where creators, fans, and brands all connect.

DAY 1 ←

VIP WELCOME MIXERS

By Invite Only: Come celebrate the start of TrendCon with our Founder and Host, Kelly "Sparkles" Chemerinsky and other creators like you.

DAY 2 ←

SILVER INFLUENCERS: SECRETS TO EMBRACING YOUR AGE

Ever wonder how the most fabulous, seasoned creators do what they do? The internet's glamparents, Ms. Mini, Buzzy Timmons, and Gorgeous Gregory, will show you.

DAY 3 ←

GLITTER EXTRAVAGANZA

More is more when it comes to glam. Learn how to get yourself camera, photoshoot, and night-out ready with Sterling James and special guests.

DAY 4 ←

LET THE GEEK GAMES BEGIN

Come show off your trivia skills with your favorite geeks, including super reader Emmie Kristoff, opera baby Pretty Callas, and gamer great Jimi Jester.

DAY 5 ←

YOU LIFT, BRO? POWERLIFTING EXHIBITION

Don't be intimidated by the weight room anymore. Let Ande Azad, Dakota Hunter, and Brawny Becks show you what it takes to master those attempts and deadlifts like a pro.

DAY 6 ←

(NOT SO) PITY PARTY

Parting is such sweet sorrow . . . luckily, partying isn't. Instead of shedding tears, let's send this year's TrendCon out in style with a farewell pool party. Until next year. XOXO

DAY 1: IT'S VEGAS, BABY

CHAPTER ONE

"PLEASE, DON'T FREAK OUT."

"They can't sit near us." BamBam's voice echoed through the entire airport terminal, drowning out my whispered plea for calm.

"It's not a big deal, Bam—" I caught my grandma's warning look and switched to her Public Grandma Name, hoping it would magically make her less inclined to turn into a cartoon villain. "Mini, it's not like she's sitting next to you."

"How do you know that?" BamBam growled.

I glanced down at my shoes, unsure if this was a real inquiry or one of my grandma's world-famous rhetorical questions, designed to get you in trouble. BamBam was a lot of things: a popular #Granfluencer, expert in all things over-fifty fashion and beauty, Chicago area reigning pai gow poker champion, and my biggest fan. What she wasn't was patient. BamBam suffered fools with about as much grace as a panda in a packed space.

After a beat, I decided to take a risk and answer the question. "Statistical probability. There will be hundreds of people on this plane. That, and I'm already in the middle seat."

"Probability, my foot." BamBam used her I'm-in-public curse, then snatched up her purse and grabbed the handle of her roller bag. "Out of all the flights leaving Chicago O'Hare, of course she would choose mine."

So much for calming her down. Exhaling slowly, I tried not to notice that people were staring. More specifically, the two people who had just gotten off the moving walkway. I could almost feel Buzzy Timmons's eyes burning into me as I hurried to keep up with my grandma.

"Jamie, come here, please. This nice young person needs to see your ticket." I walked the last few feet over to where Bam-Bam stood laying on the charm with the airline attendant, her slight Alabama accent thick as honey when she was trying to get her way. BamBam winked and smiled at the haggard gate agent as I held out my phone for them to see my boarding pass. "Isn't it lovely? We were able to upgrade our tickets to first class. This young person is giving us a deal, too. And while you can't have champagne, you know I'll have a glass."

"I think my mama would be disappointed in me if I didn't give Ms. Mini the very best." The gate agent smiled.

"Well, Jamie here will have to take a picture of us. You can text it to your mama when we're done. And you tell her hi from me." BamBam laughed, and I almost groaned. Of course someone at the airline would be a fan of Ms. Mini's Makeup Counter. While they chatted, I peered over my shoulder toward the source of our problems.

Buzzy Timmons, sworn enemy of my grandma and a fellow #Granfluencer from Chicago, was engaged in what looked like the same not-that-woman process with her grandson, albeit in a more passive-aggressive fashion. Her gray hair was pulled back by a large fabric bow as she furiously pecked at her phone with one finger. Her coral-colored sweater was wrapped around her shoulders like she was a country-club tennis pro, perfectly matching the suitcase set that her grandson, Ethan, was trying to drag off the walkway toward a row of seats far away from us. I couldn't see much of him from where I stood, but he seemed different from the last time we'd crossed paths. Taller, maybe?

Buzzy's expression grew pleased, and she said something I couldn't make out; then both of them turned in our direction. My whole face got hot as my eyes shot down to inspect the carpet. I was praying they hadn't caught me staring. Not that I was staring. I totally wasn't. More like trying to memorize what this grown-up Ethan looked like for self-preservation purposes. I hadn't seen him in at least three years. Back then, he'd been almost the same height as me and skinny, with a close-cropped haircut. If he and Buzzy were going to be at TrendCon this week, I needed to know who to steer clear of or risk getting caught in the cross fire. That was the only reason I was looking. Obviously.

"Jamie, can you take a picture for us?" BamBam's voice rang out as if she were making a flight announcement for the terminal.

"Um . . . sure," I said, hoping the color had left my cheeks. Stepping forward, I took the gate attendant's phone and began snapping photos, changing my angle slightly to crop other people out of the picture and mitigate the shine coming from the fluorescent lighting. I could tell BamBam was getting impatient, but she'd be grateful later when this person, or their mom, posted these online.

"And maybe a quick video, too? You could say that line? My mom thinks it's so funny. She is always quoting you," the gate attendant said.

"Of course, honey. What's your mama's name?"

"Sherry."

"Got it." BamBam nodded at me, and I quickly switched the phone to video, then gave her a thumbs-up so she knew I was ready to record. Pulling her shoulders back, BamBam winked at the camera, then said, "Sherry, I'm here with your baby, and I heard you're a fan. Real Bad Mama Jamas recognize each other. We've both been fine since your kid was in pajamas. Stay bad, Sherry." BamBam blew the phone a kiss as she delivered her signature catchphrase *Stay bad*, then laughed as I cut the video off.

"Here you go." I adjusted my baseball cap and pushed my long braid over my shoulder before handing the phone back to the gate agent. "Hopefully, one of those pictures will work."

"Oh, they will," BamBam crooned. "Jamie doesn't like when I brag, but she is very good with cameras."

"Well, thank you," the gate agent said, waving the phone in my general direction. "Ms. Mini, you just sit right there until we start calling first class to board."

"Thank you," BamBam said, honey still coating her words. Winking at me, she tilted her chin up, then began strutting toward an open chair. Once we were out of earshot, she whispered, "That two-bit, wannabe-me, knockoff Buzzy can enjoy herself at the back of the plane. We're getting leg room."

While BamBam cackled over her victory, I glanced back at Buzzy and Ethan. Buzzy was grinning at Ethan and holding on to his arm as they walked toward where he'd stashed their carry-on suitcases. I wondered if he still had freckles or if he'd outgrown them . . .

Not that I needed that information. I gave my head a little shake. BamBam had her reading glasses on and mini-keyboard out. Her phone screen was blown up, so I could see her answering fan questions on her most recent video, about removing makeup stains from white shirts without bleach.

Without glancing up, BamBam asked, "So did you look at that list I sent you? What'd you think?"

BamBam had recently decided it was time for her to reach a younger audience. As she put it, there was more money in marketing to young people without money than there was in marketing to women over fifty who got money. When she'd been invited to be on the Silver Influencers panel at TrendCon, the biggest content creator's convention of the year, she'd taken it as a sign that it was time to start collaborating with more beauty influencers who were closer to my age. In true BamBam fashion, she'd spent the week before the con studying the videos of younger beauty creators and whittling her top-tier "to work with" list down to six names. One of them, Sterling James, was also a Chicago-based influencer. If only he were on the plane instead of Buzzy . . .

"I think any of them could be good. Except that Jackie person who does Halloween makeup."

"You don't think that could be fun for me?"

"On Halloween maybe? Goth girl is not your vibe, BamBam." I laughed.

"If you say so." She shrugged and looked up over her bifocals at me. "So, you'll do a bit of scouting when we land? Try to make some new friends for your grandma?"

Technically, this was a question, but I didn't dare answer no. She considered it part of my job to track these creators down and speak to my "fellow young people" until we met someone it made sense for her to collaborate with. Never mind that I personally knew almost nothing about beauty. Not to mention no one knew who I was, which was how I liked it.

"Yup." I nodded.

"That's my girl." BamBam smiled and turned back to her keyboard.

I sighed and started digging through my bag for my laptop. I'd shot some footage of BamBam going around the airport so I could do a travel recap of her getting to TrendCon. Might as well start editing it now. Sticking on my headphones, I put on the soundtrack to one of my current favorite movies, *Direct Mail*, and got to work, hoping the magic of the music would inspire me to do something new and cool with otherwise mundane images of moving walkways and BamBam's cheetah-print jacket.

"What?" I nearly dropped my laptop when BamBam tapped me on the shoulder, startling me out of my concentration.

Waiting for me to take my headphones off, she smirked. "Time to go."

"Oh." I looked over at the boarding line. The gate agent was already scanning in an early-boarding family. "That didn't take long."

"It took twenty-five minutes. You were just focused." Bam-Bam waved her hand in a hurry-it-up gesture, but she was smiling. My grandma was about the only person in the family who didn't really care how much time I lost trying to get an edit right.

Leaving my headphones around my neck, I slipped my laptop back into my backpack and stood just as the attendant started the call for our group.

"Hurry up. I want Buzzy to have plenty of time to see me in line." BamBam cackled. "That upgrade cost me a vital organ, but it'll be worth it to see her face."

"Maybe we should get really obnoxious luxury luggage next time. Go full-on flashy." Despite promising myself that I was not going to encourage this stupid rivalry, I giggled.

"You get me to one million followers on YouTube, and then we'll talk." BamBam smirked at me until something over my shoulder caught her eye. All the humor left her face, and she suddenly looked like she smelled something foul.

"Once again, now boarding our Group One passengers. That's those passengers seated—"

"Oh hell no." BamBam's voice cut through the announcement, and my heart stopped.

In the movies, moments like this were in slow motion so

the audience had time to recognize the horror of an impending train wreck. I would have killed for even an extra thirty seconds to process the sight of Buzzy and Ethan walking toward us. Buzzy's expression as sour as BamBam's. Next to her, Ethan was furiously whispering something that looked like *It's not a big deal* over and over.

"BamBam, get in line first." I nudged my grandmother forward and prayed that a one-person buffer would be enough to keep the two of them civil during the boarding process.

"I'm Mini, remember," BamBam said as she strutted to the front of the line with far more speed than one would expect a sixty-seven-year-old to have.

"Right. Well, Mini, keep it cool, okay?"

"Baby, I'm always cool. Unlike some people." BamBam fished a pair of sunglasses out of her purse pocket and put them on, then turned to face forward in the most dramatic fashion humanly possible right as Ethan and Buzzy approached.

"Grammy, why don't you let me go first so I can deal with all the luggage?" Ethan stepped in line directly behind me, clearly sharing my body-block strategy.

"Of course, darling. I have such a thoughtful grandson." Buzzy beamed at him, her voice loud enough for BamBam and half the airport to hear. Sounding like she'd been asked to eat nails, she added, "Hello, Mini. Funny running into you here."

"Hi, Buzzy. Small world, isn't it?" BamBam turned as if startled that anyone behind her would have the impunity to speak to her. My grandmother's voice had the tone of someone who would rather drink motor oil than exchange niceties with this person. To me, she said, "Jamie, make sure you have your boarding pass ready," then marched toward the gate agent, who hadn't asked her to step forward.

"Nice to see you again," I said to Buzzy, my expression somewhere between a smile and a grimace. At the rate things were going, this would be the most awkward flight in the history of aviation. To her credit, Buzzy glanced at me with more pity than disdain, which, while not exactly how I wanted anyone to think of me, was good enough for now. I nodded in Ethan's general direction and avoided eye contact. Talking to him was a bad idea for about 453 different reasons, not the least of which was that I'm not the most extroverted person. If I was going to make awkward small talk with anyone, it would absolutely not be the grandson of Buzzy Timmons.

Turning away, I scanned my boarding pass, then hustled to catch up to BamBam, who was already halfway down the jet bridge.

"She always has to copy me," BamBam said through gritted teeth. "That woman has never had an original idea in her entire life."

Part of me wanted to point out that, for all BamBam knew, Buzzy had booked her first-class tickets months in advance. She probably thought BamBam had copied *her*. Not that I'd ever say that to BamBam. I value my life.

The smell of recycled airplane air interrupted my thoughts, and I stopped just short of walking right into BamBam. The family that had boarded in front of us was trying desperately to herd two toddler twins down the aisle with little success.

Instead, the tots kept pausing to wave at literally the entire plane, including empty seats and each other.

BamBam started waving back, which made the twins wave harder. My grandma loved kids. And unlike the twins' parents, BamBam had no qualms about holding up an entire plane, so it could be a while before we made it to row six. I smiled, then took out my phone to text my parents that we were boarding our flight.

"'Come to Vegas,' they said. 'It'll be fun,' they said." A low voice came from over my shoulder, startling me. Leaving my text unsent, I whipped my head around to find Ethan, half a smile tugging at one corner of his mouth. "You got suckered into this, too?"

His mop of sandy-brown hair curled at the edges, just a little too long, so it framed his pale face and hung in his eyes when he looked down at me. He'd gotten taller and filled out, the once-gangly line of his shoulders replaced by muscle. His face was still round, but the edges of his jaw and cheekbones had sharpened. Even with his eyebrows raised at our precarious situation, there was no other way to put it: Ethan had gotten hot.

I nodded, an awkward laugh forcing its way out of my throat as I tried to get my brain to function while standing this close to him. We were not supposed to interact. I was only supposed to admire him from afar and hope my grandma, or his, didn't catch me ogling him. Instead, here he was making jokes while my brain gave off *danger* signals mixed in with useless bits of information like the fact that he still had freckles sprinkled across the bridge of his nose.

The sound of a shrieking kid hit me like a jolt, and I checked over my shoulder to make sure BamBam hadn't heard him. Luckily, she'd abandoned her luggage and was squatting halfway down the aisle, presumably to get a better waving vantage point. The three of them were now waving at a baggage loader outside the window who also didn't seem to have concerns about holding up a flight.

Turning back to Ethan, I said, "If someone gets murdered in Vegas, does that still stay there?"

Ethan blinked at me, and I kicked myself. Really, who makes murder jokes with strangers? Why couldn't I be a normal person? I waved the hand clutching my phone at him as I flailed around trying to explain the death joke before he thought I was threatening to murder him or something. "You know, because—"

"What happens in Vegas stays in Vegas. I get it." A full-blown smile swept across Ethan's face as he laughed, the sound low and rich as if the joke were a secret between the two of us. "Jamie, right?"

I arched an eyebrow and leaned to the side so I could see around him. Buzzy was talking to a flight attendant as other passengers remained stuck behind her, crowding the mouth of the plane. Meanwhile, BamBam and the waving children were also holding up the plane. We weren't getting to Vegas anytime soon. Catching my hesitation, he looked down the aisle toward my grandma before saying, "I'm Ethan. You probably don't remember, but we met a few years ago at—"

"I remember," I said quickly as I stretched toward our row,

attempting to dump my backpack off into my seat, trying not to shudder at the memory of the last time our grandmothers were in close proximity. "I'm hoping to avoid a repeat of last time."

"I guess it is kind of hard to forget about that . . ." Ethan's voice trailed off as he rubbed the back of his neck, clearly thinking about the same incident. I won't go into the gory details, but I will say that a thrift store, a can of Mountain Dew, and some discount glitter were involved. It hadn't ended pretty for either grandma. The dry-cleaning bills were enormous. After a beat, his smile returned. "This time won't be so bad—everyone is older and wiser."

"Older, yes. Wiser?" I narrowed my eyes at him before lowering the handle on BamBam's carry-on bag. I tried, then failed to heft it over my head and into the bin.

"Do you need help with that?" Ethan laughed, and my face got hot all over again. Great, I was having a messy hair day, and the fact that I had almost no upper-body strength was on full display, too. The zipper on my pants better be up, or I would officially be on a losing streak.

"Um. That would be—"

"No thank you, young person." BamBam's voice came from over my shoulder, causing me to jump about six inches out of my skin. Whipping my head around to face my grandmother, I caught the full force of her very best keep-your-distance glare. "Jamie, why don't you sit by the window? I'll take care of the luggage."

With that, BamBam picked up her suitcase like it was a dish towel and hoisted it overhead while I dove into our row and

Ethan backed up two steps to get out of swinging distance. For a brief second, he looked at me, a mischievous grin playing across his face that I prayed neither grandma noticed. If they did, this was going to be a very long week for both of us, and I certainly didn't need that.

I tried to smile back in the noncommittal way strangers in a grocery line smile at each other, then turned to face the window as Ethan moved on.

"Stay away from that boy, baby. He's probably just as bland and unoriginal as his grandma. You don't want him to steal your ideas."

"Okay, BamBam," I said, making sure I giggled at her joke.

Cute or not, I was going to Las Vegas for work. Ethan was about twelve kinds of distraction that I didn't need. Not to mention he could potentially get me fired from BamBam's business or worse. As far as I was concerned, my mission for the next week was to avoid Ethan Wyatt at all costs.

CHAPTER TWO

"HERE WE ARE," BAMBAM SAID, TAPPING HER CREDIT CARD TO
the cab's reader. By the time our taxi reached the hotel—
BamBam refused to take the hotel shuttle, because Buzzy would
be on it—I was both the most comfortable and the least relaxed
I'd ever been. I had so much room on the flight over but couldn't
sleep knowing that Buzzy and Ethan were one row back and
across the aisle.

Somewhere over Colorado, BamBam reiterated to me in
unequivocal terms that I was to avoid "fraternizing with that
insipid woman or her young person at all costs." Of course, that
directive didn't stop my mind from spinning a million scenarios of all the things that could go wrong with those two here.
Okay, and one absolutely impossible scenario where Ethan and
I became friends and Buzzy and BamBam let their rivalry go.
I know, I know. Don't judge me based on one moment of mis-
placed optimism.

Dragging our suitcases toward the entrance, I felt a blast of cold air and general overwhelm hit me as soon as the doors to the Stonereel Casino and Resort opened. It was giving exactly what the commercials for Las Vegas promised—upscale and tacky all at once. White marble covered every surface, and a massive chandelier hung in the entryway above an oversized white table with a gigantic yellow orchid growing in a glass dome. But what commercials could never have prepared me for was the sound. A wall of pings and dings from a casino floor I couldn't even see yet, squeaky suitcase wheels, and helpful employees with chipper voices all trying to get my attention at the same time.

"We're gonna have some fun this week. You know they have twenty restaurants in this hotel, and I have good luck with pai gow. Grandma is gonna win some walking-around money. Might even share it with you." BamBam gave me a side squeeze, then, standing up straighter, she added, "Alright. Time to go be Mini."

I had just enough time to think about how weird it was that my grandma had a semifamous alter ego before a few people began to approach her for pictures. I wheeled our suitcases around and found a spot to film where BamBam wouldn't be backlit and tried to capture a few seconds of video for her travel-recap post.

I'd taken another two steps to the side to get a clear shot of BamBam's smile as she gave someone a hug, when a shriek echoed across the lobby.

"Jamie!" Nittha Suparat drew out the *e* sound in my name so that it was about forty-five syllables long and squeezed me hard enough that she nearly knocked me off balance. "I missed you."

"Hi, Nittha." I gasped, trying to free my arms from her death grip so I could hug her back.

"I'm extremely glad you are here. This whole week would have been tragic without you," she announced to the entire lobby while still holding on to me.

"No one would ever accuse you of hyperbole." The voice of Gabriela Avila came from somewhere over my shoulder. Craning my neck, I could see Gabby making her way toward us in her trademark black faux-leather miniskirt and combat boots, her usually big, curly reddish-brown hair worked into two French braids. Gabby's personality was what you'd get if a sass machine married a goth girl and had a baby in Florida. Half Afro-Cuban and half white, the girl never met a black nail polish that she didn't like. Gabby was a dyslexia-and-reading-differences creator who loved all things vegan-fashion and was currently dabbling in judo. Most importantly, she was the kind of loyal friend who'd help you hide a body even as she told you how stupid you were for being in the situation in the first place. Tapping Nittha, she said, "Let go. You're hogging Jamie, and I want to hug her now."

A knot of people watched us, trying to figure out if we were famous enough that they should want to take pictures with us, too. My face got hot, and my friends grinned.

"Still shy. Don't worry. No one cares about us." Nittha laughed and waved a hand around dismissively, her hot-pink manicure flashing against the white walls of the lobby. Nittha and I were the same height, but that was about where the similarities ended. While I was a quiet, skinny, Midwestern, half-Black, half-white girl from Chicago, she was a spunky, curvy, first-generation Thai American from Los Angeles. Where I was understated and a bit anxious, Nittha was all about bright colors and big, exaggerated emotions. Where I was a straight-A student who went to every class like my life depended on it, Nittha had convinced her parents to let her go to online high school so she and Cricket, her dog-turned-social-media-star, could work whenever and wherever they wanted. As ridiculous as she could be, she was also like sunshine in human form.

When I first started coming to influencer events with Bam-Bam, I kept mostly to myself. Nittha, on the other hand, was a friend-making magnet. She basically wouldn't leave me alone, until one day, we were legit friends. The following year, she'd done the same thing to Gabby once Gabby had started going to Nittha's online school during the pandemic. Now our little friend group was like an island in a sea of sometimes-cliquey and drama-filled content creators who we tried to steer clear of.

"Where is Cricket?" I asked, searching for Nittha's ever-present sixish-year-old one-eyed Yorkie. We didn't know much about Cricket's life before Nittha, but whatever it was it couldn't possibly hold a candle to how spoiled she was now.

"Oops! I left her on the chair when I saw you come in." Already bouncing back to where she'd left her dog, Nittha asked, "What happened on your flight? Your text sounded dire."

"I literally texted 'in the cab with BamBam. Long story, be in the lobby in twenty.' How is that dire?" I asked Gabby as Nittha wandered out of hearing range to retrieve her dog.

Gabby rolled her eyes, and I tried not to laugh. "You know Nittha. Why read it as a regular, totally innocent message when you can add drama?"

"Here she is!" Nittha appeared at my side, holding up an unfazed Cricket.

"I like the hat." I glanced down at the dog, who was wearing a giant sun hat, as if dogs, or anyone, really, need to worry about the sun while indoors.

I was scratching Cricket's chin when I caught sight of BamBam scowling at the sliding glass doors right as Buzzy stepped off the shuttle.

"Uh-oh," Gabby said, following my gaze.

"Yeah." I winced as some of the people talking to BamBam realized that Buzzy was also in the lobby. Ethan stepped out behind her.

"Guess that is part of the long story?" Gabby asked.

"Is it? What happened on the plane? No more catastrophic makeup challenges, right?" Nittha asked, then added, "Do you need to hold Cricket? She is good for emotional support."

"I might need her later, depending on how today goes." I giggled. Cricket was a lot of things: Adorable and fluffy, yes. But emotionally supportive? That was a stretch.

Out of the corner of my eye, I could see Ethan wandering away from the collection of people who had formed around his grandmother and strategically willed myself to forget about him.

"Should we talk about it at the pool without the dueling grannies present?" Nittha tried, and failed, to whisper. "Cricket,

Gabby, and I were going to grab a couple of bottled waters from the drinks stand, then go. Those pool prices are outrageous. Want to come?"

I'd planned to work more before the convention officially started with a VIP reception tonight, but now that I thought about it, I could take my laptop to the pool and—crap.

"I forgot a swimsuit." I sighed. Despite my best intentions, I noticed Ethan saunter toward a group of kids our age stationed in the lobby, then stop suddenly. He waved awkwardly at them before meandering in our direction. "I'm sure BamBam would let me get one this afternoon but—"

"Don't worry, you can borrow one of mine." Nittha followed my gaze before I could tear it away. "Is it me, or is that cute guy walking this way?"

"He's probably going to sit over there." I gestured to some lobby chairs before catching sight of Nittha's sly expression. Belatedly, I remembered that Nittha could invent a love story out of thin air, and it was clear that she was already working on one for me and Ethan. I kicked myself, then added, "And no one said Ethan was cute."

"You know his *name*? That must mean something." Nittha giggled, then shook her hair out of her face. "And clearly he thinks you're cute, because he is coming over here."

"What? No he isn't." The back of my neck began to prickle with nerves that I assigned to Ethan being foolish enough to stroll in my general direction and not to anything Nittha was saying. Any minute now, he'd pivot toward the chairs and prove my point.

"For the record, I'm not agreeing with Nittha on this par-ticular made-up romance, but he is almost here." Gabby angled her body away from Ethan so she could talk to us without being overheard. "Why do you look super freaked out?"

Ugh. Gabby was right. He walked right past the chairs and was still on track to run into us. I gritted my teeth and said, "That's Buzzy's grandson. He clearly has a death wish."

"A sexy death wish, maybe." Nittha wiggled her eyebrows at me.

"Pretty sure that's not a thing," I growled.

"Totally is." Nittha's voice bubbled with excitement.

"Wait, that is Buzzy's grandson?" Gabby asked, whipping around to look at him again. Turning back to us, she said, "Why do I feel like I recognize him?"

"G and I should go. Don't want to overwhelm him when he's trying to make a move." Nittha grinned.

"One, there are no moves being made. My parents won't even allow me to date until college, remember?" My body was officially breaking out in a cold sweat. Buzzy and BamBam were close by, engaged in a battle over who could smile the hardest at fans. Surely, Ethan wouldn't stop to talk to me. But if he did . . . I looked from Nittha to Gabby with pleading eyes. "Two, don't leave me."

"Again, I want the record to reflect that I don't think there are moves being made either. But also, I need to use the bath-room. Sorry, Jamie." Gabby smirked. I very much doubted she needed the bathroom that bad. More like she wanted to see what would happen if Buzzy or BamBam caught us.

"Really. I insist. It'd be much better if you stay."

"Nah. Let's go, Gabby." Nittha held up Cricket and waved her little paw at me, smiling over the top of the dog's ridiculous hat. "You better tell us everything at the pool."

With mischief written all over her face, Gabby started walking backward. "Text us your room number. We'll bring you a swimsuit."

With that, the two of them walked away, leaving me with the terrifying prospect of having to interact with Ethan without being murdered by our grandmas. Panicking, I pulled out my phone and pretended to be very busy, because now was 100 percent the time when that trick would finally start to work.

"Hey." I felt myself jump—yep, pretending to be busy on my phone still didn't work—then faced Ethan. He'd stopped a little farther away from me than people who were friends would stand, but close enough to make it clear we were speaking to one another. Beneath his shaggy hair, a crease in his brow formed as he watched me. "Sorry, I didn't mean to scare you."

"He-hey," I stammered, embarrassed by the sudden onset of jumpy awkwardness caused by the combination of awareness and fear that had started to snake through my veins. I reminded myself that technically he'd approached me. In the eyes of the law and, hopefully, my grandma, I was innocent. Clearing my throat, I tried to level my best stern look. "You really shouldn't be speaking to me."

"Or what?" Ethan laughed. "Your grandma will put away your suitcase again?"

Belatedly, I tried to turn my laugh into a cough. No matter what, I could not get caught laughing at his jokes again.

"I don't want to be forced to sleep out on The Strip tonight."

"I'm sure my grandma would be happy to take you in. It'd give her a reason to gloat." Ethan's smile was slightly crooked, as if he was enjoying this conversation more than he wanted to let on.

"I wouldn't accept that even if the alternative was a pit full of snakes," I replied, trying to keep my expression neutral.

"That feels dramatic."

"That's because Mini would dramatically kill me in the morning."

Ethan laughed that same low, warm laugh, and I fought to keep the sound from making a permanent home in my memory. "Somehow, I can't see Ms. Mini doing that."

"Okay, fine. Mini would never murder me." I bit down on my lip and tried to suppress the smile that seemed determined to betray me. "She would, however, put me on an early flight home if she smelled even a whiff of shenanigans."

"Literally no one has ever accused me of shenanigans." He stepped a half foot closer to me. Little red lights started flashing in my brain. We were definitely in the friends-talking zone now.

"There is a first time for everything." I shrugged and took a casual half step backward. "I'm gonna go get us checked in before Mini sees me within fifty yards of you. Have a nice convention."

Have a nice convention? Could I be any less cool? I turned and started wheeling our suitcases away as quickly as I could, hoping that the giant chandelier would fall from the ceiling and flatten me before Ethan had the chance to process how profoundly uncool I was. Not that I cared if he thought I was cool. Clearly.

"Nittha dropped this off for you." BamBam held out a small bundle of cloth as soon as I stepped out of the bathroom. The sight of her already sprawled across the fluffy white comforter of the bed closest to the window with a perfect view of the pool made me smile. Before BamBam had retired and become the queen of all things mature beauty, she had worked as an elementary school administrator, makeup counter rep, and hairstylist, respectively. Years of standing all day had left her with a deep and unapologetic love of putting her feet up whenever she could. At this stage, it was a running joke in our family. If BamBam wasn't going a mile a minute, she wasn't going at all.

"I'm about to take a nap, but before I do, your daddy texted me to remind you to finish up that application for SISU's business administration program, then send him the draft so he can read it over," BamBam said as I started across the room.

At the mention of Southern Illinois State University's business administration program, any joy I'd felt since we'd made it to our room melted away. I knew my dad meant well, but I had no interest in getting my college degree in business. And even less desire to send that essay to my dad, who would red-pencil every sentence because my word choice was "too juvenile" or something equally perfectionist. Then again, if I didn't send him the essay soon, he'd only find something else about my future to obsess over.

Honestly, BamBam convincing Principal Danvers to let me out of classes three weeks into the new school year seemed like nothing compared to the backflips she had to do to get my parents to agree to this trip—and not just because she and Principal Danvers were pai gow buddies. BamBam had promised my parents that I wouldn't miss a beat of my senior year if they let me come to TrendCon with her. In the end, she'd secured my freedom in exchange for a series of college visits, vigilance in maintaining their no-dating-until-graduation rule, forty-five minutes of SAT prep and college application work every day, and no missed homework.

"You know this is your parents wanting you to have a solid chance at getting into a good school." Whatever expression I wore on my face, BamBam must have known that this wasn't exactly the text I'd hoped my dad would send. That was one of the reasons I loved BamBam: Her years of spending every afternoon with my siblings and me after school meant that I didn't need to explain how I felt to her. She just knew.

"Or, it's my parents trying to plan my entire life for me by making me go to the college they went to in order to study exactly what they studied." I raised an eyebrow, then flopped down on the edge of my bed. "Last week Mom literally said, and I quote, 'Business is a practical major to have on your résumé if you decide to pledge my sorority.'"

"That sounds like your mother." BamBam's tone was crisp,

her lips pressed into a thin line as she forced herself to swallow whatever less-than-nice thing she wanted to say about my mom and her college affiliations. "I'm sure she won't be too upset if you don't join her sorority."

"I doubt that." I exhaled and slouched over.

"Well, no need to think about the application right now. You've got all week to work on it." BamBam held the suit back out to me and smiled, as if a trip to the pool would erase the fact that my parents were as excited about my interest in film as they were about the possibility of an alien invasion.

"Thanks, BamBam." Fixing a smile on my face, I took the swimsuit from her and held it up. "Where is the rest of it?"

"What do you mean?" BamBam sat up a little to see the suit, then leaned back and started cackling. Of course Nittha would have the most absurd, tiny hot-pink bikini in the world.

"Is it me, or is this like really small?" If I wasn't careful, I was going to end up with a sunburn on my butt or an endless bikini wedgie.

"You know what they say, what happens in Vegas . . ." Bam-Bam managed to hold it together long enough to shrug and wiggle her eyebrows before she started laughing again.

"I know what happens here stays here. I'm more concerned about my swimsuit trying to stay here while I'm wearing it." I eyed the strings suspiciously.

"Oh, baby, I wore those all the time back in the day. They are sturdier than they appear. Your parents may not want you dating, but you can live a little. The suit is cute, and it'll show off what you got." When I didn't immediately budge, BamBam grinned, then waved a hand at me. "Go get changed. Grandma needs you to get out of here so she can take a nap."

I bit my bottom lip and headed toward the bathroom, the sound of BamBam's giggles following me to the door. This trip was already full of surprises. I just hoped a wardrobe malfunction wouldn't be the next one.

CHAPTER THREE

"WOULD YOU STOP PULLING AT THAT?" GABBY TUTTED, SLAPPING my hand away from my bikini bottom. "You look cute."

"I look like a half-naked highlighter," I shot back, stepping out of her reach so I could adjust my swimsuit in peace.

"No one wearing a swimsuit of mine would even remotely resemble a highlighter. I have impeccable taste," Nittha teased, setting the handbag containing Cricket down so she could spread her towel out on the chair next to Gabby's. Through some miracle she'd managed to sneak Cricket into the pool area, so we'd picked chairs at the quieter end, away from the other people our age, hoping that the lifeguard wouldn't immediately send Cricket, and us, back inside the second she came out of the bag.

I spread my towel out on the other side of Gabby, then set my laptop on the little table between us before busting out a bottle of sunscreen. My mother was extremely white—like blond-eyebrows-level pale—so that meant that sunburns were a real possibility for me, even with my melanin and frequent trips to Lake Michigan over the summer.

"Can someone help with my back?" I asked, rubbing sunscreen into my arms.

"I'll help in exchange for details on the Lobby Hottie. What did you say to make him fall in love with you so quickly?" Nittha said, walking over and plopping down next to me.

"I swear, if someone even blinks at me, you see a crush." I laughed, then handed the bottle to her as Gabby came to sit on my other side.

"Not true. You and Gabby simply refuse to acknowledge when people like you. That's why you need me." Nittha dumped a blob of cold lotion onto my back, then paused. "I did some speed internet sleuthing—"

"You mean stalking?" I interjected, a shiver running through me as I tried to adjust to my skin being two different temperatures.

"It isn't really invasive if his videos are public."

"Isn't it, though?" I tilted my head, giving Nittha a skeptical eye. "It's not like he created the videos with the intention that you would memorize every detail of his life."

"Ugh. Save your internet ethics speech. We all know how you feel about social media, and we have all week for that soapbox." Gabby rolled her eyes as she took the sunscreen from Nittha.

"I don't think the entire world needs a central location to watch me, or anyone, make a fool of themselves on the internet."

I sighed. "Nor do I think it's reasonable for everyone to have access to my every thought."

"Who is sharing their every thought?" Nittha groaned, sounding put-upon. "And do you think you'd make a fool of yourself? Or, is that what your parents are worried about?"

"Both." I shook my head like the distinction was irrelevant. Much like their approach to my nonexistent dating life, my parents were inclined to overmonitor even a whiff of me on social media. One video of me and my friends dancing together in the seventh grade was enough to convince me that I never wanted that level of my parents' scrutiny again.

"It is okay to not be perfect, you know. That's what curation and the delete button are for," Gabby pressed.

Last year, the two of them came to visit me in Chicago, and I got an earful of my mom lecturing me about my "smudgy eyeliner" when Gabby posted something to one of her accounts. In her defense, Mom didn't want me to regret my appearance later on, but as Gabby pointed out, the comment came too late to be helpful. The video was already up, and it hadn't bothered me until Mom pointed it out. Needless to say, these two were never letting that particular boundary overstep go.

"Nothing is ever really gone on the internet." I sighed, returning to the present when Gabby handed the sunscreen back to me.

"You want to be a filmmaker, yes? How is anyone supposed to hire you if they can't see you and your work?" Nittha asked. "Issa Rae got her start on YouTube."

"I know, I know. I'll put together a private channel with my portfolio when I make something worth sharing." This was the one place Nittha, Gabby, and I fundamentally disagreed. They couldn't understand why I refused to have my own social media, and I couldn't find a way to make them understand that I didn't have anything good enough to withstand my parents' opinions. Someday I would. Maybe. But not now.

"Don't put down your videos with Mini. They help and entertain people. If you won't be a collaborator, you should at least put your name in the captions when you post them." Nittha crossed her arms. For a second, we all sat staring at each other in the kind of stalemate that only friends can have. Finally, coming to a decision to let it go for the moment, Nittha perked up. "Whatever, we can fight about this later. Back to Lobby Hottie—"

"You know his name is Ethan."

"Yeah, but nicknames for crushes are way more fun!"

"Plus, this place is packed with people who know him. We don't need rumors starting." Gabby grimaced.

"The only one spreading this crush rumor is Nittha." I laughed.

"Right now. But pretty soon, everyone will see it," Nittha teased.

"Because you told them to," I said.

"No, because you are star-crossed. This is meant to be." Nittha's eyes were wide with earnestness. If anyone ever invented a prize for the best hopeless romantic, she'd win. Her social media basically doubled as a timeline of every girl she'd ever dated. If they lasted more than two weeks, she was also dressing them in outfits to match Cricket. "*Anyway*, I did a little internet sleuthing, because I thought I recognized him, and he is, like, mildly car proficient. His channel has thirty thousand followers. That's not bad."

"Mildly car proficient. What does that even mean?" Gabby asked.

"He talks about cars and stuff," Nittha said, waving a hand, as if the gesture would summon the details for her, then she frowned. "Whatever. You know I don't drive. His channel has car parts in it, okay? And I didn't have that much time to watch. I was trying to get Cricket dressed."

I laughed at the thought of her trying to fit Cricket into a bathing suit. "Nittha, I love you so much, but what do you think I'm even going to do with that information?"

"Talk to him about cars. Obviously." Nittha shrugged, then picked up her phone. "Smile!"

Gabby and Nittha both leaned in at the same time. I pretended to smile, only to stick my tongue out and make a silly face right as Nittha snapped the picture.

"Aw, we're cute!" Nittha said, showing us the picture. "Are you okay if I post this?"

"Sure. It's not like I have to see myself looking ridiculous again." I giggled. Unlike Nittha and Gabby, I had the benefit of anonymity. No one cared what I looked like on vacation other than my mom, who only checked my friends' social media when her curiosity outweighed her wish to pretend that I had privacy, which was all the time. Fortunately, unless I was wearing or doing something truly egregious, Mom would act like she had no idea what I'd been up to. Even though I *knew* she was lurking.

"Very true. And it wouldn't be the first time you've shown up on Cricket's account being ridiculous," Nittha teased as she stood up and walked back to her chair. Glancing around for anyone watching us, she stealthily pulled Cricket out of her carrier. She and Nittha were wearing matching bright-blue swimsuits and sun visors. "Okay, we need to take a couple pictures, then we'll come back. Gabby, will you help me, since Jamie is being all serious and brought her computer?"

"Happy to." Gabby grinned and peeked over the edge of her sunglasses at me. "Who works at the pool?"

"You two are technically working right now, too." I laughed and leaned back in my chair. "Have fun."

As soon as they were in the pool, I reached for my laptop, letting the lazy sun soak into my skin as I worked. I'd started playing with the placement of a text box on a thumbnail of BamBam holding up about fourteen different makeup brushes, when a voice I didn't want to recognize interrupted me.

"Is someone sitting in this chair?"

I closed my eyes and willed anyone other than Ethan to be standing there. Why was he so determined to speak to me? Couldn't he go be cute somewhere else?

"Jamie?"

Opening my eyes, I found Ethan looking down at me from behind a pair of black Wayfarer-style sunglasses and a blue baseball cap.

"I'm awake. You should not sit there." I threw him some side-eye.

"Why?"

"Because my grandma's window faces this direction."

"It isn't like she is gonna see us from all the way up there."

"That's what you think. She probably has a spy at the pool." When he didn't budge, I tried a different tactic. Turning back to my computer, I added, "Besides, don't you want to go hang out with all the other people our age who actually make content?"

Ethan snorted and looked over at the other end of the pool, where Sterling James, one of the beauty creators on BamBam's list of potential collaborators, and this guy who made prurient skits were splashing unsuspecting passersby. If I was smart, I'd get up and go try to talk to Sterling instead of sitting here watching as Ethan shook his head and began spreading out his towel next to mine. "Yeah, I'm good here."

In movies, when a guy takes off his shirt, the film starts going in slo-mo so you can watch everyone around him react without him being aware of the effect he is having on the hapless pool denizens. I made the mistake of glancing up right as he peeled the white T-shirt from his body, revealing a thin pink scar running down his chest . . . and muscles. Nothing bulky or overly defined. Less like he was spending hours in the gym and more like a combination of genetics and someone whose job included manual labor.

This moment was nothing like the movies. I mean, I stared, alright. But unlike in a movie, he knew exactly what effect him being shirtless and two feet away from me was having on my otherwise-rational mind.

Ethan smirked. Tossing the shirt on the edge of his chair, he asked, "You doing okay?"

A little spike of panic coursed through me, and my brain temporarily disconnected as I cast about for a way to recover any chill that he might have thought I had. My eyes landed on my sunscreen, and my ability to think kicked back in. Throwing my braid over my shoulder, I picked up my bottle of sunscreen and held it out to him.

"My mom is as white as you are. You are gonna burn in fifteen minutes," I said, doing my best to seem totally unfazed, like cute boys took their shirts off in front of me all the time.

Ethan looked down at my hand, then back at me. His confidence didn't falter whatsoever as he sat down. "I'll put it on in a minute."

"You truly are full of bad ideas." I tossed my sunscreen onto his lap.

"You wound me." Ethan threw a dramatic hand over his heart and slouched. "You don't know me well enough to know that my ideas are incredible. Yet, anyway. We'll be friends, eventually."

"Name one good idea you've had since we met."

"Sitting next to you." He grinned as if I'd walked right into his trap. "See how fun this is?"

I rolled my eyes. "Someone is going to tell our grandmas, and then it'll be like TrendCon Miami all over again, only without my dad here to break up the shouting match before mobility devices get tossed around."

"I was at a soccer tournament last year, so I don't have the same emotional baggage from Miami—although I heard my grandma really took more of a swing than a throw, which was still impressive, of course."

"Uh, her cane was lightweight, and she wielded it like a bat. Plus, BamBam was in a walking boot, so she couldn't get out of the way fast enough, although really Buzzy's cane just grazed her thigh." I shook my head and wondered how I let myself get sidetracked instead of encouraging him to go away. "But that's not the point. If you don't want the trauma of seeing your grandma take her earrings off for a fight, you should leave."

"Who is going to recognize us? It's not like I wear a swimsuit on my channel."

I arched a skeptical eyebrow. Somehow, I doubted that people would forget a face like his enough to have him go completely unrecognized. But maybe his main audience consisted of stereotypical cishet men drooling over engines.

"Trust me." Ethan gestured to his bare chest. My eyes started to follow the motion but stopped as soon as he pointed at me. "And you literally don't exist on the internet. You're like a ghost."

"You were looking for me?" I wrinkled my nose at him.

"I—" Ethan blinked at me for a second, his cheeks turning a shade of pink that had nothing to do with being in the sun.

"You're telling me you didn't look for me?"

"Nope." I shook my head as he raised an incredulous eyebrow at me. It was almost adorable watching him squirm. I sighed. "But Nittha did. She says you're into cars."

Ethan's face erupted into a grin. "Oh, I see. You got someone else to do your dirty work."

I rolled my eyes. "It's not like I asked her to."

"Sure. I believe you." Ethan's gaze followed in the direction I nodded, where Nittha was holding Cricket above the water for a photo. "Don't worry. I won't tell anyone how you research the competition."

I shook my head and tried to focus on my computer. "So, you admit that we are in competition, then? Do you always fraternize with the enemy?"

Ethan studied me. "We're not enemies. Our grandmas are."

"But you just said we were." I grinned as an idea turned over in my mind. If I couldn't make him go away, maybe I could make Ethan useful. Tilting my chin toward Sterling, I asked, "Do you know that guy over there, the one with bleach-blond hair?"

Ethan's gaze followed the direction I'd pointed him in. "You mean Sterling?"

"Yeah." I nodded, fighting the urge to get too excited.

"I do. Did. Kind of. We're friends-ish. We used to play soccer together in Portage Park." Ethan stumbled through his explanation of his relationship with Sterling, then readjusted in his chair slightly, as if the question made him feel uncomfortable. Pulling at an invisible loose thread on his shorts, he added, "He works with someone I used to date, so it's complicated. We don't talk as much anymore, but we were close. If you are asking because you think he is cute, bad news: He is gay."

"Google already told me that, but thanks for lookin' out." I laughed, then explained. "My grandma thinks she might want to work with him, but I wanted to do some reconnaissance before she talks to him. Don't tell her I told you."

"Wouldn't dream of it." Ethan's frame relaxed a little. He said, "Don't let the glitter fool you. Sterling is supersmart, highly competitive, and dead serious about his business. The guy is twenty-four/seven thinking about his brand and how he positions it. Honestly, he'd probably be the perfect match for Ms. Mini. They both have big personalities."

"Thanks for the intel," I said before returning to my work.

Ethan leaned back in his chair, ostensibly soaking up sun. Meanwhile, I tried to focus on BamBam's content schedule, so I could figure out where I wanted to slot her latest brush video into the plan. She had a sponsored video for a hydrating face cream going out soon, too, and I wanted to time the brush video's release so that it didn't draw potential viewers away from it—

"So, you and Nittha seem close. She was with you in the lobby." Ethan's voice interrupted me. I faced him only to find him watching me, tension tracing his jaw as he tried to sort out how to say whatever it was he was getting at. Ethan took a deep breath and gestured in a circular way as if the motion would help me connect the dots. "Is she your friend . . . girlfriend . . . platonic life partner . . ."

For a moment I blinked at him, and then I started laughing. Ethan's face looked like he might crawl into a hole at any moment. This happened a lot with Nittha and Gabby. They were both so pretty and outgoing. I couldn't really be mad at people for asking the sidekick friend if they were single, even if Ethan's attempt was clumsy.

"We're just friends. But, bad news for you. She typically dates girls. And trust me, right now, she's got a whopper of a girlfriend."

"I wasn't asking about her for me." Ethan looked shocked

39

that I would think he was asking about the dating status of an objectively pretty girl for benign reasons.

"Sure. You and everyone else who's ever asked me."

"No, really." Ethan sputtered. Clearing his throat, he tried again. "You're not interested in her?"

"Girls aren't for me so far, but even if I was interested, I'm not Nittha's type. Everyone she dates is about a foot taller and ten times louder than me." I laughed, envisioning Nittha's current girlfriend. That girl was basically a walking megaphone. Anytime she needed to do anything, the entire world got an announcement about it: tying her shoe, losing a pen, changing a tampon.

"So, what would be your type?" Ethan asked, drawing out the *o* in *so*.

I snorted. "Nice try. You seem like the kind of guy who'd flirt with a light post if it were in front of you."

"Nah," Ethan said, suddenly very interested in the seam of his swim trunks again. I pursed my lips together and waited. "Can't a guy ask his new friend about her life?"

"Again. We're not friends. You're the one who said we were competition, remember?"

Ethan laughed, and I caught myself smiling even as I tried to scare him off. "Okay, then how about we know just enough about each other to be cordial when our grandmothers aren't around? What's your favorite color? It's probably dark purple."

Great. He'd noticed my nail polish, and now my imagination was working overtime to bring the whole friend scenario from the plane back again. That couldn't happen. Sometimes fibs were for the greater good . . .

"Actually, it's—"

"Miss, you can't have your dog in the pool area." The lifeguard's voice rang out, startling both Ethan and me. We paused to see Nittha looking like she might try to argue and get all of us banned from the pool, while Gabby looked like she'd commit homicide if Nittha did that.

"Well, that's my cue." I stood and started packing up my stuff as Gabby pushed Nittha to start walking. Throwing my sundress over my head, I then glanced over at Ethan. "Keep the sunscreen."

"You're leaving?" Ethan said, looking between me and my friends, who were slowly wading out of the pool as if the delay would make a statement about the rules. "I can bring it back to you."

"Keep it. You're gonna need it more than me." I laughed and started cramming Nittha's stuff into her bag right as she reached the chairs.

"Can you believe . . ." Nittha stopped midsentence, noticing that Ethan was sitting next to me. A Cheshire cat grin spread across her face as whatever romance she was spinning in her head started to kick into high gear. "Hey, I know you from—"

"Nope. No small talk, the lifeguard is coming. We gotta go," I said, taking Cricket from her arms and handing her a swim cover-up.

"Jamie didn't tell us your name." Gabby jumped in where Nittha had left off, enjoying the fact that I was squirming. "I'm Gabby, this is Nittha."

"I'm Ethan. Nice to meet you both."

"Okay, great introductions. Time to leave." I cut in again.

Gabby's face turned from mischievous to surprised as she watched me pick up her and Nittha's bags. Apparently, she had underestimated how quickly I could get myself out of an awkward situation when highly motivated. I passed Gabby a tote and tucked the dog back into her carrier, then looped my arm through Nittha's and said, "Bye, Ethan."

He smiled at the two of them as if they were old pals, then turned to me, wearing an expression every bit as mischievous as Gabby's, and said, "See you later, new friends."

"Not if I can help it." I rolled my eyes and tugged on Nittha's arm to get a move on.

"What was that about?" Gabby asked, ducking her chin to try to catch my eye as I steered us toward the exit.

"Nothing," I said, shaking my head. "Ethan was trying to get us both disowned by our grandmas. Again."

"Ugh. You're gonna tell me that you sat there the whole time and had no fun? Who doesn't want a little forbidden love?" Nittha giggled and took Cricket's bag from me.

I was halfway through denying it when a sneaky little voice in the back of my head pointed out that I *had* had a smidge of fun with Ethan.

"Nope. No fun. And, I value my life, so don't get any ideas." I said that last part to myself as much as Nittha. I certainly didn't need to be getting any ideas about Ethan either.

CHAPTER FOUR

"OH GOOD, YOU'RE BACK," BAMBAM CALLED OVER HER SHOUL-
der as I walked into our room. "How was the pool?"

Ethan's words floated back to me. *No one will recognize us.*

"Uh, you know." I plugged my laptop in to charge before answering so she couldn't see the trepidation on my face. "Fine
until Nittha got us kicked out for bringing Cricket to the pool."

"Shoulda seen that one coming." BamBam laughed. "Bringing a dog to the pool. I'll bet it was in a swimsuit, too."

"It was. And they matched."

"Nittha is always getting into something. That girl cracks
me up."

"Also, I saw Sterling James. I didn't talk to him, but I talked
to someone who knows him. It sounds like you two might
have something in common," I said, sidestepping the name of
my informant. I didn't like to lie to BamBam, but sometimes a
lie by omission was necessary for self-preservation's sake. To

43

BamBam, loyalty was everything. She once gave my dad the cold shoulder for a week for mentioning my late grandfather's funky feet in public. Me being in close proximity to anything Buzzy-related would crush her. Better to tell a little lie and keep my grandma speaking to me than break her heart over one random conversation.

"Hmm. He uses a lot of glitter, which isn't really my thing." BamBam paused, her face pensive. Shrugging, she stood up. In one hand, she held her toiletry kit. In the other, her favorite snuggly blue bathrobe. "Then again, your grandma can learn new tricks. See if you can talk to him tonight and let me know if he seems interested in collaborating. I'm gonna go get in the shower and then get ready for the reception."

"Alright." I yawned and flopped onto my bed, suddenly jealous of her nap.

As if reading my mind, she said, "If you want to get some sleep, I'll wake you up when I'm out of the shower and lotioned. Then we can talk strategy while we put our faces on."

"Thank you." I smiled. BamBam still called doing your makeup "putting on a face." At this stage, I was pretty sure she was using the expression because she knew my siblings and I poked fun at it.

No sooner had my head hit the pillow than it felt like BamBam was gently shaking me awake. Groaning, I cracked one eye open to see my grandmother in her pink leopard-print shower cap hovering over me. "Baby, time to go get cleaned up."

"A few more minutes."

I tried to roll over, but BamBam's firm hand on my shoulder

stopped me. "You've been asleep for forty-five minutes. Up and at 'em."

I made a sound in response that could only be described as somewhere between *mhurg* and the pterodactyl noises my baby cousins make in place of speaking.

"Let's go, kiddo. No more lollygagging." BamBam shook me less gently this time.

I tried to swat her hand away but had no luck. She didn't stop rocking me until I sat up, pushing flyaway hairs out of my face. "I'm up. I'm up."

"Finally," BamBam said, giving me just enough space to get up without leaving me room to lie back down. As I shuffled toward my suitcase to find my shower stuff, she started talking like my brain wasn't still trying to power up. "So, how do you want to cover the Silver Influencers panel tomorrow?"

"Mmm . . . Who is on it?" I asked, mostly to give myself time to think. I wanted to try something new, to challenge myself filming-wise.

"You know, they were supposed to send me an email, but I didn't see one come through . . ." She trailed off as she settled herself in front of the mirror that hung above the desk and flipped on the nearby lamp for extra light. "I'm sure Gregory will be on it. He's on all the panels these days."

"Are the two of you still going to that show?" I asked.

"You know it." BamBam chuckled. She and Gregory were friends from way back in her early video days. He was a retired sociology professor with expertise in the history of drag culture. The man could find a way to link literally anything to drag queens—slang, Disney villains, pop-star stage aesthetics, even the repopularizing of sequins. If it existed in the broader culture, Gregory knew where it existed in drag history first and why we were seeing it now.

Mysteriously, BamBam had announced that she and Gregory were going to a show, but she wouldn't say what it was about. Dad thought it was drag; Mom thought it was magic; my older sister was convinced it was some concert that was so expensive, she didn't want to buy me a ticket; while my older brother thought they were going to watch a raunchy comedian. My money was on Chippendales or *Magic Mike*. The super popular, campy strip shows were often set to disco songs and therefore the perfect nexus of BamBam's and Gregory's interests.

BamBam smiled as she put on her moisturizer. "So, what about the video?"

"Let me think about it in the shower," I said, already halfway to the bathroom.

By the time I'd finished washing my sunscreen off, I had a plan. It was totally different from what people would expect from her page. For it to work, I'd have to try a couple new things, starting with borrowing some lighting from Nittha and relying on BamBam's questionable camera skills. But if I was right, her audience would love it. And if they loved it enough, there might be a new sponsorship opportunity in her future.

"I got it!" I shouted as I opened the bathroom door, steam from the shower billowing out. BamBam jumped with surprise, smudging her eyeliner slightly.

"Got what?" She tutted and picked up a cotton swab to fix the wobbly line on her eye.

"An idea for how to shoot the panel." I busted out of the bathroom still in my towel and shower cap. If I were at home, Mom and Dad would have told me to stop dripping everywhere. Then again, if we were at home, Mom and Dad would have thought this idea was a bad one, so whatever. "Actually, the whole trip, really."

"Okay, let's hear it. What are you gonna do with a fashion grannie in Vegas?"

"That's the thing. We are gonna do what anyone does in Vegas. I feel like it's a three-part day-in-the-life series, including a get-ready-with-me where people watch how you put on your makeup and pick out an outfit to go onstage, panel highlights, and then a go-out-with-me video where people see you having fun with your friends and whatnot. We can connect them thematically by using the hotel's mirrored hallways so your plans feel extra glam. Imagine, every time you walk through one, we blend the transition from one event to the next. Gregory could do it, too, and the two of you could cross post."

"Okay . . ." BamBam drew out the vowels in the word as she thought. "Ripping and running around town isn't really my brand. Would my audience really care about me playing pai gow or going to dinner? What about something like a watch-me-try-lipsticks?"

"That's the thing. It's the perfect time to test out new content, because everyone knows you're on a trip, and the Vegas videos will stop soon if they hate it. Besides, you can do both. The resort is basically a giant mall. We can film a lipstick-wear test at midnight if we want." I shrugged and hoped the argument would work.

I'd always wanted to try filming a person moving around in mirrors like in *Enter the Dragon*. It was notoriously difficult to film without the audience seeing the camera and breaking the fourth wall. While I wasn't about to build a mirrored hallway back in Chicago, Las Vegas was full of them. Even filming Bam-Bam getting into the elevator without the audience seeing me or my camera would be tricky, but I'd always wanted to try and pay homage to the classic.

"Plus, this fits the goal to expand your range, show brands that you can do more than apply eyeliner or pick the perfect dress. You can travel, go dancing, review restaurants, and have fun just like the young people with all the sponsors. Think about it, BamBam."

She nodded. "Alright. But going out in this city? Old people play slots all the time. That's not special."

"It is if you are having fun with other older people! Plus, you're the cool, well-dressed grandma everyone wishes they had. People like your version of retirement. It's inspiring and re-latable. Why not grow that beyond makeup?" I grinned, trying not to look too smug as I tied my pitch up in a neat little bow.

A smile crept across her face, and I knew then that BamBam was going to agree. "Alright. Let's try it. What's the worst that happens?"

"Yes!" I started bouncing on the balls of my feet and clapping like I was a cheerleader at a football game.

"You know, your folks sending you to those business camps is really paying off. That was a good little pitch."

BamBam chuckled, and I felt my mind split in two. I guess

I did have two years of SISU business camp to thank for the power of persuasion. And on the one hand, I was excited that she liked my idea. On the other, it made me nervous. What if my parents were right and the skill that I had was less about entertaining people and more about the ability to sell something? The idea that my parents might have a point scared me, and I pushed the thought away before it could do any more damage to my enthusiasm. Looking at BamBam, I said, "I need to borrow some gear, but I'm sure Nittha will have it, and—"

"I'm sure you do, baby. But you'll have to grab it later. We need to get going, or we will be the last people to get to the reception." BamBam checked her phone clock. We had plenty of time, but to BamBam, the difference between fashionably late and just plain rude was about five minutes in either direction. Smiling back at me, she said, "What are you gonna wear? And I still plan to help you put on your face, so we have to hurry."

"Who cares what I look like? I'm behind the scenes, remember?"

"Being behind a camera is no excuse to disappear." BamBam shrugged and picked up her dark-brown eyebrow pencil.

Ouch. What was with everyone today? Just because I wasn't out there in flashing lights didn't mean that I was hiding. I wanted to let my work speak for itself. And it would, when it was good enough.

"I'm not disappearing. I'm letting my work do the talking."

BamBam snorted as if this was the most ridiculous thing she'd heard all week. "Well, you gotta take credit for the videos if you want your work to speak."

Okay, that part I didn't have an argument for. Yet. "I'm not—"

BamBam arched an eyebrow, as if daring me to come up with an explanation that she couldn't put holes in. I shut my mouth. A few heartbeats later, her face relaxed into a smile. "Plus, if I'm gonna start doing going-out videos, I've got to practice going-out makeup. Who knows? Maybe you'll like those videos enough to put your name on them? Or at least let me say 'videos by my grandbaby' in my bios, like the other gran-fluencers. Gregory brags about that all the time."

"Fine. You can do my makeup." I fought the urge to point out that Gregory was referencing his drag grandchildren, of which he had half a dozen, so of course he was constantly praising and working with them. His biological grandkid was nine and there-fore not helping with anything, unlike me. I sighed and added, "But only because you need to practice. And I'm picking my own outfit. I'm on vacation from any and all dress codes, too."

"You are gonna be so cute!" BamBam said, jumping up from her chair and pulling me toward my suitcase. "I won't tell you what to wear, but let's see what you've got in here."

CHAPTER FIVE

"SEE WHAT A BIT OF MASCARA CAN DO?" BAMBAM BEAMED OVER at me as I checked my appearance in the elevator's mirrored walls. She laughed and came to stand next to me, pulling out her phone and striking a pose so the two of us could take a picture. Holding out the phone, she said, "Your parents will love this."

"Nice work." I smiled up at her. She was getting better at doing stuff like not taking photos at bizarre upward angles, which was good. It meant I wouldn't have to worry about her as much when I went to college next year.

"I love that dress on you, BamBam."

"I look good, right? I do wish they had it in pink or something, but the black is alright." BamBam grinned, giving the calf-length, form-fitting beaded dress a shimmy. It had modern flapper vibes, which BamBam played up with a cute little headband and long pearl necklaces. "I still can't believe Lady and

House sent me something from next season's collection. I feel like I'm officially a celebrity. My wardrobe is ahead of the trend."

"I can. Lady and House knows you're a badass." I smiled. "I'd want to give you early access, too."

The elevator dinged right as BamBam reached out to give me a quick hug and a kiss on the side of my head. Keeping her arm wrapped around my shoulders, she steered us off the elevator, smoothing my carefully revived curls back into place as the sound of a party in full swing washed over us.

"Hello," said a broad-shouldered bouncer with an extremely slick ponytail and an even slicker suit. "Welcome to the Trend-Con mixer. I'll need your names, please."

"Of course. I'm Eugenia Webb from Ms. Mini's Makeup Counter, and this is my assistant, Jamie," BamBam said, instantly flipping into Mini's honied voice. I knew why BamBam called me her assistant. Saying *director* or *producer* would've seemed ridiculous. After all, what seventeen-year-old was a director? Still, the title irked me. BamBam kept her own calendar, answered her own emails, and got her own coffee. Usually. Okay, sometimes I got coffee, too, but that wasn't my main job and she knew it.

"Right." The bouncer began tapping away on a tablet, not missing a beat. After a few more taps, they said, "Here you are. Thank you both for joining us. If you could hold out your right wrist, please.

"This one will let you order alcohol at the bar if you would like," the bouncer said, snapping a bright-orange bracelet around BamBam's wrist. Taking my wrist, they snapped a dark-green band on it, then scowled at me. "And this one will only get you a Coke. Don't even try to swap. Got it?"

A tiny part of me thought about pointing out that I was with my grandma, and as a compulsive rule follower, there wasn't a snowball's chance in the desert that I was ever going to try swapping, but then I realized that the bouncer was big enough to tear me in half and thought the better of talking back.

I nodded. "Got it."

The bouncer's face relaxed again. "Alright, you two have fun. Don't forget to pick up your VIP goody bags on the way out."

"Thank you," BamBam and I said at the same time. Glancing at each other, we giggled as we walked past the bouncer and around the corner, then froze.

"Oh wow." My voice felt small next to the view from the roof. The city spread out in front of us, sparkling like stars in a clear sky. The lights from The Strip gave the night an endless quality, making everything feel limitless and full of possibilities. It was stunning.

"That is something else." BamBam whistled low. Peering down at me, she winked, then squeezed my hand. "Come on, kiddo, let's have some fun."

With that, we stepped into the party. A DJ was situated on one side of the terrace, lit up by a bunch of blue and purple lights. On the other side was the bar. In between was the pool, also lit up with blue lights and surrounded by white couches and red chairs that wobbled like eggs.

"There's Myra. Let's go say hello." BamBam waved at a woman with streaked black-and-gray hair. I'd never met Myra, but I knew she reviewed BamBam's contracts. Listening to a conversation between the two of them sounded about as interesting as watching paint dry.

"Actually, if it's okay, I want to look for Sterling and ask Nittha to borrow her lights."

"Alright, but don't leave the party without telling me."

"Say hi to Myra for me."

BamBam nodded, then headed off toward her friend, leaving me to try to find mine. I was about to go check over by the bar, when I spotted a group of people about my age huddled around one corner of the pool. A few feet from the larger group was Nittha, talking about a mile a minute to Gabby.

"Hey," I said as soon as I was within earshot.

"You look gorg." Nittha gestured at me.

"All cutesy in that dress." Gabby grinned.

"Thanks, it has pockets, and it's stretchy." I smiled and jumped into a split stance so they could see what I meant. The dress hugged my body, but it felt more like sweats than something I couldn't sit down in. "It's basically the only fancy-ish thing I brought."

"Love a dress with pockets." Nittha giggled, then added, "There are more parties, by the way, so if you seriously didn't bring anything else, get ready to go shopping in Gabby's suitcase. She packed enough for three weeks."

"Only enough for two and a half weeks." Gabby laughed as if the convention being six days had been a minor consideration in her packing plans. "And it's good you look stunning, because the boyfriend Nittha insists you have just walked in."

"I don't have a boyfriend."

"Tell Ethan that." Nittha nodded toward the elevators. "He and his grandma are right there."

I shifted in the direction of the elevator bank in time to see Ethan and Buzzy entering the party. My heart stopped.

Ethan wasn't wearing anything particularly special, just jeans and a plain black collared shirt. In fact, the outfit wouldn't have been remarkable at all if it didn't fit him so well. Unfortunately, Ethan wasn't why I was breaking out into a sweat right now.

Buzzy was wearing the same dress as BamBam.

"Oh no."

"Don't want to see him?" Gabby teased.

"No, that's not why—" I shook my head, then tried again when Gabby raised an eyebrow. "His grandma and my grandma are wearing the same dress. How did she even get that dress? It was supposed to be for BamBam. It's next season."

"Oh, that is bad." Nittha's eyes went wide.

"What's the deal with them anyway?" Gabby furrowed her brow as she tried to keep up with the glances Nittha and I were exchanging.

"They used to be part of a shared channel when they were first starting out. I think it was just poorly organized, but basically my grandma and Buzzy seemed to have too similar of content. Since BamBam posted on Tuesdays and Buzzy on Fridays, BamBam decided Buzzy was a no-talent copycat who pretended to be her friend but was actually re-creating all her videos for her white-lady, sweater-sets-and-pearls crowd. I've never asked her personally, but based on what her followers say in BamBam's comments, Buzzy probably thinks my grandma is a bougie bossy-pants who has deluded herself into thinking she invented fashion."

"That is a very specific feud." Gabby snort-laughed.

"It sounds funny, but you didn't see them on the plane." I frowned.

"And then there is you and Ethan. He's a handsome grandson pining away for the granddaughter of a rival family and trying to find ways to be with her, like Romeo did Juliet," Nittha added unhelpfully.

"None of that is true. He only wants to be friends."

"Why, if your grandmas are beefing like that?" Gabby asked.

"I don't know," I said, throwing Nittha a don't-try-it look.

Nittha smirked. "Doesn't matter now—your friend is walking toward us."

"What?" I tried to position myself behind Gabby. "Maybe he won't see us."

Nittha waved at him, then smiled at me as he waved back. "Bad news. He sees you."

"Because you signaled him," I hissed, heat creeping up the back of my neck as he got closer.

"Pretty sure he saw you before." Nittha laughed.

"You might be on your own." Gabby snickered, leaning away. "Maybe I'll get popcorn and watch this mess—"

"Hey, Ethan."

Gabby, Nittha, and I all jumped as a short white girl with a chin-length bob and perfectly applied winged eyeliner detached herself from the group of kids close to the pool and planted herself firmly in front of Ethan.

"Who is that?" Gabby said, sounding unreasonably offended that anyone would interrupt the potential train wreck she'd been waiting for.

"Emmie Kristoff," Nittha breathed, as if that name would mean anything to Gabby or me. It didn't. Still watching, Nittha's eyes went wide as Ethan's face sank. "I can't believe she's here. And talking to him."

"Again, who is that?" I asked, echoing Gabby before I could stop myself. I was not supposed to be interested in Ethan or his life. And I was definitely not supposed to care about anyone who put their hand on his arm in a way that implied comfort or familiarity, which Emmie was currently doing.

"She started out as a super popular BookToker, but she's branched out. Like posting about handbags, makeup, travel, you name it—she markets it all now." Nittha shot me a smug expression. Apparently, my interest had not gone unnoticed. "She's also Ethan's ex."

I wanted to look away but couldn't. Whatever Emmie had said, Ethan didn't appear happy. If anything, it seemed like talking to her was draining his battery.

"So, what happened with them?" Gabby half whispered.

"I don't know all the details yet, but I know they broke up because she cheated on him, and the internet is upset."

"I can't imagine having to break up in the public eye," I whispered as Emmie reached out to touch Ethan again. He crossed his arms in front of his chest, leaning ever so slightly away from her hand. I couldn't see Emmie's face from this angle, but she must have noticed him flinch, because she froze mid-gesture. She said something, and Ethan sagged. Not enough to be noticeable to anyone who didn't know him. In fact, if you'd never met him and you saw his face, you'd think he was having a conversation about the weather. But even with what little I knew about him, something seemed wrong.

Gabby shook her head. "I guess it's the hazard of dating someone in our line of work, but—"

"Friends, if I may have your attention, please." The sound of the DJ's voice cutting through the moment made half the people on the terrace jump. I glanced over at the DJ, who was signaling for everyone to quiet down, and then quickly back at Ethan and Emmie. Ethan turned to walk toward where his grandma was seated. Then, standing beside her, he resolutely faced the DJ booth. Emmie continued to watch him from a distance. So much for figuring out what they were talking about . . . Not that it was any of my business.

"I'll get back to the music in a minute, but before I do, I want to invite our fearless leader and founder of TrendCon to the stage. Everyone, please give it up for Mr. Kelly 'Sparkles' Chemerinsky." The DJ put "Sparkles" in air quotes as he referred to maybe the internet's first and biggest influencer. A stout, middle-aged white man in a loud suit jacket, with hair that was a little too disheveled to be casual, jogged onstage and took the mic.

"Hey, hey, hey! How's it going, party people?"

The terrace of people erupted into cheers, and I caught Gabby's eye. Both of us started to roll our eyes. *Party people* felt like a bit of a misnomer for a group of roughly a hundred and fifty people on a business trip.

"Some of you may know that I have a little thing going on where I like to make people's day. And I want to do that again, here, at TrendCon."

The room went silent. Sparkles was notorious for doing things like hiding ten thousand dollars somewhere and letting a hotel clerk find it, or partnering with a car manufacturer to give away cars to an entire bus of people. A small part of me wondered if we were all about to get five hundred dollars' worth of credits to a ritzy hotel restaurant. Next to me, Nittha held her breath.

"This year, I'm announcing my biggest influencer prize yet." The terrace was so still you could have heard a pin drop. Sparkles scanned the room, keeping everyone on edge for way longer than seemed even remotely reasonable, then shouted, "One hundred and fifty thousand dollars for the person who makes the best video about this year's con and Las Vegas!"

It felt like someone had shut off the volume on the terrace. I could tell that people were talking. Some of them looked excited, others disinterested, likely already making more than that on sponsored videos. The rest seemed disappointed. They were probably the weirdos hoping for a scavenger hunt or some other physical activity.

Whatever. None of them mattered. I wanted that prize.

No. I *needed* that prize. With that kind of money, I could make the sort of movie that film schools couldn't ignore. Maybe as important: If I could win that prize, my parents would be done encouraging me to go to business school or join my mom's sorority to build "lifelong connections." A prize like that wasn't just money. It was an endorsement. This prize would prove that I could support myself. Something that would make my parents see me, exactly as BamBam said they would.

"Now, I'd like to invite some friends on the stage with me. Jasmine Ortiz, mayor of Las Vegas; Eric Vanderway, owner of the Stonereel Resort; and Lenny Hampstead, the most famous Elvis in town. If you're getting married here this week, Lenny is your guy," Sparkles said as a stiff-looking woman in a pantsuit who used a lot of hairspray, a man wearing sunglasses in the dark and with a neck that had been done so many times it looked stretched tighter than a drum, and a, well, man dressed as Elvis jogged onto the stage.

Sparkles cleared his throat, then waited for the crowd to quiet before he continued, "Some logistics, and before I forget, please visit the contest website as well for a full listing of rules and other legal jargon. To claim the prize, you'll need to post a video that's no more than a minute and a half on your channels with the hashtag TrendConSparkles—"

"Stupid hashtag." Gabby laughed. I gave her a quiet-I'm-trying-to-listen face.

"—winners will be announced at local screenings held on a Saturday two weeks after the con ends. Be sure to sign up for your region's specific TrendCon newsletter and follow my TrendCon YouTube channel for contest updates."

Next to me, Gabby snorted at the plug for Sparkles's other businesses, but this time she didn't try to talk to me. Usually, I found it exhausting to sit through his pitches, too—Sparkles also led a creator academy, content studio, and networking groups that people could pay to join—but today, I didn't care.

"Our collective audiences will vote for the top three videos. Then myself and our esteemed judges' panel will pick a winner. The winning video will also be run as an ad by the Las Vegas tourism board and be seen by millions of people for the next year. Good luck, everyone!" The room erupted into more cheers as Sparkles jogged offstage waving and smiling and the DJ kicked the music up again. Everyone around me went back to enjoying themselves, but I couldn't.

Just as quickly as Sparkles had given me hope, he'd thrown a wrench in my plans. If people's followers could vote, there was no way I'd win. A video like this was as much a popularity contest as it was about art, and without a social media following, I couldn't even pretend to be popular. For the first time in my life, I wished I had even one account. But maybe that didn't matter. All I needed was a partner. And I was sharing a room with mine—she just didn't know it yet.

DAY 2: RAISING THE STAKES

CHAPTER SIX

YOU KNOW THAT PART IN MOVIES WHERE THE MAIN CHARACTER wakes up thinking about the exact same thing they were obsessing over the night before? I used to watch scenes like that and think they were totally unrealistic. Welp, I was wrong. By the time we went to bed, BamBam had already said no to half of my arguments for entering the contest, but I'd stayed up most of the night dreaming up more of them, and I'd be damned if I didn't attempt those, too.

"Good morning, BamBam," I said as soon as she opened the bathroom door.

"Bah!" BamBam shouted, and clutched her chest in surprise, then blinked at me until she gathered her composure. "You scared me. Why are you up? It's seven a.m. Don't you need to sleep through lunch?" BamBam laughed at her own Jamie-always-sleeps-in joke as she walked toward her bedside table, where her phone was plugged in.

"Ha. Ha. Cinematic genius needs rest," I said, rearranging myself on my pillows.

"Considering how much you sleep, it seems a lot less like genius at rest and more like genius in its final resting place." BamBam started laughing at herself again, then added, "You could sleep through a train on the Blue Line rolling past your window."

I snorted. In reviewing my failure last night, it occurred to me that begging BamBam to please, please, *please* participate in the TrendCon video challenge right after the thirty-seventh person that evening told her that she and Buzzy were wearing the same outfit was probably not the best way to set myself up for success. But today was a new day.

"Speaking of cinematic genius, I know I mentioned the TrendCon video to you last night—"

"You call that mentioning? I'd have called it badgering." BamBam raised a skeptical eyebrow at me.

"Tomato, tom-ah-to." I shrugged, hoping that BamBam would find my answer charming. It worked . . . kind of. Okay, she half smiled, but that was enough for my desperate little mind to keep going. "Anyway, I understand what you were saying about TrendCon not getting free exposure from you—" BamBam opened her mouth to object, so I rushed on, my voice sounding artificially bright as I heaped an extra dose of positive spin on it. "And I totally understand you feeling like Mom and Dad worked hard to set aside funds for SISU, so a prize entry is unnecessary, but there are other reasons besides the money. This could be another great opportunity for us to showcase a different side of your business."

"Baby, how would this be different than any of the other brand partnerships I actually get paid to do?" BamBam pursed her lips to the side, her tone a little less patient than it had been a few moments ago. "That Sparkles man threw a VIP party to try and trick some of the country's biggest creators into giving TrendCon and Las Vegas free advertising. Grandma wasn't born yesterday. Besides, a contest entry at my level just cheapens the brand. That's something creators who are just getting started do, not veterans like me."

Grasping around for something that made an unpaid advertisement sound like a good idea, I cleared my throat. "Maybe they would want you to become the new face of TrendCon."

"Because Kelly Sparkles is eager to retire all of a sudden?" BamBam didn't even try to sound like she was humoring the idea.

"Maybe not TrendCon Las Vegas, but maybe the Chicago regional creator's network could—"

"Jamie." BamBam tilted her head at me as if she couldn't believe that she had to point out how obviously ridiculous that idea was. "I love that you are always looking for new ways to grow my platform, but honestly, we already have a good plan. And I don't want to be the face of a con, not even TrendCon. Just yesterday you pitched me on a much more reasonable way to branch out. I'm not cut out to be the face of an event or a whole city, but a makeup brand? The more I think about it, the more I'm convinced that you are onto something with that."

"But—"

"Baby, if you really want to enter, why don't you and one of your little friends do it?" BamBam's voice sounded exactly like it had when she would watch my siblings and me after school and we got too rowdy. If I didn't give up now, there was a real chance she'd send me to go play in the yard or give me a chore to shut me up.

"Okay. Fine. I'll ask Nittha."

"There you go." BamBam gestured at me and grinned. "Speaking of Nittha, did you get what you needed from her for the video? We should probably start setting up soon, since the panel starts at ten."

"I forgot to ask last night. I'll text her now." My heart sank even though I tried to keep my face neutral as I picked up my phone to text my friends for an emergency coffee. Getting the equipment had slipped my mind because I was excited about the TrendCon prize.

A hint of desperation started to creep through me, and I pushed it back. Maybe Nittha and Cricket would want to partner? I'd never collaborated with anyone other than BamBam. Nittha and I had totally different styles, but this could be a good learning experience. Plus, filming a dog would be a new directorial challenge for me to add to my résumé along with TrendCon prizewinner. Shoving the covers away, I popped out of bed and rushed over to my suitcase so I could get ready for the day. Bam-Bam saying no was only a minor setback.

"Jamie, your phone is ringing," BamBam called, pulling me out of my thoughts.

"Coming," I called back, still surveying the contents of my suitcase.

"It's your mom. I'm gonna answer," BamBam said, this time

truly getting my attention. I turned to sprint back toward my nightstand, trying to catch BamBam before she picked up the phone. I did not want to talk to my mom right now, or almost any other time, for that matter.

"Bam—"

"Hello, June." BamBam's voice sounded too animated to be genuinely excited, but she smiled all the same. "Uh-huh. Jamie is just coming out of the bathroom. You know it's early here." BamBam raised one eyebrow at me in an are-you-ready-to-talk gesture, then said, "Yes, we are really having a blast. And she's already so excited for those college tours. Oh, here she is. We'll catch up later. Yup. Bye-bye."

Holding the phone out to me, BamBam mouthed *S-A-T*. While I appreciated the warning, I would have appreciated her ignoring the call more. Holding my breath, I pulled my shoulders back and took the phone from her.

"Hi, Mom."

"Hi, Messy."

I cringed at the nickname. I was Mom and Dad's messy third child—the one who seemed to constantly need correcting. Then again, they called my older sister Buffie—short for buffalo—because she was big as a kid, so it could be worse. Kind of.

"How's Las Vegas? Are you having fun? Do you like the hotel? I saw pictures online. It looks amazing. I'll bet it's fun." Mom asked and then answered her own questions in rapid succession.

"It's been fun so far. I've mostly been working, so I've only been to the pool once. But Nittha and Gabby are here, which has been cool." Immediately, I regretted telling her they were here. I loved my mom, but if there was an annual prize for helicopter parents, she and Dad would win every year. The internet was her greatest tool, and the fact that I didn't have my own social media was probably killing her. Not because she wanted me to document my life per se, but it meant that she couldn't watch my social life and make sure it was on track for the future she and Dad had planned for me. As it was, without social media, she had to stick to refreshing my grade portal at school and watching my phone's shared location dot not move all day.

To my parents, my future was to attend a well-respected, affordable college—ideally studying for a degree with good practical application, like economics or business. While there, I'd meet my husband, so I could be married by twenty-seven with a house close to them. Also, I would join Mom's sorority, as my sister had, or my dad's community service organization, like my brother. And above all else, I would do this without embarrassing them.

"Working, huh?" Mom said, sounding half distracted. She was likely making her way over to one of Cricket's pages so she could stalk me. After a beat, she added, "What's on the docket for tonight? Something fun, I hope."

"I'm gonna go to dinner with Gabby and Nittha, since Bam-Bam is going on her mystery adventure with Gregory." I grinned over at BamBam, who was watching me from the mirror over the desk as she organized her lipsticks.

"Well, that seems nice. If you find out where BamBam is going, be sure to text the family chat." Mom's tone sounded like she thought it was about as nice as a trip to a crowded supermarket. "Listen, I don't want to keep you long since I know you've got plans, but I happened to check the SAT practice test portal, and it looks like you haven't logged in yet, so I wanted to remind you. If you have free time, check in there. Fifteen minutes of practice is better than no minutes. Also, I talked to Dad, and he said you still hadn't sent him your essay for SISU."

"I'll get to it." My heart slammed around in my rib cage as I tried to think of a way to wiggle out of her plan. "Actually, I meant to talk to you. I was thinking I might try something else this summer instead of the internship at your office."

"Oh? What's that?"

"Maybe something film related, like seeing if I could work on-set for a commercial filming company. You know, to try something new."

There was a long pause on the other end of the line, and I imagined my mom's face as she processed what I was saying. Anytime I mentioned doing something that didn't seem sufficiently business-y with my time, her expression grew tight, as if she were sucking on a lemon.

"Well, we can talk about it more later." Mom's voice was artificially bright. "After all, you can never have too many accolades on your résumé when looking for that first job. Why don't we focus on applying to college, getting that B up in physics, and working on that SAT prep for now?"

Mom kept talking, but her voice had gone fuzzy. I did not want to talk about SAT prep while I was taking time off school for a work vacation, especially when it felt like I was practicing to go to school for a thing I didn't actually want to study.

Glancing over at the table where BamBam was sitting, I

caught her eye. She raised an eyebrow at me, and I shook my head to indicate that things were not going well.

BamBam nodded once like a Mafia don in a mob movie and then projected her voice. "Jamie, I hate to interrupt but we've got to go."

On the other end of the line, Mom paused, clearly hearing BamBam from across the room. After a moment, she said, "That's your cue."

"Yeah, BamBam says it's time to go." I tried to keep the relief out of my voice.

"Okay, well, try and sneak in a little homework. Do it by the pool! I saw a picture of you on Cricket's profile. Where did that swimsuit come from?"

"Tell your mama you love her." BamBam started again as soon as my eyes got wide at the mention of Cricket's socials. Called it.

"Okay, Mom, I'll try to work on physics love you bye." I said all of this in one fast breath, my finger already hovering over the red End Call button.

"Alright. Love you, too. Have fun."

I pressed the button as soon as she got that last word out, then chucked my phone toward the other side of the bed. Leaning back on a stack of pillows, I closed my eyes, the gnawing pit in my stomach opening up wider. I had to find a way out of Mom and Dad's plans, or I would spend the next five years of my life doing things I didn't want to do and living a life that made my parents happy and me miserable.

I was officially desperate to win this contest. They couldn't say no if I was a winner.

"I'm so sorry, but I'm way too slammed. I have a big branded post coming out next week, and I'm super behind," Nittha said, sounding genuinely disappointed as she took a massive gulp of the caffeine-free, sugar-free, dairy-free, coffee-ish drink that I'd gotten her from Beginners Luck, the coffee bar in the hotel's lobby. I'd hoped to bribe her with an overpriced drink. Apparently, my idea of a bribe needed some work.

"It's okay." I sighed, trying not to look like I was going to cry, which I low-key felt like doing. Instead, I shrugged and focused my gaze on my own coffee-free drink.

"What about you, Gabby? Maybe you two could be partners?" Nittha perked up.

I turned to Gabby and smiled hopefully right as her face fell. "I wish! A couple of other disability and difference creators asked if I wanted to join their group while you were dealing with the whole Buzzy-BamBam-dress snafu. We figured there'd be strength in numbers. Sorry."

"It totally makes sense for you to team up with them. No big deal," I lied. It felt like a very big deal, but slowly melting into a pathetic heap on the highly polished floor of a coffee shop seemed a little dramatic, so pretending it was fine was my only remaining option. "Don't worry about it. I'll figure it out."

Gabby's brow furrowed. "Is there a reason why you don't start your own social media account for this?"

"I thought about it, but with the audience voting, I'd basically be a long shot." I slumped to the side as Nittha nodded in agreement.

"Oh, duh." Gabby stopped and shook her head to indicate that she knew the question was silly. "I'm sure we have to know someone with a sizable following who wants to enter but doesn't have a plan yet." The unusual brightness in Gabby's tone confirmed that I was screwed, even if no one wanted to admit it.

"Who knows, maybe your future husband, Ethan, will want to work with you, and this will be how you fall in love," Nittha said, her voice sounding dreamy.

"Oh god." Gabby sighed, clutching her lemon-berry iced latte, which had also been my treat and another useless bribe. "Not that again."

"Seriously, don't think about it anymore. I'll figure it out," I said, ignoring the little voice in my head that was almost desperate enough to partner with Ethan or Buzzy at this stage. Nittha and Gabby exchanged glances like they didn't entirely believe me, and I jumped to change the subject. "Are you two gonna go to that go-kart thing?"

"Yes," Gabby replied too quickly. I had forgotten how much that girl loved fun-complex games. Give her a claw-and-stuffie machine, darts and balloons, or anything that dispensed tickets, and she would be happy for the rest of her days.

"If Gabby wants to, I'll go, I guess," Nittha said, with the appropriate amount of enthusiasm for an under-twenty-ones TrendCon activity planned by the convention organizers to keep us out of the casinos and looking like we were having a moderately fun time should anyone decide to post about it. "You?"

"Maybe. It's right after BamBam's panel, so I'll see if she

needs me to do anything first." At this rate, I might have to go go-karting to find some niche creator to step in front of my camera. Noticing my friends exchanging another set of pitying glances, I changed the subject again before my desperation started to waft off me like a smell in a cartoon. "Nittha, should we go get those lights? BamBam seems to think she'll need over an hour to do glam."

"Why does she need more than an hour?" Gabby raised an eyebrow as the three of us started to make our way to the elevator bank. "She must be really serious about taking this rivalry to the next level after she and Buzzy showed up in the same outfit."

I smirked. "Oh, you have no idea."

CHAPTER SEVEN

THE JOKE WAS ENTIRELY ON ME. AS IT TURNED OUT, BAMBAM DID need a lot of time to film her beauty routine. In fact, she needed so much time that I finally had to show her how to turn off my two cameras and Nittha's lights, then go down to set up to film the panel. I'd only just finished begging the con videographers to let me put a GoPro at the back of the room with them when attendees and panelists started arriving for Silver Influencers: Secrets to Embracing Your Age.

Picking a spot toward the right-back of the room, I walked a few seats in and dropped into a chair, then took out my phone so I could both monitor my video feed and film BamBam from a different angle once things got started. Maybe, if I won the TrendCon challenge, I'd buy myself another camera. Clearly, I needed one if BamBam was going to film more of these kinds of day-in-the-life—

"Funny seeing you here." Ethan's voice was tinged with humor as he slid into the seat next to me.

Fifteen thoughts slammed through my mind simultaneously. Why was he here? Was Buzzy here, too? The room wasn't full, so why was he in my row with his camera out? And why did he smell good? Spicy and clean at the same time.

Okay, the answer to that last question wasn't entirely necessary for my survival. I shook my head and tried to refocus on getting the answers that might keep both of us alive. "Why are you here?"

"Same reason as you." Ethan shrugged. "On the upside, they aren't wearing the same thing today."

"What?" I glanced over at the little knot of people BamBam was standing near more closely. In her bright-yellow sleeveless kaftan she was easy to spot. Sure enough, there was Buzzy in her customary taupe shirtdress. The two of them were as far apart as humanly possible from one another and sending each other intermittent frosty glares. I whipped my head around to face Ethan. "Do you want to be excommunicated from your family? Don't sit so close to me."

"It's the best angle." He said this with a completely flat affect, but behind his deadpan expression, a smile was lurking. "Are you going to enter the contest?"

"A, you can't sit here, so don't try and distract me. B, I'm trying but Mini doesn't want to enter," I answered, ticking points off on my fingers.

"A, I'll move once the panel starts. They are too busy hating each other to notice us right now." Ethan paused, a half smile finally surfacing when I laughed, then continued looking at me like he'd won a little victory. "And B, why won't Mini do it?"

"About twenty-seven reasons, some of which are valid. Free

advertising irks her. Plus, she won't admit it, but even if we split the one hundred and fifty grand, it's enough money that I'd have options outside of being beholden to my parents after graduation. That would probably put her in a tricky spot with them because they don't exactly see filmmaking in my future, but—"

I cut myself off as I watched his expression become pensive, as if he was actually thinking about my predicament. Why was I telling him this anyway? Shaking my head, I pivoted. "Actually. The details don't matter. She won't do it. I don't have an audience or accounts to win on my own, obviously. I tried Nittha, but she's too busy with another project, and Gabby's already working with other people. Hence, I'm still figuring it out."

"Alright, gentlefolk, we are gonna get started here if you could settle in. A few housekeeping rules . . ." someone in a TrendCon staff T-shirt said into the mic, calling the room to order.

I raised an eyebrow at Ethan, in case he'd missed his cue to get up, then unlocked my phone to check my camera feed. Hopefully, no one had knocked into it and messed up my angle. The event camerapeople would not be happy with me if I tried to sneak back there to fix it.

I glanced over right as Ethan leaned forward to catch my eye, placing his elbows on his knees.

"I'm gonna enter. If you want, we could work together and split the prize." His voice was soft, as if he hadn't proposed that I break literally every rule my family had ever laid out for me.

I searched his face for any hint that this was a joke. It had to be. He held my gaze, his honey-brown eyes showing no signs that this was a trick. Instead, he appeared perfectly comfortable. Hopeful, even.

Maybe it was the way he was watching me, but for a brief moment, a tiny sliver of my mind wondered if it could work. If the idea wasn't as obviously bad as it sounded. After all, we both clearly thought our grandmas were ridiculous for holding this grudge. And he did seem genuinely nice. And a little funny, even.

Ethan nudged my knee with his, the touch sending sparks across my skin. I pointedly ignored the prickling sensation where my body was trying to memorize his touch.

Stay away from that boy. BamBam's words from the plane crept into my thoughts. I didn't know anything about his style. I hadn't even seen his videos. Looking over at him, I said the thing I knew I had to say all along. "That is another terrible idea."

Ethan's face faltered, and then his easy smile returned. "Well, if you change your mind . . ."

He shrugged and leaned back in his chair. The shift in his expression happened so fast that if it hadn't been for the way his eyes changed, like he didn't make the baseball team or something but was trying to be chill about it, I would have thought I imagined it.

Trying not to let his disappointment become my own, I reassured myself that I'd find another way to enter the competition. This really was for the best. I turned my attention to my phone, just in time to see a text from my dad.

Dad: What do your grandma and a 90-degree angle have in common?

Ever since I'd gotten a phone, my dad had become the king of corny math jokes. I was pretty sure he had a book of them somewhere. Right as I started to text back an answer, his response popped up.

They are both always right. Ha!

I snorted at how bad that one was as another text rolled in, taking my smile with it.

Wanted to send a little math joke since your mom said you are working on your physics and SATs today.

Hope you are having fun with BamBam!

The corner of my brain that was desperate to get away from my parents' all-consuming life plans began to scream that I had to find a way out, while the part of my mind that was logical seemed to disappear altogether. Ethan's words echoed in my head. *If you change your mind . . .*

"Actually. Yes, let's work together." The words were out of my mouth so fast that I barely had time to process what I was thinking, let alone what I was saying. I watched as Ethan's head jerked to face me.

"What?"

"I need a partner, and for whatever reason, you are willing to share prize money, so let's work together," I said, forcing my tone to sound matter-of-fact and not like the rush of panic I was feeling suggesting this.

"No, I mean, I heard you." Ethan shook his head, his hair falling into his eyes. "It's just . . . you literally said no thirty seconds ago. Are you joking?"

"Totally serious," I said, surprised by the resoluteness in my voice. "I've had a chance to think about it, and us collaborating makes sense."

"I don't . . ."

"Do you want to work together or not?" I pulled up the camera feed to check it one more time before I started using my phone to film the panel, trying to sound like I wasn't the one who had to get down off my high horse.

"Yes, I guess. I'm confused, though—"

"Are you going to the go-kart thing after this?" I whispered over the sound of Evelyn, the middle-aged moderator with a voice like a worn-out gym sock, who began asking the panelists to introduce themselves and share their journeys to influencing.

"Yes?" Ethan's answer sounded like a question, as if he was trying to figure me out.

"Good. We'll plan there. You should move now." A small, bemused smile crossed Ethan's face, as if all of this was a little funny to him. It was the kind of smile that felt like we had an inside joke, a secret, or some other special thing between us. I gave my head a shake and faced the front of the room, then held up my phone. I didn't need to think about what that smile meant right now.

"You've got a good angle. My grandma will be jealous," Ethan whispered. I turned and found his face a few inches from mine as he leaned forward to see my screen.

"Why are you still here?" I whispered back, tilting my phone away from him.

"It's too late to move now. They've already started." Ethan grinned mischievously. He opened his mouth to say something right as Evelyn asked the second question.

"Now that we all know how you got into this business, I want to ask—new tech can feel daunting, not to mention all the jargon. How are you staying up-to-date with the changes?"

"Such a good question," Gregory jumped in. Without thinking, Ethan and I looked at one another, his face echoing exactly what I was feeling. This was everyone's favorite question to ask older people, like somehow the answer would be any different coming from younger people.

"You know, I often search for how-to videos. Or sometimes I ask a friend. If I'm still in the store where I bought my phone or computer, I'll check and see if there is someone there who can show me the basics . . ." Gregory began rattling off all the ways literally anyone would learn how to use a new piece of technology. Clearly too nice for his own good. It must have been all those years of teaching.

I focused on filming the panel. The footage would be shaky since I didn't have anything to stabilize the camera, but it would be good enough to use as B-roll to hide cuts later. I invaded Ethan's space to get a better view, then realized that BamBam was speaking about me.

". . . and, y'all, don't be afraid to ask the young people in your life. I'm extremely blessed to have three wonderful grandbabies who help me out all the time. One of them is here now. Jamie, baby, where are you?" BamBam craned her neck as she began to scan the room. My nerves rattled. I could not stand up with Ethan next to me.

"I agree with Mini. I have a delightful grandson who is here as well," Buzzy said, causing BamBam to throw her a sideways glance. I grimaced. BamBam had so little subtlety in her facial expression that it felt like the entire room could practically hear her yelling, *Get your own ideas*, without her having to say it.

"Y'all, I don't want to spoil anything, but Jamie has some great video ideas, too." BamBam plowed on, ignoring everything Buzzy said. "Jamie, why don't you wave so the people can see you?"

I felt Ethan stiffen. Meanwhile, I began to wonder if a sinkhole would appear and swallow me if I prayed hard enough. With each second that that didn't happen, the room got quieter. Finally, I gritted my teeth and raised my hand as Buzzy said, "Ethan, hon, where are you?"

Next to me, I could almost feel Ethan's energy joining me in my silent sinkhole prayer. To his credit, he wasn't foolish enough to raise his hand when mine was already in the air. The most desperate part of my brain hoped that BamBam didn't have her contacts in and therefore wouldn't be able to see who was sitting next to me, even though I knew that was impossible. She wouldn't have even made it into the room without—

"There she is. That is my brilliant granddaughter Jamie . . ." BamBam trailed off as she registered the exact thing I feared.

"And there is my handsome grandson Ethan." The generally chipper tone of Buzzy's voice died off somewhere around the second syllable of Ethan's name as she processed what BamBam had figured out roughly two seconds earlier. While I can't prove this scientifically, I'm almost certain that my heart stopped, and my entire body went cold for a full minute. When I finally heard BamBam's voice, it was as if I were outside of my body. Like she'd already murdered me, and I was a ghost hearing her words.

"Young person, you want to tell me why you are sitting next to my grandbaby?" BamBam arched an eyebrow. As if suddenly remembering she was in front of an audience, she put a you-know-better smile on her face and said, "Jamie, this is like school. You gotta watch out. He's probably trying to copy off you."

"Ethan would never." Buzzy's voice was miffed, like she'd just missed out on a good flash sale. "No one in this family has ever copied anyone."

"I wouldn't go that far," BamBam grumbled. "You were wearing my outfit last night."

Half the room erupted into chuckles as Buzzy sputtered. Ethan glanced over at me, as if we had received the same telepathic message. The only hope we had of salvaging this panel was to separate and pray that they got distracted. Giving me a quick half smile, he feigned complete surprise and jumped up. Raising his voice loud enough for the room to hear, he said, "So that's who you are! I won't copy your outfit if you don't copy mine, okay?"

"I'll be watching you," I called, pointing two fingers at my eyes and then back at him as the room laughed. Ethan slowly backed away.

"I didn't copy your outfit," Buzzy said, still clearly irritated by my grandmother's accusation. "Lady and House sent—"

"Oh, Buzzy, don't get your nose out of joint. We all know it was an accident. We're joking around." Gregory frowned. "You two are so dramatic, and I say that as someone who is an expert in drama." He rolled his eyes. "Evelyn, what's the next question?"

Evelyn laughed, then cleared a dirty sock from their throat and asked, "So, as about everyone here knows—other than the two grandchildren in this room—we get tired a little more easily as we age. How do you all manage your energy and your filming schedule with the needs of an aging body?"

The space next to me felt surprisingly empty without Ethan. I tried to fight the urge to see where he was in the room. If he was badgering some other poor unsuspecting grandchild in a different row or if he'd snuck out entirely. I waited until Bam-Bam, Buzzy, and Gregory were thoroughly engaged in a discussion about managing their energy levels—they were all big fans of the micro-nap—then threw a quick glance over my shoulder.

As soon as I did, I regretted it. Ethan was standing at the back of the room, staring directly at me. Feeling my face flush, I mouthed the one thing I knew would give me the upper hand. *I told you so.*

Ethan raised an eyebrow and leaned against a wall, a small smile crossing his lips, before he mouthed back something that looked suspiciously like *Worth it.*

He turned his attention back to the front of the room, leaving me with more questions and absolutely no upper hand. I started filming BamBam again but couldn't focus. By the end of the panel, I realized that the only thing I knew about him for certain was that there was more to Ethan Wyatt than I'd anticipated. And that I'd just agreed to something that could get us both into a lot of trouble.

CHAPTER EIGHT

I SAT IN THE TRENDCON CHARTERED PARTY BUS AS WE HURTLED toward Kart World and tried not to feel sick. When I'd agreed to Ethan's proposal, I'd been peak desperate. Now, with a few hours and one absolute disaster of a panel behind me, I was starting to second-guess our plan. It wasn't that I didn't want the money; I just wasn't entirely sure how I was going to pull this off.

"I'm glad you're here," Nittha said, turning around in her seat to grin at me as the bus's party lights twinkled above her head. "I was so sad Cricket wasn't allowed to come, but then you surprised us, and BamBam clearly needed an emotional-support pup after this morning's 'incident,' so this all worked out perfectly."

Nittha put air quotes around the word *incident* as if that would somehow soften the blow of mentioning what the internet was already calling #GrannieGate. What Nittha didn't know—and I had no intention of telling her—was that while BamBam was upstairs with a cold compress on her forehead and Cricket snuggled at her side, drafting a rage email to the con organizers about including Buzzy without telling her, I was preparing to go behind her back with Ethan.

I glanced in Ethan's direction. He was sitting a few rows up from us, crammed between the window and Sterling James, who was chatting with him a mile a minute. It struck me as strange that Sterling wasn't sitting next to Emmie, but then again, if Sterling was as savvy as Ethan said, he was probably trying to avoid being in too many pictures with Emmie while hoping to be seen supporting her jilted ex. Empathy was good for brands. Messy friend drama, less so.

"We're here," Gabby sing-songed, an uncharacteristically large grin spreading across her face as we pulled up outside a small, tired-looking purple-and-red building labeled **Kart World**. Next to the building stood a zigzagging racetrack with a few karts already running around it. Nittha and I exchanged surprised glances as Gabby popped out of her seat, nearly knocking other people out of the aisle. Briefly looking over her shoulder at us, she waved. "Hurry up. Fun awaits."

"It's only fun if you know how to drive." Nittha sighed and pushed herself out of her seat.

"I'm not sure it is that fun for anyone other than Gabby, even if you do know how to drive," I whispered.

Nittha stifled a giggle as the two of us stepped off the bus. Unlike literally everyone else who lived in Los Angeles, Nittha didn't drive, which meant she was here strictly as moral support for me and Gabby. Okay, Gabby mostly. I wasn't planning on doing much driving. Catching sight of Gabby at a coffee cart, she perked up and pointed. "I'm gonna get one. You want?"

"I'm good, but thanks." I smiled and waited until Nittha had bounced off in Gabby's direction, then scanned the crowd of people for Ethan and Sterling. I spotted Sterling almost immediately, his bright-red shirt billowing as he gestured emphatically at a group of people, including Emmie. Like the last time I'd seen her, she was perfectly made-up. Even sitting on the edge of a picnic table in the parking lot of a fun complex, she looked stylish. She didn't seem upset this time, though. If anything, she appeared to be in her element, surrounded by people who looked equally flawless.

Not that Emmie's feelings were any of my business. Hell, Ethan's business wasn't even my business if it didn't have to do with this video. I shook my head to clear my mind, then spotted him. He was alone in a quieter corner of the outdoor complex, leaning against the go-kart track railing with his back to the party. He was standing mostly in the shadows, wearing a tie-dye gym tank top that had big armholes, white shorts, and sneakers with bright-green high socks. This was what he wore when it was hot outside?

His outfit looked ridiculous, but with the dappled sunlight filtering through the racetrack's shade overhang playing across his face, he was cast in the kind of glow that was typically reserved for people in art house films. His jaw and cheekbones took on a harder edge while the breeze tossed his hair around carelessly. Watching him from this distance felt different. Less like he was the boy next door and more like he was the kind of forbidden fruit that you were desperate to taste.

Then he turned, and recognition crossed his face as he aimed that casual smile at me. A thousand butterflies in my stomach tried to make me sick. Taking a deep breath, I waved at him in a weird, jerky little burst, then immediately stopped. Why was I waving? It wasn't like I was on a ship going out to sea. Ethan could clearly see me.

Exhaling, I started walking toward him, weaving my hands together in front of me and demanding that the butterflies in my system pull it together. I didn't need to be nervous. This was a business deal, nothing more.

"Hey," he said as soon as I approached him.

"Hey." I did my best to lean against the railing, careful to keep enough distance between us that it could seem like an accident if someone snapped a picture that BamBam happened to see. I waited for Ethan to say something, but instead he just looked around as if the parking lot of a fun complex in the middle of a Vegas strip mall was the most fascinating place on earth. Finally, I broke down and asked, "Before we officially do this, something's been bugging me. Why did you offer to work with me?"

"I think you're cute."

My brain malfunctioned a bit before I came to my senses. I snorted. "Sure. What's the real reason?"

Ethan took in a sharp breath, then exhaled slowly. The expression on his face said he hoped I'd be distracted by that joke, even as he prepared to answer the question. Checking over his shoulder, he turned his attention back to me. "I don't really want to hang out with the group I used to go to these things with. You and your friends aren't close to my old circle."

He paused, moving his head from side to side as if debating how much more he should share. If what Gabby and Nittha said about his breakup was true, it made a lot more sense that he was hanging around us. "You need help, and I need new friends."

I nodded, deciding not to pry any further. "So, we're a match made in desperate-people heaven?"

"Pretty much." Half of Ethan's mouth turned up in an ironic smile.

I sighed. "So, how do you want to do this?"

"Do what?"

"Make our video."

"I guess we should figure out our idea before we do anything else." Ethan's forehead wrinkled as if he was surprised that I hadn't tried to backtrack on our agreement. "How do you usually work with people? Any deal-breakers?"

My brain went fuzzy with nerves as Ethan kept asking questions. I had absolutely no experience directing anyone other than myself and BamBam. Worse, I didn't know if I could describe what I did to anyone else. For someone who wanted to be a director, this seemed like a massive oversight.

"Truthfully? I have no idea how I like to collaborate. The only person I've ever worked with is BamBam." Ethan's eyebrows disappeared underneath his hair, and heat flooded my cheeks. "Don't judge. I don't have my own social media, remember?"

"Not judging." Ethan held his hands up in a pacifying gesture. "Just surprised. At the pool, you seemed so serious about editing that I assumed you had a bunch of partnerships and projects going."

"I wish. I want to study to be a director someday." I watched him for a moment, trying to decide if he was being sincere. Nothing about his expression felt like he was waiting to spring a mean joke on me. "Anyway. I don't actually know what I'm doing—I mean, I know what I'm doing with a camera, but not with other people and . . ." I paused as Ethan's expression shifted from surprised to confused. Taking a steadying breath, I tried again. "What I'm trying to say is, I'm new to working with people, so you might have to tell me stuff sometimes."

"Communication. Got it." The corner of Ethan's mouth twisted into a small smile. "If it makes you feel any better, I haven't done much collaboration either. We can teach each other."

"Thanks." For a minute, we stared at each other, an unspoken understanding passing between us. I wasn't sure how or when, but something had changed. Ethan's eye contact felt more deliberate as our quiet understanding turned into a low hum of electricity. Ethan licked his lips and narrowed his eyes at me. My pulse sped up. The urge to reach out and trace the skin along the hem of his tank top crossed my mind, and I was suddenly very grateful for the space between us.

The screech of tires on cement disrupted whatever was happening to us. Ethan blinked and cleared his throat. I pushed my sudden and inexplicable interest in his collarbone out of my mind and continued. "So, I was thinking, and you can say no, but I did some internet sleuthing, and Kelly Sparkles is from

Las Vegas. It's why he has at least one big event here every year. What if we made the theme of our video a love letter to Las Vegas?"

"Okay." Ethan nodded slowly, his face drawn in concentration. "Tell me more."

"Like, we'll take all the establishing shots of TrendCon, smiling, happy people, flashy product demos, and all that, but then we can film you doing Vegas-y stuff—not only the tourist activities, but some things off the beaten path, too."

"Make all of Vegas the star of the show since Sparkles loves it. I like it." Ethan smiled briefly. Then his expression changed. "Wait. Why wouldn't we film you, too?"

"Because I don't have a social media account or any kind of following." I shrugged.

Skepticism was written all over his face. "But you are here at the con and working on the video. It'll be weird if it's only me."

"It'll be even weirder if I suddenly appear out of nowhere." I furrowed my brow at Ethan.

"But you're not out of nowhere. You're the creative behind one of the most popular influencers over sixty."

"People will know it's me behind the camera if they read the credits. I don't need to be a director who makes cameos."

"Why not? The most famous directors in the world do that." Ethan narrowed his eyes at me. "Plus, I'm not an actor or a tour guide. I explain car trouble on the internet."

He did have a point about the director-cameo thing. But I wasn't going to give up years of anonymity and the ability to avoid an additional metric ton of parental scrutiny, not to mention the option to bury imperfect work, that easily. If my face was in it, there was no taking it back. The internet is forever. I'd be defined by this video. If we lost, it'd be a humiliating mark on my digital résumé and further proof to my parents that I should be an accountant or something. If we won, then I'd include my name in the credits.

I shook my head. "It won't be weird, and you won't have to become an actor overnight. We'll use cuts and music to make it interesting." Ethan sucked in a breath as if he wanted to argue some more, and I rushed to add, "It'll be great, I promise. I'll even do the editing to prove it to you."

For a minute, Ethan looked like he might try to disagree with me, then thought the better of it. "Alright. Did you have a first location in mind?"

"I googled unusual attractions, and the Stonereel is super close to this aquarium with a shark tunnel."

Ethan snorted. "You sure are prepared."

A goofy grin crossed my face, and I tried to hide it. These kinds of compliments were dangerous. This was a boy who snorted because of me. The sound alone should have been the least appealing thing in the world. Instead, my brain was really out here thinking it was adorable. I blamed the tank top. I gave my head another shake and caught sight of Gabby and Nittha headed our way. We needed to wrap this up quickly.

"I try. Speaking of preparation, our grandmothers cannot find out," I said, putting extra emphasis on the syllable *not* in *cannot*, just to make myself clear.

"It can be our secret, for now." Ethan leaned toward me conspiratorially. I hadn't noticed his height before. He was a full head taller than me. When we stood like this, I could see his eyes more clearly. In this light, they appeared darker, more like chestnut with flecks of amber than honey brown.

I took a slight step to the side to put some distance between myself and his eyes. "Do you think you could get away from your grandma this afternoon?"

"Yes." Ethan straightened up again. "When we get back, I could probably tell her I'm having lunch with friends. Would that work for you?"

"Yeah. I'll tell Mini the same thing."

"Cool. Meet you outside of the main hall once the TrendCon lunch starts?" Ethan smiled and leaned off the railing as he spotted my friends headed our way.

"We should both try and take establishing shots of the con until then."

He nodded.

"Hey, friends," Nittha said, a massive grin working its way across her face as her eyes went back and forth between me and Ethan. "What ya talkin' 'bout?"

"Nothing much." Ethan shrugged, half a smile playing with the corners of his mouth as he fibbed. "Just working out our grandma-based differences."

"Oh." Nittha sounded as if that was the least interesting thing she'd heard in a week. Turning toward me, she held a drink out and said, "I know you said you didn't want anything, but they have a Beginners Luck over there. So here. Blueberry matcha latte with extra whipped cream and chocolate drizzle, iced."

"Thank you," I said, trying not to smirk. I suspected that she'd picked up my favorite not-coffee so that she and Gabby had a reason to walk over and find out what Ethan and I were talking about.

I closed my eyes and inhaled a deep whiff of sweet, earthy goodness then grinned up at Ethan, who was watching me with complete surprise.

"What?"

"Nothing," he said, pushing his hair out of his eyes. "I didn't have you pegged for a ten-dollar-coffee drinker."

"First, matcha is a tea, and second, it's eight fifty, and it tastes like gold," I said, trying not to feel judged by my drink order. "What did you think I'd drink?"

"Black coffee. Isn't that what all artists drink?"

"Only the ones who are sad on the inside," Gabby said, waving her lemon-berry iced latte at him.

Ethan snort-laughed. "I guess I'll be sad on the inside and rich on the outside, then."

"You don't even have plain coffee, so really you're neither right now," Nittha said, pointing her usual technically-coffee raspberry whipped-oat-milk decaf mocha at him.

Ethan opened his mouth to say something, when an exhausted-looking person with a clipboard, wearing a purple Kart World shirt whose better days had been sometime in 2017, cupped a hand over their mouth. "TrendCon group, we are ready for you. If you can step this way and grab your wristbands."

The four of us turned and joined the crowd of teens shuffling toward the wristband line as the employee began listing the rules in a way that sounded like their battery was low.

"You'll be racing in teams of four. Fastest team wins bragging rights and free food from our snack bar." The employee glanced up for a fraction of a second. "Helmets and seat belts must be worn while driving. And remember, if you post on social media, use the hashtags"—the employee looked down at the clipboard—"TrendConLV and KartWorld . . . also with an LV. Okay, go pick your teams, and we'll get started soon."

"Cool. So . . ." Ethan drew the word *so* out. "Can I be on your team? I'm a great driver."

"I don't drive, but you all should be on a team together." Nittha smiled up at me and batted her eyelashes as if she was creating some kind of romantic moment for us instead of dooming me to a high-pressure driving situation with a boy who loved cars and had only recently agreed to work with me. Not that Nittha knew that part.

"I actually wasn't planning on—" I started, when Gabby cut me off.

"Excellent. You're both on the team." Gabby's face went stone-cold serious as she did some calculation. "We just need—"

"Sorry, babes. I'm on Ethan's team." Sterling appeared next to Ethan's shoulder as if by magic. He was waving at a group of three people with bad haircuts and shoulders wide enough to make it clear they were fitness influencers. Turning to Ethan, he let his smile fall as he said, "You know I like to win, and they are clearly not equipped to do that. So, who else should be on our team?"

"I'm already on Jamie's team." Ethan shrugged and gestured to me. Sterling looked over, noticing me for possibly the first time ever and sizing me up like he was reconsidering leaving the gym rats.

"Is it my team, though?" I laughed, hoping to ease some of

the tension. Sure, I'd been wanting to talk to Sterling. But not like this. I wasn't a great driver like Ethan. The whole moving-vehicle thing still stressed me out. I'd only gotten my license last year because my parents made me so I could get to SAT classes and my piano lessons over the summer. My mom had sworn that I'd be grateful later, but I was still waiting for that moment to arrive. As it stood, I wished right now I were Nittha, who'd wandered off with my camera to film god knew what. The last thing I wanted was to be responsible for anything if Sterling didn't win. BamBam didn't need me making enemies of younger beauty influencers she might want to connect with. And she certainly didn't need to make an enemy of Sterling James over go-karts.

"And I'm also on Jamie's team," Gabby said, crossing her arms and sizing him up like she would be ready to try out some judo if he said anything about us. While I appreciated the protective instinct, her help was the opposite of helpful right now.

Taking in Ethan's and Gabby's stances, Sterling smiled and turned to me, extending a hand, "Well okay, then. Team Captain Jamie, I don't think we've met before. What do you do?"

"You wouldn't have heard of me." I smiled and shook his hand even as my nerves started to fray under the weight of his perfectly lined gaze. "I'm the producer for Ms. Mini's Makeup—"

"Oh my god, I love her. Ms. Mini is who I want to be when I grow up. Icon." Sterling grinned, then glanced over at Ethan. Toning his smile down a notch, he added, "Not that your grandma isn't great, too." Returning his attention to me, he said, "After we win, Jamie, you and I should talk."

Ethan shrugged. "You and Mini have matching energy. It makes sense."

"He gets me." Sterling smiled over at Ethan, then grew serious again. "What's the plan here?"

"I think we do this like a track-and-field relay," Gabby said, leaning in, her competitive spirit growing more intense. Great. Now I had to contend with pressure from two people hyperfixated on winning when I barely had the skills to parallel park. When no one immediately responded, she rolled her eyes and said, "The person who goes first is the second fastest and the one with the best reflexes for the start signal. I'm gonna guess that is you, Sterling." Gabby paused for confirmation and Sterling shrugged, a smug smile tugging at the corners of his lips. "Alright, then your third fastest goes—that would be me. Our goal is to give the slowest, Jamie, a head start. Fourth is your fastest. Ethan, since you are a car guy, that's you. You'll have to make up any ground we lose on Jamie's leg." Gabby grimaced at me, then added, "Sorry, James, but you know it's true."

"It's okay. I know—"

"But you won't lose ground, will you, Jamie?" Sterling interrupted me with a smile, but it sounded like a threat. He had his phone out, ostensibly filming us for his channel. Noticing me noticing the camera, he added, "Don't worry. I'll add you all as collaborators if we win."

Great. Now I also had to contend with the fact that my mother might see me lose *and* a BamBam × Sterling video might not be in the cards. Cold sweat cropped up on my back as I tried to think of how to respond. "I'll do my best, but—"

"Jamie's gonna do fine," Ethan said, his tone perfectly even. Tilting his chin at the helmet counter, he added, "You should go get the helmets."

Sterling narrowed his eyes at Ethan for a second, the two of them having some kind of wordless conversation. Then his face relaxed. Turning, he held out an elbow to Gabby. "I don't want to carry four helmets. Shall we?"

Gabby seemed about as charmed by Sterling's invitation to get sweaty, used helmets as she would be to spend a winter in Antarctica, but she still looped her arm through his. "Sure. I want the black ones, though. No red sparkles."

"We can talk about that." Sterling smiled as the pair of them headed off.

As soon as they were out of hearing distance, I shifted back to Ethan. "I know Mini needs my help with Sterling, but I'm not a fast driver. In fact, driving makes me nervous. What if I find another way to get in his good graces? Maybe you could get that girl who does videos breaking down operas . . ."

"She is on the fitness-influencer team." Ethan bit down on his lip to hide his smile. It was the kind of smile that made me wish he'd look somewhere else. I didn't need to get used to that smile. Taking a deep breath, he added, "Listen. Your grandma wants to reach younger audiences, and Sterling is literally the most competitive person I know. We win this, you win your grandma a meeting with Sterling. He already said he wanted to chat with you. Just gotta keep that momentum going, alright?"

"Yes, but that means I have to win, Ethan."

"I know. Don't worry. I'll help you." We locked eyes. Instinctively, I started to trace a line between his freckles, memorizing the faint pattern sprinkled across his nose and cheeks.

"Okay." I took a half step back, putting a little space between myself and those freckles. "What do I need to do?"

"Depends. I think Team Gym Rats will be our biggest competition," Ethan said, glancing over at the team. All four of them were stone-faced as they gazed over at us. "Since Sterling announced I'm the one to beat, they'll likely—"

"Here we are," Gabby called, bouncing in front of us with red sparkly helmets, causing both Ethan and me to jump. Her enthusiasm was firmly back in place. The part of me that wasn't nervous wanted to know what magic Sterling worked to get her to deviate from her favorite color and say yes to sparkly red helmets.

"Let's go, people." Sterling appeared by her side, equally amped and shaking two helmets at us. "It's time."

If I had to guess, that short walk had bonded the two of them over their bizarre, ultracompetitive commitment to games. Great. Now if I let us down I'd have Gabby on my case, too.

Ethan and I each took our helmets as Sterling handed his phone to Gabby with instructions to film him putting it on and getting settled into the kart. We followed the pair of them to the edge of the track, careful to keep our distance from everyone else.

Resting his forearms on the railing that separated spectators from the track, Ethan started speaking low. "Like I was saying. We'll see how the first lap goes, but if it comes down to us and Gym Rats, your size will be an advantage."

"All the teams will be smaller than them," I cut in, eyeing the team with skepticism. I was not particularly little; the Gym Rats were just really big.

"Yes, but will they also be faster than Sterling and Gabby?" Ethan laughed as Sterling jumped into the kart with a shout that sounded like a battle cry, which Gabby echoed.

"You may have a point." I shrugged.

A beeping sound went off, and the first drivers for each team began lining up behind a big white line as a red light blinked to yellow. Besides us and the Gym Rats, there were two other teams: a group of dance influencers and a collection of self-proclaimed geek girls, including Emmie. Sterling revved the kart's engine at the starting line, taunting Emmie playfully. Then a big blasting sound went off as the light turned green. Tires screeched, and a couple of karts fishtailed, knocking into one another as the creators driving them cackled. Of course, neither of them was Sterling, who was already halfway around the first curve, yelling curses and driving like Cruella de Vil going to get the dalmatian puppies.

"Right," Ethan said, speaking quickly to try to teach me as much as he could in two minutes or less. "Because you are smaller and all the engines have the same horsepower, you'll be able to accelerate faster. Drifting to the outer edge of the track will be easier, too. Take the turns wider than you normally would. Stay in the middle so they can't pass you easily. It'll force them to either take the curves behind you, or go wide. If they do that, they'll lose time since they are too big to accelerate faster than you on the straightaways."

"Okay." I nodded. My heart was pounding as we stopped to

watch while Sterling came into the final stretch a breath ahead of the opera singer, this time alternating between yelling tips at Gabby—already in her helmet—and more curses at the other teams.

After taking my helmet from my hands, Ethan placed it on my head and gently pressed down, the world automatically getting quieter and my vision limiting. Bending down slightly so he could meet my eye, he added, "For the straightaways, cut back into the inside of the track. And accelerate out of the turn, not into it."

Moving us close to the pit where drivers would switch, Ethan kept talking as Gabby pulled onto the track, howling like a demon set loose as she cut off the Gym Rats. As Ethan predicted, everyone else wasn't taking this nearly as seriously. The third team was still a curve behind, and the fourth team had managed to stall sideways on the track. Meanwhile, Sterling had gone back to filming the action, complete with commentary on how bad the other drivers were, compared to our team's prowess.

I shook out my hands to release the tension and found him squinting at Gabby. She made Sterling look like a tortoise crossing the road. She was basically a bat out of hell, constantly checking over her shoulder and taunting the gym bro behind her, whose entire body seemed to have gone red with rage.

As Gabby rounded the curve toward us, Ethan said, "Remember, you don't have to add to the lead, you just don't want to come in last. You got this."

"Go!" Gabby hollered as soon as she was close, already unbuckling her seat belt. Taking a deep breath, I jumped off the curb and began cramming myself between the little bars that were meant to keep us safe if the car rolled over before Gabby was fully out. Even if I lost this thing, I was gonna look like I tried to hurry. Gym Rats pulled up behind us, and Gabby reached in to help me with the strap of my seat belt as I searched for the gas pedal, then stomped down.

The last thing I heard was Gabby shouting at me, then nothing but the vibration of a go-kart engine. Hitting the first curve, I did my best to take my foot off the gas and swing wide, the cart sliding sideways with the unexpected movement. I held my breath and tried to glance back. Sure enough, Dakota from Gym Rats was weaving around behind me, trying to figure out how to pass. Coming to the end of the curve, I floored it and cut back down to the inside of the track, forcing Dakota to waste time swinging wide so he wouldn't hit me.

I let out an excited shriek and focused on the road. Ethan was right. This could work. I gripped the wheel tighter as a series of hairpin curves came up. Unlike Gabby and Sterling, I wasn't about to turn around and yell at Gym Rats; instead I stuck myself in the dead center of the track and made wide arcs like Ethan said to do. From behind, I could hear Dakota holler at me to get out of the way, but I didn't care. Ethan knew cars. He'd given me a plan, and I was sticking to it.

As soon as I came out of the hairpins, I cut back to the inside of the track, then realized that I would need to get to the pit. Instead of waiting and moving over gradually, I cut over fast, forcing Dakota to swerve in order to avoid me one more time. Grinning, I took my foot off the gas and coasted toward the pit before coming to a stop.

"Yes. Good, good, good!" Sterling shouted, running around to my side of the kart. Grabbing under my arms, he hauled me out as soon as my seat belt was unbuckled. Meanwhile, Ethan swung himself through the passenger side like I had done.

I had just enough time to catch Ethan smiling at me before I was on my feet, and he was gone. The adrenaline that had coursed through my body during the race was making me shake like I was still in the kart as I tried to get my helmet off.

"Oop, let's do that on the other side of the railing. Don't want anyone to run us over," Sterling said, placing a hand on my arm and steering me and my wobbly legs to safety.

I managed to get my helmet off, feeling a bit like I'd been pulled from a vacuum hose in the process, and sighed. Giving my head a shake, I saw Sterling still standing there, watching me.

He said, "I might have underestimated you. That cut maneuver was dirty."

"I didn't—"

"Oh no. Don't get me wrong, I loved it. We're going to win because of you." Sterling grinned. "Also, I'm obsessed with your grandma. Her retirement party get-ready-with-me videos and her Cookies and Tea TV recaps are my favorites. Introduce me?"

He said all of this so matter-of-factly that it took me a moment to process what he was asking for. He liked BamBam's videos where she spilled the tea about the latest celebrity drama while making cookies with a friend like "a good grandma." And he wanted *me* to introduce him to her.

I pushed my hair over my shoulder and tried to play it cool, like I was mulling it over and not dying to accept immediately. Shrugging, I said, "Sure. She is kinda booked up, but maybe you two could have breakfast tomorrow and work something out. I could let her know to meet you."

"Perf. I'll see her then." Sterling smiled and turned to go, then stopped. Glancing back at me, his face grew thoughtful. "Hey, you seem nice, and I'm serious about wanting to work with Mini, so you should know that I'm not sure how over Ethan and Emmie are. Ethan says they are done. Emmie says they are not. Anyway, whatever y'all seem to have going on may be real for him, or a rebound, or a boomerang moment. Only he knows, I guess."

"Oh, it's not like . . . nothing's going—"

"I don't need to hear any details. In fact, it's better if I don't. Ethan is my friend even if we're in a weird place right now." The crowd cheered as Ethan crossed the finish line first, although Sterling and I were too distracted to care much. Sterling's shoulders sagged a fraction of an inch, like the rift between him and Ethan hurt more than he was letting on, before adding, "I thought you should know. Do with that knowledge what you will." Glancing up as Ethan lifted himself out of the car, Sterling adopted his usual playful expression again. Smiling, he said, "I should go get my phone from Gabby. See you soon, babes."

With that, he was gone, leaving me to wonder exactly what to do with this information. Ethan and I weren't anything other than business partners, so who was I to care if he and Emmie were done or not? I'd just have to ignore the fact that the idea of being a rebound bothered me a little more than it should.

CHAPTER NINE

I STOOD IN AN ALCOVE OF THE HALLWAY LEADING TO THE BALL-room where lunch was being served and adjusted my camera bag for the umpteenth time. Trying to quell the nervous knot twisting in my stomach, I reminded myself that it was unlikely BamBam would bust out of lunch and start checking the different casino food courts for me. It was equally unlikely that Gabby and Nittha would accidentally blow my cover by skipping TrendCon's under-twenty-one content creator pool party. They wouldn't pass up free mocktails.

That said, the longer Ethan took, the more anxious I got. I was starting to think that maybe I should find a better place to wait for him, when one of the ballroom's heavy soundproof doors swung open. I stepped back about three feet and got ready to run if so much as a hair that looked like BamBam's walked out of the door, then calmed down as Ethan rounded the corner, checking from side to side as if he were sneaking out past curfew.

"Ethan," I whispered from my hiding place, then tried to stifle a laugh as he jumped, a small, goofy squeak escaping him. Spotting me, he exhaled and walked over, still surveying the area as he crossed the hall.

"Jamie, you scared the hell out of me," Ethan whispered. "I thought you were Buzzy or . . ." He let the sentence trail off as I beamed up at him, unable to hide my smile anymore. "You think this is funny?"

"As a matter of fact, I do." I continued to grin as we walked down the hallway toward the casino floor and the exit that would take us to The Strip. "For a guy who seemed so cavalier about my grandma catching us, you sure are freaked out about someone seeing us."

"Whatever." Ethan chuckled. "Do you know where we are going?"

I watched him for a second, trying to decide if I wanted to press for details on who else he thought I was, then pushed the intrusive voice that wanted to know who Ethan thought about aside. Now would be a deeply inconvenient time to develop friend feelings for him. And that was all they were. Friend feelings.

I pulled out my phone and held up the screen so Ethan could see the little blue dots zigging and zagging across the map that we were supposed to follow. "For whatever reason, when I put in walking directions, the map is making it seem really hard to get there."

"Maybe because we're indoors?" Ethan offered.

"Maybe." I shrugged, then added, "The aquarium is in Mandalay Bay. They have that shark tunnel I mentioned earlier. When I click the car function it's only half a mile away, so I figure we should be able to walk there and back before lunch ends."

"That's perfect. My grandma is signing merch in the exhibit hall later this afternoon, and I know she'll need help. The timing should work out."

"BamBam is doing that tomorrow, I think." I paused as the two of us moved to the side to avoid a person in a fanny pack dragging three massive yellow suitcases across the carpet. I frowned at Ethan. "At least, I hope it's tomorrow. Otherwise, we may be at risk of a double homicide."

"You think everything is an opportunity for murder." Ethan laughed, stepping slightly to the side to avoid a person meandering between slot machines. "You must listen to a lot of true-crime podcasts."

"Horror movies." I wrinkled my nose. "True crime makes me too sad."

"Because horror movies are less murder-y?" Ethan asked, his brow furrowed as he fought to keep a smile off his face.

"No. Those are clearly fictional. With true crime, I feel bad, like we are all being entertained when some poor housewife in Ohio was stabbed to death with an icicle."

"An icicle?" This time Ethan didn't even bother to hide his grin as we came to the exit, both of us doing our best to ignore a hotel employee waving us over to talk about shows. "No one would murder anyone with an icicle. How did your mind even come up with that?"

"Just the first weapon I thought of. Which, you have to admit, would be a pretty good weapon, since the evidence would melt." I stepped through the revolving door and into the bright, hot daylight of The Strip.

"When you put it like that . . . Should I be afraid of you?" Ethan walked out of the spinning doors, blinking rapidly as he tried to adjust to the change in lighting.

"Not because of that. I'm bad at maps, though—that should make you more nervous." Tracing the screen to refresh the map, I held my breath. The little blue dots were still all over the place. "It still isn't giving me a direct route, but the hotel is right down the road."

Ethan checked my phone, then looked in the direction I was pointing. "I can't really see it from here, but I'm sure once we get closer it'll make sense."

Only, it didn't make sense. By the time the two of us managed to find an escalator to the street level, we were already getting hot. When we finally realized that there were no crosswalks on the street level and made our way back up to the lofted sidewalk, we were sweating. To make matters worse, we were near the hotel with the roller coaster wrapped around it, so every so often our attempts to navigate were interrupted by screaming.

But all that was nothing, and I mean nothing, compared to the level of hangry I felt coming on.

"I think we have to go through Excalibur and . . ." Ethan squinted at my phone, his face flushed from the heat, and then added, "Maybe the Luxor, too. I'm not sure. Maybe we should just call an Uber."

"Not unless you want our grandmas to know exactly where we are and what we're doing," I said, with a little too much force. Maybe his parents wouldn't freak out if they got a text saying he'd gotten in a car, but mine would. In between obsessively calling the driver and watching the safety map, my mom would almost certainly give BamBam an earful. Or my dad on behalf of Mom.

"Right. Forgot about that."

"I'm hungry." My voice sounded sluggish, and Ethan studied me like I was delicate and not with the fear that this warning should have induced.

Glancing around the walkway, his face lit up. "There is a sign for the Luxor. We can get a snack in there."

A little voice in the back of my mind tried to soothe me. Just like every casino and resort on The Strip, the Luxor had to have a shopping mall with a food court in it. Sustenance was close at hand. As soon as we got back into the air-conditioning, I'd feel a little better. I could make it another twenty minutes if we cooled down.

"Alright." I tried to smile at him, a gesture that was probably a lot closer to me baring my teeth than an actual expression of joy.

Ethan did a double take. "You okay?"

"Kind of." I readjusted my camera bag and tried not to sigh. My bag seemed to be about fifty pounds heavier, despite the fact that I had taken one of my cameras out to film B-roll, which Ethan kept ruining by waving at me or filming me while I was filming him. "I'm not good at being physically uncomfortable."

"Define uncomfortable," Ethan said, steering us around more tourists and down another walkway.

"I can't be any combination of hot, tired, and hungry, or I become . . . unpleasant." I hoped my facial expression conveyed the gravity of the situation.

Ethan eyed me as if I might start tearing at my T-shirt and become a giant, green, screaming monster. Finally, he said, "Scale of negative five to five, with zero being a true neutral, how close are you to a meltdown?"

"Two, I think." Something about the way the question was phrased elicited a small laugh from me even though we'd managed to walk into a dead end.

"My little sister, Sophie, gets like this. I can work with a two."

"Can you? Because I can tell you now that once we hit three, I can't be held responsible for my actions," I said as another question crossed my mind. "How old is Sophie?"

"Seven." Ethan winked at me as if he hadn't compared me to someone who was still perfecting the ability to tie their shoe. I scowled up at him right as something caught his eye. "Aha! There is a tram."

"What?" I asked, putting the less-than-flattering comparison out of my mind for a moment.

"I saw this shuttle from my hotel window. I wondered if it might be around here." Ethan said this more to himself than to me as he picked up his pace, navigating us toward an off-white stucco building. Sure enough, as soon as we walked inside, a tram pulled up. Ethan turned to gently place a hand on my arm. "Here, let's get on."

I took my backpack off and laid it on my lap so I could lean back as the two of us dropped into gray plastic seats while the tram waited the advertised five minutes for additional passengers to get on. Trying to distract myself from the heat and the lingering feeling of his touch, I asked, "Do you have any other siblings besides Sophie?"

"Yes. My dad had a family before us, so I have two older sisters. They are adults now—Katie and Stephanie. Then there is me, my sister Izzie, who is fourteen, and Sophie, the seven-year-old. So, I'm the oldest, the middle, and the only boy." Ethan then reached for my backpack. "Want me to carry this for a while?"

"It's heavy." I shook my head. Ethan shrugged at me like he didn't care, so I added, "And sweaty."

"Up to you, but I don't mind," he said with a wave, as if wearing someone else's sweat wasn't a sacrifice.

I was about to say no, when it occurred to me that, actually, I was really over having that sweaty, heavy thing with me. I sucked in a breath. "You sure?"

"Will it keep you from turning into a gargoyle until we feed you?" Ethan teased. I nodded, and he lifted the bag out of my lap as the nearly empty tram started to move. Everyone else knew it was too hot to walk any great distance, apparently. Eyeing me, Ethan asked, "Better?"

"Yes," I admitted, begrudgingly enjoying the sensation of air cooling my legs down. As the tram chugged toward the casino, I watched Ethan as he gazed out the window. This end of The Strip was mostly parking lots and pavement, but he still seemed to be enjoying the view. As if he was completely comfortable. I wondered what it would be like to relax like that. What would it feel like to not constantly worry about school, my parents, or the future? Or at least to not let it show. How was Ethan doing this?

He probably got a lot of hugs as a kid. That had to be why he was so chill about this whole #GrannieGate fiasco. The thought popped into my head right as the tram slowed, and I couldn't stop the silly grin from spreading across my face.

"Ready to get some food?" Of course Ethan chose that exact moment to face me. Taking in my goofy grin, he asked, "What?"

"Nothing." I managed to suppress a laugh as I imagined Buzzy smothering him in hugs.

"You are not looking at me like it's nothing." His eyebrow lifted as he pulled the backpack on and stood up.

"It's just. You seem like someone who got a lot of hugs as a kid." I giggled as we walked off the tram. "It has to be why this whole GrannieGate thing isn't stressing you out."

"I wouldn't say I'm unfazed," Ethan replied, guiding us toward the entrance to the Luxor. "But I did get lots of hugs. What's so wrong with being openly loved? All those hugs gave me too much confidence. That's why I'm the envy of everyone at TrendCon."

I snorted. "Why would you be the envy of everyone at TrendCon?"

"Because I'm here with you."

I almost tripped over my own shoes as I tilted my head up at him to see if he was serious. Ethan returned my gaze, and my mind went back to go-karting and the electricity between us.

As the seconds stretched, I wondered if that was all in my head, or . . .

Ethan leaned down, and my heart rate went up. He was so close to me now. I stepped a fraction of an inch closer, unsure of what to expect from him but also sure that I wanted to find out. His eyes searched mine; then he whispered, "And who wouldn't want to wear your sweaty backpack?"

My brain basically froze as I watched him straighten up with a mischievous cackle as he extended a hand to reach for the Luxor's door.

He'd been joking. That was why he was leaning in. He wasn't going to try to . . . well, I don't know what I thought he was going to do, but clearly it wasn't anything intimate. Which, now that my heart had stopped racing, should have been obvious. What was going on with my imagination today? Clearly, I was hot and tired and officially inventing meaningful moments between Ethan and me instead of picking up on jokes. I blamed Sterling and Nittha for putting ideas about us in my head.

I gave myself a shake as I walked through the door and laughed. "Don't forget, I'm also hangry. I have so much more to offer than a heavy, sweaty gear bag."

"Ah yes. The vague, appealing threat of being pummeled to death if we don't get food soon. Speaking of which . . ." Ethan stopped to mentally peruse the shops, until he spotted something promising. "Will ice cream work? Or they have chips and stuff at that little stall there?"

"Can we have both?"

"I think so . . ." Ethan's voice trailed off as he checked his phone and winced. "Lunch is almost over. I don't think I can get back too late, or my grandma will start to worry."

"Yeah." I thought about what little footage we'd managed to shoot so far and tried to work out a way that we could rush through the shots I had in mind. Unless we physically sprinted to the shark tunnel, what was left of the time we had allotted would more or less be eaten up by walking to the other side of the casino. I sighed, my shoulders dropping as I faced Ethan. He seemed to read the resignation on my face as I said, "I don't know if we have time to do the aquarium."

"Who knew Las Vegas was so impossible to navigate?" He exhaled, fluttering his lips as defeat crossed his face.

"The good news is, we did get some decent shots of you with all the hotels and screaming roller-coaster stuff in the background, so this adventure wasn't a total waste." Searching for something to cheer him up, I said, "And there is the Influencers Over Forty Mixer tonight, so if your grandma is going to that, we could try for the Bellagio fountain."

As soon as I said it, the reasonable part of my brain kicked in. This was a partnership, not a friendship. I'd already snuck off twice to see him in one day. A third time was really pushing my luck.

Ethan took a deep breath and rubbed the back of his head, mulling my offer over. "What we need is a car."

"Or better timing." I nudged him jokingly. When Ethan didn't perk up, I added, "Does being hungry make you mopey?"

"Maybe. A little." He chuckled begrudgingly. "Okay, yes."

"I thought so. Let's get food. Then we can figure out a better plan on the tram."

"I'll get the chips if you get the ice cream?" Ethan asked, some of his usual lightness returning.

"Works for me. What kind of ice cream do you want?"

"Anything cookie based." Saying this, Ethan seemed to give up on sulking entirely.

"Got it." Feeling strangely better now that *he* felt better, I gave him a playful salute, then turned on my heel to go get ice cream.

"Wait, what kind of chips do you want?" Ethan called, halting me in my tracks.

"Jalapeño, please." I batted my eyelashes at him as I said *please*.

"Spicy food is your solution to hanger." A lopsided smile traced his lips as he shook his head in surprise. "I'll remember that."

CHAPTER TEN

"YOU HAVE THAT MONEY I GAVE YOU?" BAMBAM ASKED AS THE elevator shot downward.

"Yup." I nodded, resisting the urge to touch the pocket of my frayed jean shorts.

"Good, you get yourself a little extra treat at dinner. You've worked so hard lately." BamBam smiled at me, and I tried not to let the guilt of fraternizing with the enemy eat me alive. Bam-Bam thought that Nittha and I were going to dinner at one of those restaurants where you can also play arcade games. Instead, I was violating all kinds of her trust. Worse, I'd be so busy doing it that there'd be no time to get myself something special. I'd probably just eat a sub sandwich before I went back to the room.

"Have fun." I waved at BamBam as she walked into the casino where the "old heads party" was supposed to be. As soon as she rounded the corner, I made a beeline for the front of the hotel, praying she didn't double back to get some forgotten item from our room.

Walking into the entryway, I spotted Ethan shifting his weight from one foot to the other and watching the lobby of the hotel. Like me, he'd changed clothes since our sweaty hike around The Strip this afternoon. Unlike me, and my plain white T-shirt, he'd actually put effort into getting dressed in a short-sleeved button-down and jeans that were neither wrinkled nor covered in holes.

As soon as he spotted me, he smiled. It was the kind of grin that could rival all the lights in the casino. Having it aimed at me was doing funny things to my ability to process anything else . . .

Which was unfortunate, because I realized too late that he was already saying words as he walked toward me.

". . . so yeah, there is that," Ethan said, exhaling heavily, that megawatt smile still in place.

"S-sorry," I stammered, my brain trying desperately to get itself in gear. "I got distracted. What did you say?"

"Oh." Ethan's expression shifted momentarily to crestfallen but then relaxed back into comfortable all over again. "Just that I'm glad you're here, and I got us a car."

"That's amazing. How?" My entire body perked up at the thought of not having to try to navigate a mile's worth of lofted sidewalks.

Turning toward the door, he started talking rapidly: "I don't usually do these kinds of vids, so I'm winging it, but basically there are a bunch of car or car-adjacent people here, including this woman, Heidi, who builds these off-the-wall cars. She

119

offered to let me borrow one for a couple hours in exchange for a collab."

"Oh, that's . . ." My mind raced as I thought about how Ethan would have had to spend his afternoon—helping Buzzy while trying to surreptitiously find a car for us. It was such a sweet gesture. I smiled at him. "You went to a lot of trouble for this. Thank you."

"It's not a big deal. And the car is kind of strange, so it won't be a luxury ride or anything. And we have to bring it back soon." Ethan's eyes went from mine then down to his feet, as if he wanted to say something more but changed his mind. Exhaling, he said, "It might be tight, time-wise."

"Got it." I nodded. Sure, I didn't know anything about cars, but I did know about product trades and tight filming schedules. "How much time do we have with the car?"

"An hour and a half."

"Okay. Let's say it takes us twenty minutes to get there and twenty to get back, plus a half hour to film the fountain." I did some quick math as we approached the doors. "That should be enough time to have some buffer if—" I cut myself off as I caught sight of Ethan's face. "What?"

"Like I said, I don't usually film this kind of stuff, and the car is unique, so I'm shooting slower than I want to be and . . ." Ethan's unsaid words hung in the air as if it was causing him pain to admit whatever he was struggling to say.

"And?" I prompted, trying to make my voice sound gentle and unhurried, but with an hour and a half to go, we really didn't have much time for dawdling. I added, "Ethan, I can't solve a problem I don't know about. We're partners, remember?"

"I need to finish filming the car. I'll try super hard to be fast. Also, I brought you a snack so you don't have to get hangry while you're waiting." Ethan said this quickly, in one long exhale.

"You brought me a snack?" I laughed, mostly because I was surprised. If I was in a hurry, getting anyone a snack would not have been on my mind.

Ethan's cheeks turned pink, and he was suddenly very interested in the way the hotel doors slid open. After a moment, he glanced back at me and said, "Well, yeah. I knew you might have to wait for me to figure out how to film this. And I know how you feel about being hungry, so . . ."

"Aw, you care about me not murdering anyone," I joked, throwing my hands over my heart. "You are so sweet."

Was he blushing? Maybe he was trying to be nice to me because he actually did care beyond being desperate for a new friend or finding a rebound, as Sterling had suggested. The thought melted a little piece of my iceberg heart.

"I mean, I'd like to think I am. But it's not really that," Ethan said, the pink in his cheeks deepening a shade. He shook his hair out of his face, as if the motion would brush off whatever feelings were behind the flush. "I actually want us to make it to the fountain this time. The way you were glaring at me this afternoon, I wouldn't have been surprised if you decided to eat me if we hadn't made it to that food court."

"Okay, I wasn't that bad." I rolled my eyes.

"You accused me of getting too many hugs as a kid." Ethan snorted.

"Because you clearly did," I said, trying to get a handle on my giggles and infuse my voice with some indignance. "I've never met anyone who comes off as well-loved as you do."

"Whatever." Ethan smirked, then pointed toward the side of the valet stand. "Car is there."

"You can try to change the subject, but—" The thought fell away as I turned to the left and caught my breath. "Wow."

Calling that thing a car might have been an overstatement. Technically, it did have four wheels, but that was about where the similarities ended. The thing looked more like an oversized ATV than any kind of car.

"I promise it drives." Ethan rushed to add, "And I'm a very cautious driver, so don't worry about the no-doors part."

Again, *no-doors* seemed like a misnomer. It was basically two hot-pink bucket seats bolted to a frame covered in the kind of LED lighting that changes colors all the time. Like if someone took one of the quads from *Mad Max* and made it the opposite of intimidating. In theory it had a roof, but the roof was made of clear fiberglass with a cartoon bird covered in sparkles on it. If I had to guess, the valet had left it out in front of the casino not because it was cool but because they were afraid to move it.

"You traded a vid for this?" I coughed, careful to keep my voice low in case anyone was around.

"Desperate times." Ethan smirked. "It's not like we had a lot of time to plan. Just wait until you hear the start jingle."

Ethan pulled out his phone and started filming little details on the car, occasionally stopping to talk directly to the camera. Internally, my brain squeezed, and I tried to keep my thoughts off my face. He wasn't mic'ed. The sound quality, given how close we were to the crowds, would be trash. I bit back a sigh.

He'd have to do all this again in a voice-over later, not to mention he didn't have a shoulder rig, so all his footage would be shaky cam or long-arm stuff, my personal pet peeve.

"I feel extremely silly right now," Ethan said, dropping the camera and facing me. "I know you don't watch my stuff, but if you did, you'd know that it is the most no-frills content that was ever created." He sighed, his shoulders slumping as he glanced back at the car. "This video is the opposite of my channel and it's going to suck."

"No, it's not going to suck." I felt the lie slip off my tongue before I'd even had a chance to think about it. "Because we can still save this. Let me help."

I flipped my backpack around and started pulling out my camera and a tripod. I was halfway through getting my camera mounted on the sticks when I felt Ethan's eyes on me. "What?"

"You really want to help?"

"I mean, yeah. You brought me a snack." I shrugged, feeling my cheeks get hot. "This feels like a fair trade."

Ethan chuckled. "Who knew that a bag of jalapeño chips was the key to your heart? I was trying way too hard before."

"Who said anything about my heart?" I took my lens cap off. "Chips will only get me to level up your filming game. Honestly, watching you struggle was killing me. Now go start the car when I tell you to."

Ethan got ready to hop in. I hit Record, then held the sticks high above my head so the whole car was in view as he walked to the driver's seat. When I nodded, the car roared to life and then began playing "Rockin' Robin."

It took every muscle in my body not to shake with laughter

so the footage wouldn't be ruined. Fortunately, Ethan had no such obligation, and his face lit up. He threw his head back and laughed. To the camera and me, he said, "That is wild."

"It's one of a kind," I said quietly.

Picking up my cue, he reset, winked at me, then took my line. "It's one of a kind."

As the lights on the car changed color, I motioned for him to get out. Once he was back by my side, I lowered the camera, my arms aching from holding it still above my head. "You and I should both walk around it a couple times with our different cameras to catch details. The sound quality here won't be great, but you'll have enough footage to voice-over and cut together later."

"You know, you're good at this." Ethan pulled out his phone and walked toward the opposite end of the car.

My breath caught in my throat. It wasn't like I'd told him all the details about my parents, or feeling trapped in a future I didn't plan, but something about the way he said it—all sincere—was like someone putting a bandage over the cracks in my heart. It both stung and felt good at the same time. Before I could stop them, his words spread through my system faster than a drug and settled into the corner of my mind where I'd inadvertently started storing memories and details about Ethan.

"Ready?" he called, pulling me away from the strange, warm, fuzzy feeling growing in my chest. He was holding up his phone and waving. From behind the phone, he said, "I'm filming you."

"You are such a dork." He was making more work for himself

by filming me, but whatever. If he wanted to waste time cutting me out of his footage, that was his problem. Holding up my camera, I hit Record and started slowly working my way around the car, careful to keep Ethan out of my shot. Once I'd completed the circle, I motioned to Ethan to go around again. This time, I stayed still, filming him filming the car, so he'd have more options. By the time he'd made it around another time, my arms were officially tired to the point of being over it.

Turning to me, he said, "I'm good. You happy?"

"I'll have to be if we want to catch the fountain." I sighed, unscrewing my camera and collapsing my tripod before tucking both safely back into my bag. The gesture bought me a second to try to get the butterflies in my stomach back under control. We were really doing this. Or we would be if the car was more reliable than our ability to navigate the lofted walkways of Las Vegas.

Both of us got closer to the car, and I could almost feel our collective trepidation about taking something that so clearly did not have airbags onto the road. As if reading my mind, Ethan said, "It does have seat belts, I checked."

I chewed on my bottom lip. "Alright."

Walking around to the passenger side, I took a deep breath and grabbed both sides of the no-doors and pulled myself into the vehicle. Once I was in, I put my backpack between my knees, praying that Ethan didn't take any sharp turns too fast, then started trying to figure out how to put on my seat belt.

It was one of those harness seat belts with a seemingly endless number of straps that all connected to one another. After a minute of buckling, unbuckling, untwisting, retwisting, and adjusting, I finally decided to copy Ethan. Unfortunately, he'd already buckled up and was watching me struggle, amusement written across his face.

"Do you need help?"

"No. I got it," I said, more out of pride than honesty. If Ethan could figure this out, then surely I could, too. I tried another buckle and almost immediately unfastened it. The thing felt like it was designed to strangle me.

"You sure you got it?"

"Mostly sure," I said, keeping my eyes focused on the task at hand so I didn't have to see him trying not to laugh.

"It's just that we are kinda tight on time, and—"

"Okay, fine." I dropped all the different buckles. "How does this work?"

"Here, lean forward," he said, reaching across the car and pulling a strap in front of my seat. "Put your arm through this part."

I rotated around to move my arm through the strap. Ethan's hand grazed the base of my neck as we both tried to adjust the belt. My skin prickled with the sensation of his touch, awareness running down my spine. I took a deep, steadying breath.

"Sorry," he said as something clicked over my shoulder and the belt dropped a few inches. He sat back into the driver's side. "You should be good to snap the front buckles now. It works like a star."

"Right." Objectively, I understood what he was saying, but my body was still stuck on the way the skin on the back of my neck was tingling, as if his hand were still there. I gave myself a mental kick to push the sensation of his touch out of my mind and started clicking buckles into place.

"Ready?" He smiled at me again, then twisted the key in the ignition. This time the car blared "Birds of a Feather" as it roared to life.

Working the stick shift into gear, Ethan eased his way out of the valet traffic, the engine's growling growing louder the faster we drove. Part of me wanted to ask Ethan what kind of person would want a car that was both extremely loud and very absurd. The other part of me knew there was no way he could hear me over the sound of the wind coming through whatever door holes were called.

The light at the end of the Stonereel's exit turned red, and Ethan took the car out of gear, quieting the engine as we rolled to a stop. For a second, we sat in semi-silence, the colors of the car changing around us. Searching for something to say that would make me feel less ridiculous, I shouted, "How'd you get so good at putting on weird seat belts?"

"Little sister's car seats. Although, she can do up her own belt now," Ethan teased, watching me through the rearview.

"Rude."

Ethan smirked as the light turned green, then moved the car back into gear. Ten very loud minutes later, we pulled up to the Bellagio's parking lot.

"We made it," Ethan said as soon as he shut off the engine.

"And the whole Strip knows it," I said, unbuckling my seat belt. Even though the car was off, it still felt like my entire body was vibrating along with the engine. "Why would anyone want a car like this?"

"What? You don't want to announce your presence to half of Chicago every time you go to the grocery store?" Ethan asked, unbuckling his own seat belt.

"Can you imagine being late to school in this?" I giggled, jumping down on wobbly legs.

"Or being late for curfew? You'd get caught by the whole neighborhood." Ethan got out of the car like he'd disembarked from a ship. Our eyes met, and we immediately cracked up. Walking around to my side of the car, he passed me a bag of jalapeño chips and smiled. "Promise me, if you need a break you'll eat, okay?"

"I promise." I smiled, taking the chips and putting them into my bag for later. As the two of us began winding our way toward the front of the hotel, I asked, "Where'd you learn to drive a stick?"

"I'm not really sure." Ethan's brow furrowed as he thought. "My dad, I guess."

"How do you not know where you learned to drive?" I asked as we weaved around a family.

"I know where. I was at my family's garage." Ethan shrugged. "I've hung around my dad, cars, and other mechanics for as long as I can remember. I don't know that anyone ever really taught me. I feel like someone asked me to move a car one day, I probably stalled out a thousand times but learned along the way."

"So, your family owns a repair shop?"

"Yes. My mom works there, too, so basically the whole family spends our time in the shop," Ethan said, a faint smile tracing his lips, as if whatever memory came with this explanation was dear to him.

"It must be fun to share an interest with your family." A tiny pang of jealousy squeezed at my heart. The kind of envy where you are both happy for someone and sad over the thing you'll never have washed over me.

"I wouldn't say it was a shared interest so much as my parents didn't have money for babysitters after Stephanie and Katie graduated, so the interest was forced upon us." Ethan laughed as the iconic dancing fountain pool came into sight, already crowded with people waiting for the show. "But yeah, it's nice. Especially now that the garage is doing well enough that I don't have to be there unless they need extra help or I want to hang out with my parents or something."

"That's sweet. You're lucky to have the kind of family that hangs out together."

"I am."

Ethan glanced down at me, and I smiled up at him as we slowed our pace, both of us scanning the pool's railing for a break in the crowd where we might be able to squeeze in and film the fountain without a bunch of heads in the way.

"There are a lot more people here than I thought there'd be," Ethan said after a beat of searching.

"You're taller than me, so if we can't find a spot, maybe—" I cut myself off as I watched a family reorganize themselves against the railing, making enough space for a person to squeeze in between them and another group. I reached out and placed my hand on Ethan's, pulling us toward the edge of the balcony overlooking the water. "There's a spot."

The gesture wasn't meant to be a big deal, merely a way to move us away from other pedestrians, but as soon as my fingers touched his skin, it felt like I was being pulled into him by a gravitational force. The electric hum that seemed to constantly hover between us returned, its spark more intense this time. Ethan glanced down at my hand, then back at me. I held my breath as the two of us stood still for a heartbeat that felt like it lasted forever.

Someone walked by carrying a baby, and Ethan moved a few inches closer to me to avoid them. He was close enough that I could smell him, clean. Like whatever soap he used had euca-lyptus in it plus some other scent that was all him. I liked that scent more than I wanted to admit. I knew I should take a step back. Being so near to him was reckless. There were only so many reasons he could be this close to me, and if anyone from the con or one of our grandmas' combined three million follow-ers recognized us, they might jump to conclusions. Then again, I wondered how much I'd care if they did.

The next moment, a woman with a toddler and a giant M&M's store shopping bag jostled us, throwing me slightly off balance. I let go of him, instantly releasing the tension be-tween us.

Ethan blinked at me as if he was as confused by whatever was going on with us as I was. He ran a hand through his hair as I cleared my throat, willing my cheeks not to flush while I took my phone out.

"I'm gonna film with this." I waved the phone at him, still feeling flustered. "It's too crowded to use my big camera."

"Um. Okay." Ethan sounded groggy as if he was reconnecting us with the reason we were here.

Turning my back to him, I carefully removed my backpack and set it on the ground, then looped one strap around my ankle so no one could scoop it up and take off with it. A hush fell over the crowd as the fountain lights came on and music started to play. I tried to focus on my camera as the first spout of water shot up, but I couldn't. At least, not the way I usually did when I was working. Ethan was standing near enough to me that I could feel the warmth of his body along my back. The smell of his soap worked its way through my memory. A piece of me wanted to lean back and snuggle into his chest. To take a deep breath and wrap myself in him.

Another burst of water shot up from the opposite end of the pool as the music crescendoed, and I was slow to pan to it. We didn't have time for me to miss shots. I was being ridiculous. If I wanted to win the contest and get my parents off my case, I needed to focus on the task at hand, not on the boy behind me. Holding my breath, I hoped that if I couldn't smell him, whatever this feeling was would go away.

I managed to film the rest of the show without any more slipups. Ethan stepped back as the crowd dispersed, giving me room to unlace my backpack from my ankle and put it back on.

"What'd you think?" he asked as I readjusted the straps on my bag.

"The show was cool. I didn't realize that it was set to music. It felt like a fountain dancing in an old Western movie."

"Right." Ethan's voice got louder as joy washed over him. "Like a guy on a horse should ride down the sidewalk or something."

"Can you imagine?" I giggled, letting the image play out in my mind. "I feel like that would be either a really good start or a really good ending to a Vegas comedy movie."

"When you become a famous director, please make that movie . . ." Ethan trailed off as he smiled down at me.

"I would have to be incredibly famous to convince people to watch that. Who would watch a Western set in modern Vegas?" I laughed.

"I'd see it."

Ethan grinned, then ran his hand through his hair. I'd been waiting for him to start walking toward the car—we only had about twenty-five minutes left—but he hadn't yet. Maybe he was waiting for a few more people to clear out of the parking lot? The air was beginning to chill, but I couldn't bring myself to suggest we go back yet.

Out of nowhere, he asked, "What's your favorite movie?"

"Oh, that's like asking what a musician's favorite song is . . ." I hummed as Ethan came to stand beside me, leaning against the railing that separated the walkway from the now smooth fountain pool.

"Everyone knows that when you pick a favorite movie, it is forever, and there are no takebacks. Whatever you choose, it's more serious than going to college or getting married." Nudging me playfully with his shoulder, he added, "You can't change your answer. Choose wisely."

I huffed. "Okay. Maybe *Seven Samurai*?"

Ethan opened his mouth to say something, when I changed my mind. Holding up a hand, I said, "No. I take that back. *His Girl Friday*."

"I don't know what either of those—"

"Ethan?"

Ethan's gaze shot over my shoulder, and the color drained from his face. I turned, then caught sight of Emmie. This close, she was maybe even a little prettier than she'd appeared from far away. My heart sank. If this girl was Ethan's type—tall, short hair, trendy—I was absolutely not. Not that I wanted to be. Nittha's romantic daydreams were rubbing off on me. Pushing the thought aside, my head swiveled from Ethan to Emmie as an uncomfortable silence settled between them.

Emmie rocked back and forth on her heels for a second before saying, "Am I interrupting? I can go."

I got the distinct impression that while she didn't want to leave, Emmie was being sincere about her willingness to go if Ethan or I asked her to.

Something about the question seemed to jar Ethan into responding. "We were just talking about movies. Do you know Jamie?"

"Uh, no. Hi, nice to meet you." Emmie waved in a short jerky movement, which came off about as awkward as I felt.

"Nice to meet you, too," I said, smiling and pulling my shoulders back to invoke an extra measure of confidence. I had low-key resented wearing braces for five years, but right now, I was extra grateful for every cent my parents spent on my orthodontia. Sure, the drive over to the fountain left my hair looking like someone had stuck me in a wind tunnel, but at least I had my smile going for me.

Silence stretched between the three of us again. Emmie seemed like she wanted to say something but couldn't decide if she should do it in front of me. Ethan seemed like he wanted a meteor to fall from the sky and crush him. Attempting to break the ice, I turned to Emmie. "I've seen you at TrendCon. What kind of videos do you make?"

"Mostly book reviews with a side of lifestyle stuff," Emmie said, her voice sounding like she was torn between being grateful for the assist and wishing that I would drop off the face of the earth. To Ethan, she said, "What are you doing here?"

"We're working on a video." Ethan's words were clipped, as if giving her information was costing him dearly. "What are *you* doing here?"

"Mall," Emmie said, as if there weren't a mall in every casino. Side-eyeing me, she added, "Ethan, maybe we could get coffee sometime and finish talking about the thing we were discussing at the pool party?"

Cryptic much? My Spidey senses tingled. What were they talking about? It had to be important if she was willing to exchange coded words about it in front of me, a literal stranger. Emmie stared at him, her face equal parts unsure and hopeful as she playfully batted her eyelashes.

"Uhm, I have to check my schedule. I'm kind of busy with my grandma and filming and . . ." Ethan's voice trailed off as he rubbed the back of his head.

"It doesn't have to take long. Maybe we could eat and talk? Like we could get dinner while . . ."

I stopped hearing what Emmie was saying as Ethan's entire demeanor sank, like strings were attached to the back of his neck, pulling him toward the ground. I couldn't watch this. Not because I cared, I reasoned with myself, but because the guy had bought me a snack. Anyone who would feed me didn't deserve whatever emotional cajoling was happening here.

"Oh my gosh!" I drew in a sharp, dramatic breath and snatched Ethan's wrist up. Squinting at the face of his watch, I feigned terror. "Ethan, we gotta take the car back. Now."

"What?" Ethan sounded confused, as if this whole interaction had mentally sapped all his energy.

"The car. We need to take it back to your friend ASAP. Like, we should probably run to the parking lot." I nodded, making my eyes as wide as possible to signal that if he wanted help, he should play along.

His eyes locked on to mine for a second. "Oh, shit. I forgot about the car." He said to Emmie, "So sorry. I told Heidi I'd have her car back by nine, and you know how she is."

Emmie looked like she had no idea who Heidi was and didn't really care about her cars at all, but she recovered quickly enough. Offering us a half-hearted smile, she said, "Of course. Talk to you soon. Nice to meet you, Jamie."

"You too," I said. Ethan and I both started speed walking toward the car. I slid into the passenger's side. Ethan waited until I had figured out my seat belt, then said, "Thanks."

"Anytime." I bit down on my bottom lip. I didn't want to

make him feel worse about whatever was going on by asking questions, but I also wanted to know what I'd interrupted. Before I could decide what to do, Ethan turned to face the steering wheel and started the car. "Three Little Birds" blared through the speakers, which typically would have been funny, but neither of us was in the mood for jokes.

On the ride home, I kept sneaking glances at him, watching for any sign that he wanted to talk about what was bothering him. Instead, he remained stone-faced, the wind pushing his hair around as he drove. It struck me as ironic that I'd spent so much time wishing he wouldn't talk to me. Now I'd give anything for us to keep talking.

DAY 3: PLAYING FORE KEEPS

CHAPTER ELEVEN

"EARTH TO JAMIE."

Nittha waved at me like she was trying to signal a ship from land. We'd skipped breakfast so I could help her film a GRWM for her and Cricket. But, so far, I'd mostly stared into space or tried not to think about last night. I thought I was good at hiding being distracted. Apparently, I was wrong.

"Sorry. What did you say?" I cleared my throat. Cricket sat next to me on the bed wearing a pink gingham dress with a matching headband. She'd managed to wedge herself so close to my leg that it was bound to wrinkle her outfit, which would irritate Nittha. I petted the pup and then picked her up, hoping that she would still feel sufficiently snuggled without putting creases in her clothes.

"What's up with you?" Nittha asked, eyeing me like maybe I was sick and she didn't want to catch whatever I had but was trying to be nice about it.

Gabby glared at her. "What she means is, you look tired."

"Nothing. I slept weird."

Nittha and Gabby exchanged a look of doubt. I actually wasn't lying. I simply wasn't telling the whole truth. I *had* slept funny . . . because of Ethan. After we'd made it home, curiosity had gotten the better of me, and I'd finally checked out his channel. I'd told myself I'd only sit through one video, but then I got sucked into watching him explain how to clean dirty car parts, change windshield wipers, and talk to everyday people about why they bought certain cars.

It wasn't so much the car knowledge that was interesting—although I knew next to nothing about cars, so his channel was more useful than I'd expected—it was more him. I could see why thousands of people watched his videos even before I'd read the comments. He had this reassuring enthusiasm as he talked. He wasn't using fancy camera angles or editing programs. He was simply a fresh-faced Midwestern boy in his family's garage holding up car parts and talking to you in this we're-already-friends tone. It was relaxing. Like ASMR for car lovers.

"Clearly something is wrong. What aren't you telling us?" Gabby asked, the soothing expression she'd worn earlier wearing off.

Shoot. I'd spaced out again. Twice in a row was bad.

"Also, you and Cricket are cute in this picture. Can I post it?" Nittha said, holding her phone out to me so I could see it. I wasn't sure I was particularly cute, but Cricket was smiling in that way dogs sometimes do when they are getting a particularly good tummy rub.

"Sure." I nodded, hoping that her putting the photo online might distract her and Gabby from asking any follow-up questions.

"I'm gonna say, 'Auntie's helping me get ready.'" Nittha sat on the bed next to me, leaving Gabby to hold the giant light-reflector screen that she was supposed to be in charge of. Nittha added, "So, you gonna tell us what is on your mind?"

My resolve cracked. "Okay. But, Nittha, if BamBam asks, we went to dinner last night. Got it?"

"Why do I need to lie to your grandma?" Nittha asked, her eyes going wide.

"Now I really want to know what happened." Gabby grinned and leaned forward. "Why is Nittha covering for you?"

"It's not a big deal, it's— Don't look at me like that, Gabby." I stopped and eyed my friend.

"Like what? I'm not looking like anything." Gabby was absolutely looking at me like something, as a poorly concealed smile pulled at her lips.

"Wait. Are we lying to BamBam because you and Ethan are secretly in love and sneaking around?" Nittha asked, her voice hovering above a shriek.

"No. I mean, yes. But not like that." I rolled my eyes.

"So, what was it like?" Gabby gasped.

"Tell us everything," Nittha demanded at the same time. She started bouncing on the bed with excitement, causing Cricket to sniff at her as if she was irritated by all the fuss. I'd never felt more understood by an animal in my life.

Taking a big breath, I started from making my deal with

Ethan to the mess of our attempted walk to the aquarium, then going through the absurd car he'd managed to get us, to watching the Bellagio fountain show and running into Emmie, who he very clearly did not want to talk about. The further I got into the story, the bigger Gabby's grin got and the more she had to shush Nittha to let me keep talking.

"I can't believe you didn't text us about this immediately after," Gabby said once I paused to take a sip of my blueberry matcha latte.

"I know. But there wasn't really time." I shrugged. "And now you know why I need your help with BamBam. She cannot find out."

"I'm fully freaking." Nittha fanned her face. "We could have helped you get ready."

I snorted. "Get ready for what? Being sweaty? Riding in a toy car? Drowning in the awkwardness of seeing his ex while we were working?"

"Your date," Nittha said with a little shake of her head, like it was obvious.

"Where in that story did you get date?"

"The part where you went to the Bellagio fountain. Literally, the most romantic spot in all of Las Vegas," Gabby said. Her smile was absolutely massive.

"First, that is not true. *Sharknado 4*." I set Cricket in my lap so I could use my hands to number my list.

"There are four of those?" Nittha asked.

"Better question: Why did you watch all of them?" Gabby added.

"Yes. And my dad wanted to," I answered, then toyed with the silver ring on my index finger that my parents had given me for making the honor roll my sophomore year. "Second, not a date. We didn't even get dinner. And third, we are literally working together on the project neither of you would partner with me on, remember?"

"He bought you chips, which low-key feels like dinner. So basically you had a dinner date." Nittha bounced on the bed, ignoring my entire list.

"I don't have any dating experience, but I'm pretty sure that is not how dinner dates work." I pushed a flyaway curl out of my face.

"Hate to agree with Nittha, but I do kinda feel like that was a date," Gabby said, her lips pursed to one side. "Like one of those sneaky dates. You know, like where you thought you were only going to the movies with a friend, but then they have their arm around you and suddenly, you are making out with them instead of eating your overpriced Swedish Fish and—" Gabby cut herself off as she looked between Nittha and me. "What? That hasn't happened to you?"

"Nope." Nittha shook her head.

"I can't say that it has." I wrinkled my nose at her.

"Huh." Gabby tilted her head to the side as if this was the first time she was hearing that this wasn't a universal experience. After a moment, she shrugged and said, "Regardless, I'm sure you know what I mean. Everyone has been out with someone and then realized that it might not be the sort of hangout they thought it was."

"Okay, that has happened to me." Nittha nodded and pointed at Gabby. "When my girlfriend invited me to go glow-in-the-dark mini golfing, I thought it was going to be a whole group thing, but it was just us."

"But that didn't happen here," I protested. The memory of whatever electricity seemed to pass between us yesterday—the smell of him, the feel of his body near mine—managed to fight its way out of the expanding corner of my mind where Ethan details were stored. Looking back on it, maybe that wasn't as in-my-imagination as I'd thought? Maybe my friends were right, and it was a sneaky date?

I replayed the night and felt my face flush all over again for a different reason. It wasn't like he'd tried to hold my hand, or wrap his arm around me, or even extend our night past when we needed to have the car back. Indeed, I'd picked the location, so unless I was subconsciously planning dates, there was literally no sign of a sneaky date. This was Nittha and Gabby getting in my head.

Looking first at Nittha then Gabby, I said, "I know that wasn't the case, because we ran into his ex, and there is clearly something going on there, since he—"

"Wait. You still haven't googled their breakup?" Gabby stopped me.

"Why would she do that?" Nittha said, sounding like Gabby's question was the silliest thing she'd heard all morning. "She doesn't internet."

"I internet." Nittha threw me a don't-lie face, so I added, "Kind of."

"But like, you've googled him, right?" Gabby asked, her mouth dropping open when I shook my head no. "See. This kind of behavior is why I know you don't know when you are on a sneaky date. I pity anyone who has ever had a crush on you."

"I mean, I watched some of his videos last night. I'm still playing catch-up." My voice sounded a smidge defensive and a part of me wondered why I was trying to explain myself. Giving Cricket a calming scratch behind the ears, I added, "I'm not dating Ethan, so why would I Google-snoop on him?"

Nittha rolled her eyes and started listing on her fingers back at me. "Maybe because he is a boy you don't know, he randomly decided to be your friend out of nowhere, you were getting in a car with a relative stranger, who for reasons you're not clear on is smitten enough with you to risk murder-by-grandma, or that he—"

"Fine, tell me about the breakup," I said, cutting Nittha's list off before she managed to convince me that googling everyone on the planet was reasonable behavior.

"It was bad," Gabby said, pursing her lips. "She cheated on him with some gaming guy and then the guy revenge posted all about their relationship, with pictures, when he got mad at her over something."

"Yeah, and the internet was mad. Like big mad. Because like E squared were the cutest," Nittha said, using her best Valley-girl voice. "Most of his followers are a bump that came from her. Before they dated, he was more or less under the radar. Like a normal car fix-it person with 10K followers."

"Ethan's not saying what happened, and obviously Emmie

145

keeps apologizing for letting her fans down, but people are not letting it go. Then you know how the responses get." Gabby shuddered. "And not like unhinged comments. Full-blown conspiracy-theory style response videos where people are combing through everything she's ever posted for proof that she is evil, fake, and messy, and should never have been trusted."

"Oh no," I breathed, thinking about how awful both of them must have felt. I'd seen BamBam's replies when she posted a controversial use for cotton swabs. People were truly nasty over a beauty tool. I couldn't imagine what something like this would make fans do. "That must have been miserable."

"Yeah. And since she is way more popular than him, she had a lot more people get upset with her because she got dumped for cheating on a golden retriever," Gabby said, her words coming faster as she got into the story.

"When did this happen?" My heart sank as I asked the question. If Ethan and Emmie had gone through all this recently, then no wonder she wanted to talk to him, and of course he was being weird about it. Hell, I'd want new friends, too, if basically everyone I knew only wanted to know me because of my ex-girlfriend. It crossed my mind that Sterling was truly trying to be nice and warn me. How could I not be a rebound for Ethan after all that?

"Like two or three months ago." Gabby shrugged. "I'm sure there are fan timelines out there somewhere, but honestly, there's a lot of super creepy misogyny around it, so I haven't gone that far down this particular rabbit hole."

"Oh yuck." I swallowed the lump in my throat. "Now I feel

bad for both of them. I can't even imagine breaking up in front of the whole world."

"Then, of course, there is the die-hard E-and-E-Forever camp, hoping that the two of them will reconcile at TrendCon, then move in together after high school to build some sort of online-couple empire. There was also that picture of them talking at the VIP Party," Nittha added with a shrug.

"It was supposed to be a closed party. Who posted?" I asked, my chest tightening. Was everyone watching them all the time?

"Emmie and Sterling James did a series together, plus they have that eyeshadow palette with bookish shade names like Cinnamon Roll and Book Boyfriend. So they are basically internet besties now. Only Sterling loves to insert himself on the periphery of drama, so of course, he posted a 'selfie' at the pool that 'accidentally' had the two of them in the background," Nittha said, making it clear that she thought Sterling's behavior was very much intentional.

I laughed, the tightness in my chest easing. Sterling might like to stir the pot, but seeing as I wasn't even a little bit famous or recognizable, I didn't need to worry about him. Even if he thought Ethan and I were getting married tomorrow, he wouldn't post about me. There was nothing to gain from it. "See this is why I don't have socials. I want zero part in whatever this kind of nonsense is."

"You should probably get used to it, given who your boyfriend is." Nittha giggled.

"Again, we are not a thing. And don't joke about it online, or you know my parents will lose it and—"

A knock on the door cut me off, surprising all three of us. Too late, Cricket jumped out of my lap and started barking at the door, as if the delayed warning that someone was approaching were helpful to us now.

"Cricket. Shhh," Nittha said, scooping up her dog and snuggling the still-barking pup to her chin. Glancing from me to Gabby, she called, "Coming."

She sauntered toward the door, peeked through the peephole, then whipped her head around. To me, she whisper-shouted, "Holy shit. It's him."

Who? I mouthed.

At the same time Gabby whisper-shouted back, "Ethan?"

Nittha nodded, a delirious grin spreading across her face.

"Ha ha." I rolled my eyes and leaned back on my arms, swinging my feet around on the edge of the bed.

"Not joking," Nittha hissed. I stopped fidgeting. Studying her, I realized this wasn't a prank. Still grinning her face off, she said, "I'm gonna open it."

"Don't." My heartbeat stilled while all the heat in my body rushed to my armpits, and I started to sweat.

"I thought you said nothing was going on?" Gabby cackled, and I wondered why my friends were so bad at whispering.

I tugged down my shirt, nervous energy crashing through my veins. "There isn't."

"Then why do you care?" Gabby asked, her smile mirroring Nittha's.

"I don't—"

"Y'all, he knows we're in here. I have to answer," Nittha

said, using her hand to give us the pipe-down gesture. She gave her shoulders a shake, practiced her most winning smile, then turned back toward the door. Meanwhile, Gabby grinned and adjusted herself in her chair so she could better see the door.

My hand immediately flew to my hair, and I tried to smooth a few of my more renegade curls back into my braid. Too soon, Nittha opened the door. I fully froze in panic like an animal caught in an automatic driveway sensor light.

"Hey, Ethan." Nittha's voice sounded like she was still smiling too big to be casual.

"Hey, Nittha. How are you?" Ethan asked, his eyes flicking over her shoulder to where I sat on the bed. One of my hands was still hovering over my hair like some kind of dorky statue. I slowly lowered it to my braid, like maybe that would make the fact that my hand was weirdly hanging in midair normal.

"Good. Filming a vid with Cricket." Nittha held Cricket out to him so the little Yorkie could get a good sniff.

"That's cool. I was hoping I could talk to Jamie." Ethan's voice sounded unsure as his shoulders crept toward his ears. Before Nittha could answer, he added, "I'm asking in the least creepy way possible. I know it's weird for me to just show up, but we are working on a project, and I don't have her number, but then I saw on your stories that you two were here, and you and me are on the same floor, plus our grandmas are both at breakfast right now, and I knew your room number and—"

"Chill, it's fine." Nittha stepped aside so Ethan could fully see into the room.

"Hey, Jamie." Catching sight of Gabby, Ethan drew his lips

into an awkward smile as he added, "Sorry to interrupt. Hi, Gabby."

"Hey," I said, and Gabby waved. The panic I'd felt thirty seconds ago dissipated as I watched Ethan flounder. Something about seeing him flustered was oddly adorable.

"I don't think anyone thought you showing up here was creepy until you started overexplaining." Nittha laughed.

"Oh good. And all three of you are here to witness this extremely not-creepy, very smooth interaction," Ethan said, rubbing the back of his head as his cheeks turned a deep-pink color.

"Super smooth, bro." Gabby chuckled, then glanced over at me, widening her eyes as if that would communicate something. Finally, she jerked her head toward the door.

Taking Gabby's hint, I jumped off the bed and walked over to the door. As soon as I reached Nittha, she turned to face me, raised one eyebrow, and smirked. Nudging her to stop, I focused on Ethan, who was still standing in the doorway. "What's up? Got another car that plays bird songs and needs filming?"

"Not that lucky." Ethan laughed. He looked down at his shoes for a second, a nervous habit, I realized. Once his eyes came back up, I caught them as he took a deep breath, then exhaled. "I was wondering if you wanted to film the DJ party with me tonight?"

"Oh, um," I said, surprised as I tried to remember what BamBam had asked me to do this evening. DJ parties were quintessential Vegas. Shooting a video about the city without the flashing lights and crowds was basically not a video about Vegas at all. The fact that he found one for the under-twenty-one crowd was even better.

"Tickets are dirt cheap for TrendCon guests, and it's at one of the Stonereel's pools, so no risk of us walking somewhere and getting stranded."

"I mean, it could be good . . ."

"I'll bring more chips if you're worried about your hanger." Ethan half smiled, and a little piece of my heart melted, until I remembered what I was supposed to be doing. BamBam had texted me earlier. Apparently her breakfast with Sterling had gone well, and I was supposed to help her with his makeup master class tonight. Of course, now I really didn't want to. The DJ party sounded so much more fun. Plus, spending a little more time with Ethan wouldn't be a bad thing. He was certainly more fun than studying for the SATs or finishing up my SISU application, which was my plan for after the class.

Ethan's smile fell as he watched me. "It's okay if you don't want to go. I thought—"

"No, it's not that I don't want to go." I stuck my hand out to catch his arm as he leaned back on his heels. He glanced down at it, and the memory of last night at the fountain washed across his face, pulling me with it. When his eyes met mine again, his expression was unreadable. My hand tingled, and I released his arm before this strange pull could go any further. Clearing my throat, I forced myself to pretend we weren't remembering the same moment. "I promised BamBam I'd go with her to Sterling's master class tonight. She's the surprise guest, so don't tell."

"Got it." Ethan's voice sounded like he was taking a gentle hint I definitely wasn't trying to give. This wasn't going how I wanted it to go. I looked over my shoulder at Nittha and Gabby, trying to figure out what to do. Nittha blinked at me, while

Gabby attempted another round of rapid-eye-movement communication. Both of them were useless.

Turning back to him, I asked, "What time is the party?"

"Technically, it starts at seven." Ethan's voice sounded nonchalant as he added, "But the popular DJs won't go on until later, so I think we could get there whenever."

"Okay, BamBam and Sterling's panel is supposed to end at seven-thirty, and then she and Gregory are going to try an Emeril restaurant and see *Magic Mike*." I paused as Gabby started snickering. Immediately, Ethan perked up. I shrugged. "When in Vegas. Anyway, if we go a little late, I could do it."

I bit down on my bottom lip.

"My grandma has late dinner reservations. She isn't gonna be back until after nine, so this could work if we don't stay out too long."

My heart did a backflip, and I forced it to pull itself together before I could think too hard about what that meant.

"Maybe we meet at the end of the conference hall, near where they have the water station, at seven-forty-five in case BamBam hangs around to talk to people?" I added.

"Sure." Ethan nodded, tucking his hands into his pockets as he rocked on his heels again. "I should get going before my grandma comes back from breakfast and wonders where I am. But see you tonight?"

"See you." I moved away from the door as he started to walk backward down the hall, that disarming smile returning to his face.

"Wait." Ethan stopped abruptly, then jogged toward me with

his phone out. "Can I have your number?" A hint of pink returned to his cheeks as he shrugged and added, "So I don't have to turn up at your friends' rooms like a weirdo to talk to you."

I smirked. "I kinda want to see how you explain this the next time you have to track me down at my grandma's room or something."

"I feel like explaining how I found you to your grandma might get my ass kicked," Ethan joked. "I'd rather just text you and keep all of my parts intact."

"I guess you have a point." I snickered and handed him my phone. I took his and smiled at the background. Holding the phone up, I asked, "Is that your dog?"

"Yes. That is Shelby, the most ancient and smelliest basset hound on the planet." Ethan's voice sounded completely devoid of warmth, but his smile gave him away. The dog probably smelled like Fritos, but he loved it.

Ethan said, "For a girl who claimed *Lady Friday* was her favorite movie, your phone screen says otherwise."

I winced, remembering the background of my phone was set to the poster for my current obsession. An extremely cheesy action movie sequel starring Teddy Flunder, the hottest actor of the moment, and an animated purple monster. Holding my head high, I said, "It's *His Girl Friday*, and I refuse to apologize for appreciating *Death Ship Five*. It had a clever fusion of animation and camerawork."

"Right," Ethan said, pressing his lips into a flat line to keep from laughing as he passed me the phone. "I'm sure that's the reason."

"It is." I nodded a little too much to be convincing as Ethan backed away from the door, still skeptical. "Watch it, and you'll see what I mean."

"No need." Ethan shook his head, mock sincerity on his face. "I totally believe you, Webb."

"See, this is why we aren't friends," I called down the hallway. "A real friend would believe me."

"But I do believe you." Ethan threw his hands over his heart, feigning hurt. "Why do you insist upon breaking my heart when you know how much I care?"

"Whatever." I rolled my eyes and stepped back into the room. "See you tonight."

"See you soon, friend," Ethan's jovial voice came down the hall right before the door clicked.

Turning around, I caught Gabby and Nittha exchanging massive, floodlight-level-bright smiles. Narrowing my eyes at both of them, I tried to stem the incoming tide of excitement. "Don't get—"

"Oh my god. This is your second date!" Nittha bounced up and down on the bed, disrupting Cricket's regal repose. The poor dog rushed to the other end of the bed and settled on a pillow, irritated.

"We are filming for the contest together."

"Girl! He was basically falling apart trying to explain himself to Nittha. He was nervous about talking to you because he likes you." Gabby drew out the word *like*, so it sounded as if it had about fifteen syllables in it.

"I think he was nervous about turning up randomly, not talking to me." I shrugged, then walked over to the bed and flopped down next to Nittha, which turned out to be a mistake, because my friend started nudging me with her elbow.

"Would it be so bad if this was a sneaky date?" Gabby asked, wiggling her eyebrows.

"No one is showing up with Swedish Fish, Gabby," I said, keeping my voice flat. "You know my parents' no-dating-until-graduation rule. Even if BamBam didn't disown me over this, my parents would ground me for life."

Nittha rolled her eyes. "But what they don't know—"

"Anyway, I have to be at BamBam's merch signing soon. Are we gonna finish filming or what?" I cut her off before she could try to make lying to my parents seem like a good idea, too.

"Fine, fine. But we are gonna talk about this more at lunch," Nittha said, lunging across the bed to get to Cricket.

"And we are helping you pick out an outfit to wear tonight. I love you, but your jean shorts are kinda killing the date vibes," Gabby said, lifting herself out of the chair.

"We aren't talking about it at lunch, and no one is dressing me." I sighed and walked back to where the reflective screen was.

As the two of them started talking about how to arrange Cricket on the dresser next to the mirror, I let my mind wander. Objectively, I knew tonight wasn't a date. Ethan and I would be working. But now that Gabby had put the thought in my mind, I was having a hard time letting the idea go.

My phone buzzed in my pocket. I took it out, my breath catching in my throat as I watched Ethan's number come up on my screen.

> **Ethan:** On a scale of -5 to 5 with 0 being a true neutral, I'm level 5 excited to hang out with you tonight.

Rolling my eyes, I typed back the same answer I'd given the day before, fighting the urge to read too much into his text. *This isn't flirting*, I told myself. This was merely a callback to yesterday's misadventures. I checked to make sure Gabby and Nittha were still engaged in arranging Cricket before answering.

> I'm still a 2

A moment later my phone buzzed again, and a smile crept across my face. I bit down on my bottom lip to try to get ahold of it.

> **Ethan:** I can work with a 2. See you tonight.

CHAPTER TWELVE

I SHOULD HAVE KNOWN THAT SOMETHING WAS OFF. WHEN BAM-Bam overheard Nittha and Gabby begging to get me dressed up at lunch, she insisted I let them. More alarm bells should have gone off when she offered to press my hair instead of going to the afternoon panels. BamBam didn't typically care what I wore unless we were going to one of her church functions or something. Gullible me, I did as BamBam asked, happy to have yet another viable reason I couldn't take the time to apply to that stupid business school.

Now, sitting onstage in a beauty salon chair at Sterling James's Glitter Extravaganza, wearing Gabby's black faux-leather minidress with BamBam tying purple hair-tinsel to my scalp, the warning sirens were blaring GET OUT. But it was too late. BamBam's evil plot was already in full swing.

"That is amazing, Ms. Mini. You are such a natural," Sterling crooned into the mic as he reviewed BamBam's work.

"Thank you, sweetheart. Us old heads know a few tricks." BamBam winked and beamed out at the audience, conveniently failing to mention that she was good at this because she used to braid hair back in the day to make extra money while she was going to school. Tying a piece of glitter into my hair was nothing compared to that. In fact, I doubted she even needed her glasses to do it.

I waited until Sterling and the event videographer were out of earshot, then looked up without moving my head. "BamBam, what are you doing?"

"If Buzzy Timmons can drop in on the Knot a Problem panel and show off her knitting skills, then I can show mine." BamBam's grin was unnerving as I put the pieces together. This was supposed to be a beauty workshop for beginners, but BamBam was no beginner. Instead, she was styling circles around the other participants and stealing the show. Something Buzzy had done yesterday when she pretended to stumble upon a group of knitters and offer them her so-called "grannie tips." Of course someone just happened to film her "surprise visit," and the internet ate it up.

"Mini. You are better than this." I tried to make myself sound disappointed even as a giggle escaped me. "You had me get all dressed up to make me an accomplice to your rivalry. I don't want any part of GrannieGate."

"Well, I wasn't about to go to a wood-carving class, so it was either trick you into this, or we do a workshop on power-lifting. I think we can both agree this is preferable." BamBam harrumphed.

"I guess you have a point." I shrugged.

"Don't move," BamBam tsked at me. "These little pieces of plastic are slippery."

"Alright, while we give our amazing participants another five minutes to finish up hair, what questions can I answer for you, darling audience?" Sterling crooned, spreading his arms wide and circling the stage.

If BamBam were anyone else, I'd have warned her that a friendship with Sterling was basically one giant internet fight waiting to happen. But after #GrannieGate, what creator in their right mind would pick a fight with BamBam? Sterling was smart enough to only start trouble when it wouldn't hurt him. BamBam would eat him alive if he stepped a toe out of line. And that's if she felt generous.

For another minute BamBam worked in silence as the audience members asked questions about what hair tinsel Sterling recommended (his own brand, duh!) and where to buy it (any Beauty BB's will carry it, and be sure to tell them Sterling sent you, personally!).

My mind wandered to the DJ party and what I was going to tell BamBam in order to sneak off, when I heard her whisper, "Baby, I've been meaning to tell you, because I don't think I said it the other day. I know your parents are worried about you, but I'm not."

I peered up at her, forgetting that I was supposed to stay still. This time, she didn't admonish me. Instead, she ran her hand down the back of my head and smiled. "You're just a different spirit than your parents, but I have every confidence that you will be great at whatever path you choose. Your mama and daddy will come around to it, too. Give them time."

"Thanks. I know you are on my team." I tried not to let the guilt strangle me. Of course she would choose now to remind me how much she loved and supported me, right after I decided to throw loyalty out the window and work with her enemy's beloved grandson.

The muscles in my chest tightened as the lines between BamBam's eyes relaxed. Giving my shoulder a pat, she said, "That's all I wanted to say. That, and I love you."

I started blinking rapidly as my eyes got misty without my permission. It was a good thing that the makeup portion was the second half of the workshop. "I love you, too."

BamBam opened her mouth to say something else, when Sterling's voice cut in again. "Alright! Let's move on to the main event . . . the Glitter Extravaganza!"

He threw his hands in the air and posed for the camera while everyone in the room erupted into cheers. Well, everyone in the room but me. I'd spent more than a few minutes dreading this part and eyeing the roughly seven hundred kinds of glitter that were lined up for us on a table. Turning back to us participants, Sterling pulled a series of thin packages from his makeup apron and waved them at us, adding, "And y'all I have a surprise—my new line of eyelashes!"

Looking at one pair of lashes, I almost screamed. They looked like rainbow-covered caterpillars had fallen into a jar of sparkles. I might love BamBam, but this was really pushing the limits of granddaughterly fealty.

My heart slammed around in my chest as I fumbled through my phone, trying to find Ethan's number. There was exactly no way in hell I was showing up to the DJ party like this. If I didn't get laughed out of the venue for looking like I'd been the victim of a glitter bombing, the amount of sparkle on my skin would probably blind everyone.

"Ahh!" I growled in frustration and attempted to tilt the phone down to an angle where I could view the screen through my false eyelashes. I really did not want Ethan to see me like this. With my free hand, I tried to adjust Gabby's stupid minidress. Tripping over myself and toppling sideways into a wall, I hissed, "Are you kidding me?"

"Jamie?"

Icy dread trickled down my spine as Ethan's voice came from behind me. For a wild moment, I imagined that I'd made up the sound of him calling my name. Maybe I was experiencing some sort of glitter-induced hallucination.

"Jamie, is that you?"

No. No, no, no. No. This could not be happening. I shut my eyes and willed Ethan to turn around or go somewhere else. Never mind that the only place to go was back down the hallway toward where my grandmother was making small talk with Sterling and a gaggle of fans. Right now, him wandering into that scenario was far preferable to him seeing me like this.

A little voice in my head reminded me that I wasn't supposed to care what Ethan thought. We were working tonight. I didn't need to look cute to film. However, I did need to appear human and not like a glitter-factory reject.

"Oh." Ethan's voice came from in front of me, and I cracked one eye open to see his face. Stunned was probably too gentle a word for his expression. He whistled low, then said, "Wow."

I gritted my teeth and opened my other eye, then did my best to glare at him through my eyelashes. "Don't say anything."

"I wasn't going to." Ethan bit down on his bottom lip and tried to swallow the laughter rolling through his body. "It's just, it's not every day I get to see a human disco ball."

"I thought you weren't going to say anything?" I tried to seem irritated and failed as I caught sight of myself in one of the mirrored hotel walls and shuddered. "So much glitter."

"What happened? And how did you get glitter in your hair like that?"

"It's hair tinsel. I've been told it will wash out eventually."

"Probably not." Ethan chuckled. "Glitter is Satan's favorite device. You'll be wearing it forever."

"Would you like a hug?" I held my arms wide. "Join me in glitter hell, Ethan. The weather here is much warmer."

Ethan shook his head and took a step back. "Tempting, but I'll pass."

"Fine, but you are missing out. I give great hugs. The glitter is a bonus."

"Rain check, then." Ethan grinned, looking me over. His expression shifted as he took in my outfit, as if he'd realized that there was more happening on my body than sparkles. Before, he'd been playful, but now there was an intensity to his gaze. Almost hungry. As if there wasn't enough of me to take in.

Tingles ran across my skin. My breathing felt shallow, like my whole body had forgotten how to work while he was looking at me. The small shred of reason I had left kept me rooted to where I stood. The rest of me imagined what it would be like to do something about that look. To feel his hands on my skin. The warmth of his body close to me. His lips on mine. Heat rushed to my cheeks as I let my arms fall to my sides, a buzzy feeling filling my head.

My movement must have jarred something, because Ethan blinked twice, his gaze jumping back to my face before he anchored it firmly to the floor between us. Clearing his throat, he mumbled, "Nice dress."

"BamBam . . . we . . . I wanted to dress nice, not for any reason but then also . . ." I tripped over my words and desperately wished that I could make my brain work the way it had before he'd looked at me like that. I took a deep breath, then tried again. "Gabby picked it out. For tonight."

Too late, it dawned on me that saying *for tonight* made it sound like I thought it was a date. Which I clearly knew it wasn't. And I didn't need him thinking I was desperate. The adrenaline in my system was slowly working its way out of my nerves and doing me exactly zero favors on the way. *Good god, get it together, Jamie.* Gesturing toward the pool, I added, "For the DJ party. So we'd blend in. But we won't blend in anymore, and I kind of can't see anything, so I was trying to text you not to meet me right now. I don't even know how to remove all this."

Ethan's face lit up as if he was finally connecting the dots around what I was trying to say, which was great, because I certainly didn't know where I was going anymore. "I think I know how to get that off you."

"You do?"

"Yeah." He nodded, his hair falling into his eyes. Using one hand to push it away from his face, he added, "I think my grandma should have what we need, and she shouldn't be back in the room yet."

"Okay." I nodded. As we started walking toward the elevator bank, I could feel Ethan's eyes on me. Glancing up at him through my eyelashes, I asked, "What?"

"Nothing," Ethan said, guilt crossing his face as he suddenly became very interested in all the pinging noises the slot machines around us were making.

"And yet, your face says it's not nothing," I prodded as we reached the elevators. "Tell me."

"I was trying to figure out how I was going to avoid getting glitter all over my grandma's room." Ethan smirked and hit the button to call the elevator.

"Oh." I glanced down at my arms, which had also been dusted in Sterling's signature body glitter and laughed. "I'm not sure that is gonna be possible."

"That was my conclusion, too," Ethan said, gesturing for me to step into an elevator as it opened up. Someone wearing a TrendCon lanyard got in with us. Giving me a once-over, they stepped as far to the opposite side of the elevator as they could get.

As soon as we got out of the elevator, we both doubled over laughing.

"That amount of glitter is repellent to everyone other than me." Ethan grinned, steering us down a hallway that was so long it made me dizzy. "I'll have you stand in the bathroom and hope for the best."

"Really?" I said, trying to make my words sound innocent. "You don't want me to sit on your bed and rub my face all over your pillows?"

"Not like that I don't," Ethan said under his breath as he unlocked the door.

"Because you'd want me there otherwise?" I deadpanned.

"I . . ." Ethan's jaw dropped, and his cheeks turned bright red as he realized what it sounded like he was implying. "That isn't what . . . I don't . . ."

"Sure. Sure," I teased. "Tell me you think I'm a bridge troll without telling me you think I'm a bridge troll."

"No. You're not—" Ethan sputtered.

"Don't make it worse." I arched an eyebrow and folded my arms.

"I mean, if you were—"

"Please, don't explain." I smirked as the flush in his cheeks deepened. Something about watching Ethan's usually unshakeable chill be, well, shaken, was amusing. "Really, there is no way to recover at this point."

"You sure?" Ethan winced, rubbing the back of his head in that way he did when he wasn't sure exactly what to do with something I'd said.

"Positive." I snorted, leaning on the wall next to the door and watching him.

"Because I could keep digging." Ethan's laugh held a touch of nerves as he dropped his hand and eyed me. "Maybe my grave isn't deep enough?"

"If you dig any deeper, you'll hit sewer pipes." I shook my head and caught bits of purple tinsel flashing in the bright hallway lights. "Put down the shovel."

"In that case, come in," Ethan said, intentionally stilting his speech so the staccato of his words could convey how awkward he felt.

"Now that I know you really don't want me here, I will." I turned to face him as he closed the door, then surveyed the room.

The layout was nearly identical to the room I was sharing with BamBam, but it felt completely different. For one, it was much neater than I'd expected. He and Buzzy had stored their suitcases upright in the little closet cubby, like they'd unpacked and actually put things away in the dressers that I'd always assumed were for show in hotels. The shared nightstand clearly delineated whose side of the room was whose. The bed closest to the window had to be Ethan's, since there was a vintage-car magazine sitting on that bed's side. On the bed itself was a small, bedraggled stuffie that might have once been a sheep or a cat; it wasn't really clear which anymore.

"For the record, I never called you a bridge troll," Ethan said, stepping around me and walking toward Buzzy's nightstand. He opened a drawer and took out a jar of Vaseline.

"I'm pretty sure it was implied, given the situation." I snickered.

Ethan followed my gaze to the bed. Frowning slightly at the stuffie, he said, "That isn't mine. It's Sophie's."

"I totally believe you." I grinned. "Anything else you want to lie about?"

"Ah, you are impossible." Ethan waved a hand at me, biting down on his bottom lip. He gestured with his head toward the bathroom. "Let's do this in here. That way the maids can hose down the whole room if they need to."

Ethan switched on the light and stepped into the cramped bathroom. He opened a large case sitting on one side of the sink and began digging around for something. Noticing me hovering in the doorway, he patted a space on the counter. "Can you sit here?"

"Okay." The air in the bathroom felt still as I slipped behind him, doing my best not to brush against his body in the crowded space. I'd never been this alone with Ethan before. This close to him, with no distractions, I could see that his hair was starting to curl at the base of his neck. My fingers itched to trace the uneven edge of his hairline and feel the soft skin there. I clasped my hands together to keep from trying to touch anything I wasn't supposed to.

"It's easier if you are at eye level," he explained over his shoulder. The sound of his voice, gentle against the whir of the bathroom fan, pulled my attention away from his hair.

"Right." I exhaled shakily. I needed to pull it together. Even if I did have a tiny crush on him, I was literally covered in glitter. Worse, we were in a cramped hotel bathroom. In action movies, any romantic moments in a hotel bathroom were because someone needed to have a bullet fished out of them. If that happened to either of us, it would be because one of our grandmas put it there.

After lifting myself onto the clear side of the counter, I crossed my ankles, letting my legs dangle as I watched him. Ethan began setting things on the surface, making sure they were all neatly lined up and visible as if he were arranging the different tools that he would need to work on a car. I'd seen him do this in his videos, but watching him do it for me felt more intimate. Like he was letting me see a secret.

"Ready?" Ethan turned to me, holding a cotton round covered in Vaseline. Nerves washed over me, and I nodded once. He stepped toward me. For a second, he just studied me, his brows knitted together in concentration, then relaxed. He set the cotton round down, then backed away, mumbling, "Actually. Hair tie."

I exhaled and tried to force myself to relax as he moved back to the case. Why did I feel so nervous? Less than twenty minutes ago, I'd had my makeup done in front of one hundred people. Surely I could have it removed by one person.

Ethan pulled out a fuzzy purple scrunchie with a big bow attached to it. Stepping back toward me, he held up the hair tie and said, "May I?"

"Uh-huh." I nodded. Ethan slowly reached for my hair, and I held my breath. I wasn't accustomed to letting just anyone touch my hair, and not totally sure what to expect. Maybe something quick and perfunctory. That wasn't this. His touch was gentle, almost reverent. As he gathered the strands together into a ponytail, his fingers brushed against the nape of my neck, sending a tingle of pleasure across my skin. My scalp had that delicious stinging sensation as he worked his fingers loosely through my hair to brush it away from my face.

"That's better." I felt him pull my hair through the scrunchie; then he stepped back in front of me and smiled. I held my breath and closed my eyes, hoping to hide how much I was enjoying his touch and how disappointed I was to lose it.

I cleared my throat and reached for something to say. Anything to help me forget the feel of his hand on the sensitive part of my neck. Opening my eyes, I said, "So, where'd you learn to do this?"

The brightness in Ethan's expression flickered, like someone had tried to dim the light in his smile. Belatedly, I remembered Emmie. She was always so put together. I had to be the densest person on earth. Of course he would have learned to do this from her. And of course he wouldn't want to talk about it. Rushing to give him an out from my big, stupid mouth, I added, "You don't have to tell me if you don't want to. We could talk about why you have Sophie's stuffie, if you'd like."

"It's okay." He picked up the cotton round and avoided my gaze. "A little bit of everywhere. Emmie, mainly. But, around the time that we were together, Izzie got into makeup, so part of it was my sister talking about it, wanting to show me stuff. She's in that phase where she doesn't really want a big brother right now, so I kind of take what I can get from her. It's clear she thought I was cooler when I was still dating Emmie, so she is back to ignoring me again. But Sophie still likes me so there is that."

"I'm sure Izzie still likes you. She probably doesn't want to like you at school, or around her friends, or alone, because she is fourteen."

Ethan laughed, but it sounded hollow, and my heart ached. Without thinking, I pressed up against his arm. "I didn't know you when you dated Emmie, but I think you're pretty cool."

"Careful. I might start to think we're friends." Reaching out his free hand, he tilted my chin toward him and took a step forward so my knee was resting low on his stomach. Leaning in, he dropped his voice and said, "Close your eyes."

I swallowed hard and did as he asked, willing myself to think about anything other than how we were barely six inches apart. If I wanted to kiss him, his mouth was right there. The cotton round slid across my eyelid, leaving a greasy trail, and I pushed away the thought of Ethan's mouth. "This probably makes us friends, doesn't it?"

"Finally." I felt Ethan's chuckle where his body rested on my knees. "I've been waiting for you forever."

The cotton round moved to my browbone, and I opened my eyes to see Ethan's honey-brown gaze studying my face again. He bit down on his bottom lip but didn't move away. My heart thudded in my chest. This was it. He was going to try and kiss me, and I was going to let him.

"Can I tell you something?" he said softly. "Now that we are friends?"

"Yes." My eyes searched his face as I waited for him to close the distance between us. I held my breath.

Ethan moved even closer to me, his voice tickling the sensitive spot below my ear as he whispered, "You look like a raccoon right now."

With that, Ethan burst into laughter, and I shoved his shoulder, mad at myself for even imagining that he was going to kiss me.

Leaning across the sink, I looked in the mirror. Ethan was correct. While he had managed to remove a whole mess of glitter, the Vaseline had smeared big dark circles of mascara, eyeliner, and eyeshadow around my eyes. In short, I resembled a raccoon.

"If I kick you right now, it'll really hurt." I huffed, sitting up straight.

"I'm sorry, I couldn't resist," Ethan wheezed.

"Give me that, and I'll do the rest myself." I held out my hand for the toner and cotton round he was holding.

"No, no. I'll finish," Ethan said, gently pushing my hand aside. "But you have to admit that you do look funny."

"I do not," I managed to say.

"Stubborn. Close your eyes one more time." Ethan's voice was still infused with humor. When I didn't immediately comply, he said, "Please. I promise I'll be nice."

"I'm no longer sure you're capable of that." He reached for my face with his free hand. His expression grew serious as I said, "Some friend you are."

"Don't say that, Jamie." Ethan's voice was low. I liked the way my name sounded when he said it. Soft, like it was a prayer. His thumb traced the edge of my jaw. Ethan swallowed. Whatever playful energy he'd put between us seemed to disappear, the room going completely still as his gaze jumped to my lips.

His eyes traced a path along the curve of my cheek and across my nose, until they met mine. Exhaling a shaky breath, he said, "And what if I wanted to be more than—"

The sound of two mechanical beeps came, indicating that the door had been unlocked and was about to open. Both of us froze. Ice water ran through my veins. Then fear.

"Shit," Ethan said.

"No," I said at the same time. I dove off the counter, the faux leather of my dress squeaking as Ethan jumped back to the other side of the sink.

"Ethan, are you here?"

He reached toward the counter and grabbed an armful of makeup-removing stuff right as Buzzy's crisp New England accent floated through the room.

For one wild moment, I considered hiding in the shower, which wouldn't have been a bad plan if the thing hadn't been made of frosted glass. My heart slammed in my chest as I searched for some escape. Literally, if there were a window I could have dangled from, I would have done it. When that didn't materialize, I turned back to Ethan, his eyes wide with panic, even as he took a breath to respond. "In here."

I shook my head violently, hoping to buy myself a second to see if maybe I could turn into a towel rack, but it was too late.

"I didn't think you'd be back so soon. I would have ordered—" Buzzy stopped midsentence as she rounded the corner to the bathroom. Her lip curled slightly as she took me in, from the tips of my tennis shoes to my head. When her eyes landed on my face, her expression changed. Then she glanced over at Ethan, who aside from looking guiltier than a kid caught shoplifting candy was still clutching all her makeup remover. Turning back to me, she simply said, "Oh my."

Then Buzzy started cackling. And I mean truly howling. She slapped her leg and leaned against the bathroom doorframe, completely ignoring Ethan and me as our eyebrows shot to the ceiling.

"I'm trying to help Jamie. She went to a makeup panel, and it went badly," Ethan said over his grandmother's uncontrolled giggling.

"I can see that," Buzzy wheezed and swiped at her eyes with one of her coral-manicured hands. Looking at me carefully, she added, "Darling, you look awful."

"I . . ." I peeked at myself in the mirror. I still had the massive, greasy raccoon eyes. Even better, the grease had started to work on the glue of my false eyelashes, so one of them was peeling awkwardly off my eyelid. Turning back to Buzzy, I said, "It looks better than it did."

That seemed to send Buzzy over the edge again. After a full minute of additional cackling, she said, "You should have used Pond's Cold Cream. Doesn't your grandma have any of that?"

"I'm not sure. Ethan found me before I had to show my face to too many more people," I hedged, careful to avoid telling her the fact that my own grandmother had covered my face in more makeup than a drag queen could go through in a month. "I should probably ask her."

I pulled on the edge of my dress and gestured to the door, hoping I could sneak by. Instead, Buzzy held out a hand to stop me. Giving me a once-over, she said, "Let me take this off you before you go. Despite what your grandma might say, we're not monsters in this family."

It took everything in me not to flinch when she reached toward my face. Instead of mauling me, she gently peeled the loose eyelash off, then set it on the bathroom counter before saying, "I have to hand it to you, Ethan. It was clever to use the Vaseline to loosen up the glue like that."

"It works on goo stuck to car windows," Ethan mumbled, as if he was worried that his response could trigger a full meltdown on Buzzy's part.

"That's my sweet boy. Always so helpful," Buzzy crooned, and it took everything in me not to laugh. Clearly, Ethan could do no wrong in his grandmother's eyes. To me, she said, "Let the Vaseline sit on the other one for a few more minutes. It'll be ready to come off soon."

"Thank you." I nodded and finally slipped past her, feeling safer now that I was out of her reach. "And thank you, Ethan. I appreciate the help."

Ethan nodded and gave me a tentative smile, as if he didn't trust himself to speak.

"And, sweetheart, if your grandma doesn't have any Pond's, come back here. That product would be faster, but what Ethan has here will work eventually." Buzzy started to walk toward the door, so I picked up my pace, careful to keep an extra foot of distance between us, in case she decided to take a swing at me with her cane. As I reached for the door, she added, "And if you don't know how to use Pond's, I have a video up on my account.

Search 'ten things grannie knows about makeup' plus my name and it should come up."

"I will." I pulled the door open. In reality, there was no way I was watching that if BamBam was in the room, but I wasn't going to tell her that. Stepping through the doorway, I caught sight of Ethan standing outside of the bathroom. "Thanks again."

"Anytime," he called.

Buzzy looked like *anytime* was a stretch for her, but she put on her best smile and said, "Night, sweetheart."

With that, the door closed, and I took off down the hall, careful to make sure I was yards away before slowing down. I'd take my chances being seen with a greasy, half-glittered face in the elevator over Buzzy coming back to try to finish the removal job. By the time I'd reached the elevator, the survival adrenaline had worn off, and I'd started to think clearly again.

What had just happened? I'd started the night with a plan. Film the DJ party and get home before either of our grandmothers knew we were gone. Instead, Buzzy now knew that Ethan and I knew each other well enough that he let me in their room. A rookie mistake. Thinking about their room made my cheeks hot for an entirely different reason. While it wasn't great that his grandmother knew that I was in her orbit, that wasn't the only mistake I'd made tonight.

Ethan Wyatt had almost kissed me.

And I'd almost let him. That could never happen again. Even if I really wanted it to.

DAY 4: GOING ALL IN

LAS VEGAS

CHAPTER THIRTEEN

SLEEP HAD NOT HELPED MY CRUSH ON ETHAN DISAPPEAR. NEI-ther had sitting through an early coffee with BamBam and Sterling—both of whom could best be described as aggressively morning people—while they debriefed last night's class and brainstormed what they might like to do next. Even trying to organize BamBam's panel footage into the start of a video didn't take my mind off Ethan. At one point, I'd almost deleted a draft instead of hitting Save.

This crush was officially turning into a distracting mess, so when BamBam asked if I would go back to the convention floor to film her saying hi to fans spontaneously, I agreed without thinking twice.

"This is so sweet," BamBam said, posing with a thirtysome-thing fan for a picture as they handed her a homemade beaded friendship bracelet.

"Thank you, honey." BamBam smiled warmly and tilted her

head in the way that meant she was ready for the next fan in line to walk over.

"Can I get a video of you saying your line?" the next fan asked, their voice shaking as they held up their phone.

"Of course you can," BamBam said, smoothing the pleats on her fuchsia jumpsuit to get herself ready. Around her the crowd of people who had gathered to get a picture while she "browsed the convention floor" took out their phones for their chance to get BamBam on video saying her catchphrase. Nodding to the nervous fan she asked, "Ready?"

When the fan nodded, BamBam busted out her most winning grin, her Southern accent a little thicker as she looked at the camera and said, "I'm here at TrendCon, still cute as the day I was born and having fun with all of y'all." Gesturing at the fans gathered around, she added, "Stay bad, baby."

Blowing the camera a kiss, she laughed and then dropped her pose.

"Thank you so much. My sister won't believe this. You totally made our day," the fan said, bouncing a little to the side, ostensibly so that another person could have a turn, while still basking in BamBam's glow.

My stomach growled. I had more than enough footage of BamBam doing these little meet-and-greets to cut together about fifty event recaps, and I was starting to get hungry. Logically, I understood why BamBam had agreed to drop into the exhibitor hall before breakfast—fewer fans made it easier for her to move and pretend this wasn't staged—but now that we'd been doing this for forty-five minutes, I was ready for a break. I could only hope BamBam would be ready soon, too.

"Alright, Ms. Mini. I have a controversial question for you. Are you ready?" the latest fan said.

"Oh, Mini loves a good controversy. Lay it on me." My grandma chuckled at the camera this new fan's partner was holding for them. These kinds of surprise interviews always made me nervous, since the person filming was likely trying to become a creator in their own right, which meant the odds that the question was designed to be a gotcha moment were much higher.

"Color combination, pink and baby blue. Do or don't?"

A little bit of the tension in my chest eased. This truly was a fashion question.

"Oh, that is controversial," BamBam said, a sly smile working its way across her face as she added, "I believe it's a do. The only rule for fashion should be wearing what feels like you."

"That's so funny! Buzzy said don't, unless you are putting together a baby's nursery," the fan said, laughing as if catching Buzzy and BamBam on the opposite sides of an argument was novel. I squinted and hoped BamBam wouldn't take the bait.

"Like I said, if you have the confidence and creativity, you can pull just about anything off. But let me not say anything bad about Buzzy," BamBam drawled, delivering her most Southern insult, aka not outright talking bad about someone while obviously implying bad things about them.

I felt my blood pressure tick up. The last thing BamBam needed was to be on camera taking shots at Buzzy . . . again. Still smiling, she added, "Pink and baby blue for a nursery feels like a tired design choice. I think there are more inspiring color palettes. But again, only if you're an original."

"I don't think I'm tired, but you might be with those same tired insults." Buzzy's voice cut through the knot of people who'd formed around my grandma. Of course she'd managed to wander over here at the precise moment my grandma was talking trash. She'd dressed effortlessly in a chic black linen suit with gold buttons and a little scarf tied around her neck that managed to match the buttons on her jacket without being a gold-lamé nightmare. Behind her, I could see Ethan grimacing, his hair still wet from the shower as he tried to weave past the growing circle of people who'd stopped to watch our grandmothers bicker.

"Are you sure about that?" The corner of the right side of BamBam's mouth lifted into a smirk. "'Cause that outfit is about as tired as your recommendations. You are either sleep-deprived or losing your touch."

"Better tired than tacky." Buzzy sputtered, an angry flush creeping up the side of her neck, darkening her cheeks. "I mean, hot pink, really?"

"Oh, I know you didn't just say that." BamBam shook her head, taking a small step forward like she was getting ready to read her for filth. "In your boring black suit, with your dull little scarf tied like you're going to a board meeting at an investment bank. News flash, Buzzy. No one's buying stocks here."

"At least I'm not a walking billboard for what happens when bright colors go bad. You look like children's chewing gum. And I'll bet you can't even go to the bathroom in that thing."

I held my breath and felt my brain start to break while three things happened simultaneously. (1) Everyone around us went dead silent and took out their phones, ready for part two of #GrannieGate. (2) I became very grateful I hadn't had breakfast, otherwise I might have thrown it up. (3) The color drained from Ethan's face as both of us processed the same threat.

Unlike the argument at the panel, this had the potential to be much worse, because there was no table or other panelists between them to prevent an actual altercation. Nor was my dad here to break things up like in Florida. Plus, I wasn't as strong as BamBam, so if things went south this was all Ethan. And I didn't doubt for a second that either grandma would take a swing at or bite him for trying to end a fight.

In short, this was bad.

BamBam ran the thumb of her left hand over her knuckles as if checking to see which rings she was wearing in case she needed to throw a punch. The gesture was subtle, but it had the same effect on my brain as her waving a giant red flag in front of my face.

I had to do something. Fast.

My mind seemed to reassemble itself in an instant as I stepped forward. "Mini, you are going to be late for that special table at drag brunch with Gregory if we don't get going." BamBam's head swiveled toward me as if she were possessed, and for a fraction of a second, I worried that I had gotten myself pulled into whatever whooping Buzzy was about to get. Taking possibly my last deep breath, I added, "No sense missing out on a once-in-a-lifetime event over a color combination."

BamBam blinked at me, as if she was waking up from a rage trance. Letting her eyes rove around the room at the sea of cameras facing her and Buzzy, she cleared her throat and said, "Right. Brunch. Hottest ticket in town." Shrugging one shoulder at Buzzy as if she'd almost forgotten she was there, BamBam added, "Sorry, Buzzy, we'll have to continue this another time. You know how it is."

"Well, it isn't as if—"

"And remember, you're going to The Kitchen to meet Chef Dang. So you two have equally good brunch plans that you don't want to miss," Ethan added, a slight edge to his voice as if anticipating his grandmother's petulant retort.

I risked a glance in his general direction, our eyes meeting for a moment. A flicker of amusement crossed his face, and I felt my lips twitch up, then immediately redirected my attention back to BamBam. Unless we wanted to risk reigniting this blood feud, Ethan and I could not be seen as colluding on this, or anything else.

Giving her head a little shake, Buzzy pulled herself up straighter. Then, moving her cane from one hand to the other in an oddly menacing way, she said, "Oh, you are right, darling. How lucky we are to have grandkids who remember our plans."

"My memory is excellent, so I don't need Jamie for that." Not to be one-upped in the gracious-recovery battle, BamBam forced a tight smile onto her face. "But we are lucky to have such thoughtful young people in our lives." Taking a quick step back, ostensibly to go but also, I suspected, to get out of reach of Buzzy's cane, BamBam turned toward me and added under her breath, "If only yours was as cute as mine. Come on, baby, let's get out of here."

BamBam wrapped her arm around me and started steering

us toward the exit as Buzzy sputtered, unable to get the last dig in as we headed for the door.

The muscles in my neck and shoulders didn't relax until we'd cleared the big exhibit hall and made it to the elevator bank. After throwing a quick glance over each of my shoulders to check for eavesdropping fans, I looked up at my grandma, who was grinning as if she were already a mimosa deep at brunch.

"BamBam, that was bad."

"For Buzzy, maybe. I got her pretty good." Shrugging one shoulder, she added, "Sometimes you gotta stir the pot. Give the people what they want. Besides, you were there to step in before anything serious popped off."

My jaw dropped as I put together what BamBam had done. Unlike me, she'd done her reconnaissance, noticed Buzzy in the room, and decided it was worth the risk to keep people talking if she could win the fight. This round of #GrannieGate had absolutely gone to her, and my grandma had officially reached evil-genius status.

The elevator dinged, and BamBam got in. Holding the door open for me, she said, "Hurry up. I've got to get my purse and get to brunch. The only thing better than Chef Dang is a whole gang of drag queens, and you better believe your grandma will be taking pictures with every single one."

BamBam winked at me as I got into the elevator. Sure, she'd almost gotten us beaten by a cane, but I couldn't argue with her there. She was about to have a great time. I, on the other hand, might spend the rest of my morning trying to get my nerves under control before I could even think about food.

CHAPTER FOURTEEN

WITH BAMBAM SAFELY AT BRUNCH, I DECIDED TO BEGIN SORTING and editing all the footage Ethan and I had collected so far. The editing software had just started to load on my computer when my phone dinged, and Dad's name floated across the screen in the family group text. The muscles in my neck tensed.

> **Dad:** Mess, checking in on that essay. Early decision deadline is coming up. Please provide an update. Thx

If I hadn't been irritated, I would have laughed. Whenever Dad was serious about something, he texted like he was writing an email to the other partners at his accounting firm and not talking to one of his kids. If he really wanted to escalate the situation, he'd send it on the group text as if he were cc'ing someone's boss. Holding my breath, I pulled up the document, took a picture of it on my screen, and typed back.

> Working on it right now.

I could almost hear the you're-not-taking-your-future-seriously-enough lecture I would get if I didn't finish this before I got home.

> **Kina:** Go Jamie! You got this. You are a smart girl and STEM needs you.

My sister's reply came in lightning fast. It was so older-sister of her that I wanted to both throw my phone at a wall and hug her at the same time. Of course, she genuinely believed that I was about to be the next Mae Jemison or something. In her mind, I would be famous and successful no matter what I did, so why not study in the science, technology, engineering, or math fields with her. If it just happened that math aligned with Mom and Dad's expectations, so much the better. Win-win for us all! It was sweet of her and also totally not what I wanted—no offense to Mae or NASA.

> **Mom:** Just think how happy you'll be when it's done.

As if reminding me that future me would be grateful for their badgering. I was not convinced she was correct about this, much like my driver's license.

> **Trevor:** Hang in there!

My brother texted, followed by four GIFs of Muppets, cats, comedians, and a coffee cup with arms typing. I suspected he was less invested in cheering me on than he was in doing a chat cleanse so he wouldn't have to be triggered by my dad putting pressure on any one of us to achieve the next time he opened up the family text. That thought genuinely did make me laugh.

> **Dad:** Good. Looking forward to reading it soon. Love you. 🩶

I smiled in spite of myself. My dad had only recently started using emojis. Much like his business-formal texting, the emojis were kind of weird but also his way of implying lightheartedness when he didn't immediately have a math joke on hand.

> Love you, all

Gritting my teeth, I closed my editing software and focused on the document containing all my supplemental college essays, blinking at the cursor and trying to force myself to finish.

Taking a deep breath, I desperately tried to think of an answer to the question on-screen.

What are your career aspirations?

None were coming to mind that weren't completely snarky, when someone knocked on the door. I jumped out of my chair and walked over to it with maybe a little bit too much enthusiasm. Plus, I was starting to get hungry again. Maybe BamBam was back and bringing me a muffin?

I threw the door open and froze. Ethan appeared startled, as if he hadn't expected me to answer the door so fast. I probably seemed startled, too. After this morning, the only person I would have less expected to see than him at my door was Buzzy.

"Hi," Ethan said.

"Hi." I tried to hide my body behind the door. I still had on my glasses and my retainer, which would have been fine if not for the still-glitter-laced messy bun, Gatorade-blue running shorts, and oversized bootleg *Doc McStuffins* T-shirt I'd stolen from my brother's throwback T-shirt collection that I was sporting as an excuse for pajamas. Unlike my brother, I did not look cool. I wouldn't even want someone to bury me like this.

"Is that a—"

"Don't ask." I cut him off, narrowing my eyes at the smirk crossing his lips.

"It's kind of hard not to." He arched an eyebrow and tilted his head.

"My brother was a fan."

"Just your brother?"

I shook my head. "You can't tell me you didn't take some of your older sisters' clothes."

"Not the embarrassing ones." Ethan grinned.

"You're a very on-the-internet person, so if that is even a little untrue, I'll find out," I threatened. I glanced down the hallway as the elevator dinged, the sound sending my pulse through the roof.

"They're probably still at brunch, so we're good," Ethan said, reading my mind. As he looked down at his shoes, his voice grew quiet. "I ran into Nittha and Gabby at Beginners Luck, and they told me your room number. I thought you might want this. It's your coffee order. Not that there is any coffee in it."

189

He held a cup out to me. I blinked at him. "You remembered my order?"

"It's kind of hard to forget."

The quadratic equation was hard to forget. A complex coffee order that nearly everyone had to write down was not. He'd remembered a thing that I liked. A grin tugged at the corners of my mouth. My stomach fluttered, and I tried to push my excitement down. This didn't mean anything.

"Thanks." I stepped out from behind the door and took the drink. Inhaling the earthy blueberry scent, I grinned. "That is really sweet of you."

"It's no big deal." Ethan shrugged. Still, a blush had crossed his cheeks. "So, I was wondering if maybe you'd want to hang out tonight?"

For a flash of a second, my heart was in my throat. A million scenarios raced through my head. Was this like a real date hangout? Friends-walking-around-the-resort-malls hangout? Or a filming-for-business hangout?

He must have read my confusion, because he rushed to add, "Since we only have like two days left to get footage, and my mentor, Michael, ate a bad fish sandwich at a gas station."

"What?" I wrinkled my nose. "Who would eat a fish sandwich at a gas station? And what does a bad fish sandwich have to do with us?"

"Michael's an expert car wrapper and he got me into making videos. He mostly works on exotic cars in LA now. Outside of bad judgment when it comes to food, he is great." I tilted my head at Ethan and he laughed, the sound shaky as he ran a hand through his hair. Taking a slow sip of his black coffee, he said, "That didn't make sense either, did it? Let me try again. Sorry."

"Please do. So far tonight sounds gross," I deadpanned. Was he nervous? Last night, he was trying to ask me something about us. But this was about filming. Why would he be nervous about filming?

Ethan smirked. "Michael, my mentor, had an agreement to make a vid about a rare car that has a custom wrap. Because of the fish sandwich, he can't drive it. He suggested the company give it to me for the evening, and they agreed. So we have a car. We can go anywhere we want." He smiled, then added, "For roughly five hours."

"Oh. I get it." I waved the hand holding my drink around in the universal gesture for *this makes sense*, even as a little piece of my heart sank. He was nervous because he was asking for my help to film another car while we worked on our project. Shrugging off my disappointment, I said, "Sure. What time should we meet?"

Ethan's face lit up, and I couldn't even regret that it wasn't about me. "Maybe six o'clock? Same place as last time?"

"Okay. I'll bring my gear."

The elevator dinged, and this time both of us looked down the hall. The same relief coursed through our veins as a parent with a very small toddler rounded the corner.

"I'd better go. I don't want Ms. Mini to impale me with a pen or something." Ethan grinned, and part of me was sad to lose that smile. It made everything seem brighter. And with the prospect of that college application waiting for me, I could use some of that brightness.

He took a step back into the hallway and gave me a small nod. "See you tonight."

"See you." I closed the door gently, then stood there, the butterflies in my stomach flapping away. He needed my help filming a car. But who was going to help me with this crush?

CHAPTER FIFTEEN

EVEN THOUGH I KNEW THIS WASN'T TECHNICALLY A DATE, I STILL got a little dressed up. In addition to my sneakers, I had on a black-and-green T-shirt and a black miniskirt. It was comfy, so I could still film, but I felt cute in it. I even let BamBam help me with my makeup, under the guise of wanting to look nice in case Nittha or Gabby decided to take pictures as we explored The Strip.

I spotted Ethan almost immediately. Or rather, I spotted the lime-green sports car with Batmobile doors parked at the very front of the hotel. If we'd been going for an inconspicuous exit, this would have blown our cover. That car could get attention from outer space.

As soon as he saw me, Ethan's face lit up. "You look nice."

"Thanks, my grandma put highlighter on me."

"Pretty sure it's not the highlighter." Ethan's gaze met mine. He stared at me like he meant every word, and my cheeks got hot. He dropped his gaze to his shoes for a second, then cleared his throat and pointed to the car. "Can you believe this thing?"

"I cannot." I tried and failed to keep a straight face as I said this.

"Okay, I know the color is a bit much, but wait till you see inside. Seriously, the seats are more comfortable than a massage chair." The absolute sincerity on Ethan's face was almost too adorable to resist. If half of the lobby hadn't been watching us, I might have actually melted into a feels puddle right next to the valet stand.

"It's got room for all this stuff, so I already like it better than our last ride." I shook my camera bag and black, oversized old-lady sweater that BamBam made me take at the last minute.

Ethan laughed. "The car got us there in one piece, didn't it?"

"Yeah, but I feel like I'll never be able to listen to 'Three Little Birds' again."

"You won't have to worry about that with this one. I can also promise that the custom lighting will not make you feel like you gazed directly into the sun."

Ethan started walking toward the driver's-side door, and I reached into my backpack to get my camera. I was halfway through trying to change my lens, when he interrupted me.

"Are you coming?"

He was standing next to the open doors, confusion on his face. "Don't we need to, like . . ." I shrugged and waved my camera at him. "You know, film this thing?"

Ethan's forehead wrinkled, then relaxed as understanding dawned on him. "No, I did that earlier. I mean, we might want to film it when we get to where we are going, but only if it'd be cool for our video."

"Oh." Now it was my turn to be surprised. "You mean, you got this car and planned out the entire shoot for us?"

"Yeah." Apprehension crept across his face. "Is that okay? If you had somewhere specific you wanted to go, we could go there instead."

"No. No. This is great." I rushed, trying to sort through the roughly fifty thousand emotions flooding my senses. He hadn't wanted my help with the car at all. He wanted as badly as I did for our video to work. Learning that put cracks in the little dam I'd built to hold back all my feelings. Smiling at him, I let the truth slip out before I had the chance to stop it. "In fact, it's perfect. Thank you."

The tension in Ethan's body melted away, and he smiled back at me. This smile felt different, quieter. This was not a smile that was being broadcast for everyone. It was reserved for me. My heart did a backflip as he motioned to the passenger side. "We should get going. I want us to get there on time."

"Where are we going?" I asked, trying not to sound like I was about to go swimming in the deep end of my emotions.

"If we timed this right, and I think I did, we should get to Red Rock Canyon in time to catch the sunset and see the city at night." Ethan beamed at me like this was a stroke of genius. "I tried to think of things that people don't automatically associate with Las Vegas, like nature."

"Clever." I nodded at him and started to walk toward the passenger-side door. I was halfway around the car when it hit me that we were going to watch a sunset. Literally one of the most quintessentially romantic things in the history of the world.

I felt like half of the people waiting for the valet to bring their cars could hear my heart pounding. Should I text Gabby to ask for the signs of a sneaky date? Would that be googleable? I could wait until Ethan was distracted and—

"Wait. Don't get in the car yet," Ethan said, yanking me out of my thought spiral. "Watch the ground in front of the door when I turn the car on." With that, he pressed the ignition, and the car roared to life. There, at my feet, projected onto the sidewalk, was an outline of a snake in green. I looked back at Ethan, who was practically vibrating with glee. "Cool, right? It's a custom door that the rare-car service installed."

"They had a snake installed?" I asked.

"Yeah, because it is a modified Viper," Ethan said, as if it were obvious. I nodded like I understood his meaning. Apparently, his bullshit detector was better than mine, because he then said, "Vipers are cars."

"I knew that." Ethan arched an eyebrow at me, and I amended my response. "I think I did, anyway."

He smirked and motioned for me to get into the car. "The company my mentor got it from customizes luxury cars and then rents them to ridiculously rich people who want to flaunt their wealth in Las Vegas."

"Okay, that I definitely understand. If you are an excessive person, why wouldn't your rental car be excessive, too?" I sank into the passenger-side seat. "Oh my god. This thing is amazing."

"I told you." The volume of Ethan's voice rose as we waited for the car doors to close on their own. "The first time I sat in the seat, I swear my entire spine realigned."

"This *is* better than a massage." I shifted around in my chair to put my bag and the sweater behind my seat, then put my seat belt on.

"They don't even make these anymore. They only ever made around thirty thousand of them," Ethan said, easing out of the valet area. Talking mostly to himself, he continued. "I still can't believe they let me take this thing."

"You really love cars, don't you?" I asked, angling my knees so I could watch Ethan and keeping my phone out for the right moment. He was so happy; I had to get a video of him actually driving.

"I was basically born in a car. I can't help myself."

"Then being a car content creator is a perfect job for you."

"I mean, I don't know that it is the perfect job for me. I sort of fell into it." Ethan frowned a little as we pulled up to the hotel exit light.

"Fell into it like how?"

He fussed with the stereo for a second longer than I suspected it normally took him to connect to Bluetooth, as if buying himself more time to think. "I started making videos to advertise my family's business. It's a long story, but after years at one garage my dad decided to start his own. I was twelve, and I didn't really think much past bringing in customers." A small smile crossed his lips. Choosing his words carefully, he added, "In fact, I was trying to copy the style of those commercials that the Chicago area big-name tire stores have on their websites. I wanted people to see we had a good, reliable garage with knowledgeable mechanics. I think I even said that in my first video, where I explained changing a headlight, which, by the way was about the only thing I knew how to do back then."

Ethan laughed gently, thinking about his younger, optimistic self. "Turns out that the one thing everyone with a car in Chicago googles is how to change a headlight on a Ford Explorer, so people saw the video and liked it. They thought the idea of a family-run garage was sweet and wholesome, and viewers thought it was cute that my dad and older sisters sort of tolerated me filming them. The more views the video got, and the more people came in and mentioned seeing it, the more it was reinforced that I should keep making them."

"This all happened because of one Ford?" I asked, incredulity creeping into the edges of my voice.

Ethan laughed again. "Well, no. I started targeting other car types that our garage works on, mostly American-made at first, but now we also work on some European cars. Anyway." Ethan shook his head to refocus. "I must have changed the headlights of every type of car that came into our garage for six months until I learned how to do other things. The videos did what they were supposed to do for us. People in Chicago learned about our business, and it grew. I started to branch out into other car content because it was helpful and more fun than watching Sophie and Izzie after school. It snowballed, and some of that has been great, but I don't know if I would do it again knowing what I know now."

"What do you mean?"

The light turned green, and Ethan began directing us onto the highway. Unlike the last car, this one was nearly silent aside from the purr of the engine. The muscles in Ethan's jaw tensed, and I realized the question might be more invasive than he wanted to get into.

"You don't have to answer that." I internally kicked myself. If this was a date, I was killing the vibe. "It's your business, obviously."

"No, I don't mind." Ethan's face relaxed as he said this, like the decision to talk about it was more stressful than actually talking. "I didn't think about what it would be like to have part of my life be so extremely public. To have people I don't know and have never met be concerned about me. They have opinions on everything: what I wear, how I talk, who my friends are." He squinted at a road sign and changed lanes before throwing a quick glance at me and adding, "Even who I date."

The memory of his pained expression while talking to Emmie returned, and I winced. "I'm guessing the internet made the breakup with Emmie worse, then?"

"Dating someone with that level of fame is hard. I thought I knew what it was like to have strangers reaching out to me or following me, because of my grandma, but Emmie was next-level. People who didn't even like cars became interested in me because of her, but we were also trapped. When you're fifteen, you don't really think about what it means to publicly date someone. You just put someone on your grid and then taking them off becomes impossible, because you aren't just breaking up with them, you are breaking up with their fans in a way, too. If I'm honest, I think that relationship was over before either of us were ready to admit it. She just moved on before telling anybody, including me."

"Oh." My mouth dropped open. It wasn't that I didn't know the story, but somehow, I hadn't expected him to say it so plainly.

"Your face." Ethan stole a glance at me and then cracked up before laying on the gas a little more. "Don't get me wrong. It wasn't funny at the time, but I can joke about it now. With you. I can't joke about it publicly. That would cause all kinds of problems." Ethan rolled his eyes, and I imagined what kind of comments he would get tagged in if Emmie's legion of fans saw it. "You know, you are one of the few people I don't have to worry about sharing any of these details on the internet."

"Perks of having a social-media-free friend." I grinned over at him as he exited the highway.

"Perks of having a friend you trust," Ethan said, watching my reaction out of the corner of his eye. My heart skipped a beat as the weight of what he'd said sank in. He trusted me. Not because I had no way to share his secrets, but because he didn't think I'd hurt him. I hoped that was true.

"What do you want to do instead? If you don't mind me asking."

"To be honest, I really don't know," Ethan said, after a moment of silence. "I stopped posting regularly. So now, when I share it's because it's a thing I'm excited about and want to teach people. My sister Stephanie is an ESL teacher, so maybe I'd like that, too?"

"I could see you being good at that." I nodded, thinking

about the way he talked to the camera, earnest and patient. Like he understood that cars could be daunting, but he had faith in your ability to figure out the whole headlight-changing thing.

"So, does Emmie know you don't want to do this forever? I feel like if she did, she'd probably give up on you two getting back together."

"She does. But she also has a different level of fame than I do. I can go back to being known only in internet car circles. At least, I hope I can." Ethan frowned, then added, "Emmie has a brand to protect, sponsorships and deals to lose. It's her livelihood, and she's trying to figure out how to make everyone happy with her again."

"Oh." When he explained it like that, I could understand her better. I lived with tremendous pressure trying to make two demanding parents happy. I couldn't imagine what it was like to try to please millions of people. "So, what does she want? For the two of you to get back together, or pretend you're still dating?"

Ethan snorted as we slowed, waiting for a red light to turn at the entrance to the park. "I'm pretty sure she has given up on that."

"Why?"

He glanced over at me like he was surprised I would ask that question. For a moment, he didn't say anything; he only scanned my face. Looking at me intentionally, he held my gaze and said, "Because I'm interested in someone else."

If it was possible to have a heart both stop and beat so hard that it might come out of a chest, mine was trying to do that. Ethan watched me, his expression shifting from playful to something with heat in it. It was the kind of look that made me want to grab onto him. To run my fingers through his hair. Feel his skin against mine. My breathing felt shallow as my imagination ran wild. I tried to make myself say something. Confirm that this new person was me.

Instead, the light changed, and he refocused on the road. "We need driving music before we lose reception."

"Okay," I mumbled as my thoughts smoldered into a useless pile. I wondered if I'd ever recover from his look. Or if I'd melt into a puddle of wanting on the floor mat if he even so much as blinked at me again. I watched as he pressed a button on the steering wheel, imagining his hand on my thigh instead of the car . . . Then cheesy music filled the air, the spell broken by a man singing about walking around in his sleep.

"What is this?" I laughed. "And why are we listening to it?"

"It's 'River of Dreams,'" Ethan said. When that didn't elicit a response, he added, "Billy Joel." When that failed to mean something to me as well, his eyes went wide. "You know, the Piano Man. You don't know any of the good music, do you?"

"This song is older than we are, isn't it?" I rolled my eyes.

"Yes. By several decades. Like the eighties or nineties, I think." Ethan started laughing as we pulled up to a little hut with a park ranger in it. He turned down the Piano Man and opened his window, taking a map from the friendly-looking ranger, who rattled off the park rules.

Falling in line behind the other cars driving through the park on the one-lane road, he turned the song back up and started howling along like we were at karaoke.

"Why is this your driving music?" I asked as soon as the song started to fade.

"It's what my dad listens to at the garage."

"Music from the eighties?" I did a little math, then peeked over at Ethan. "Wait, my parents listen to two thousands hip-hop. How old is your dad?"

"Sixty-five. Second family, remember?" He gestured to his chest before putting his hand back on the gearshift.

"I remembered. I just didn't put together that he was that much older when he had you. Isn't your grandma sixty-nine?" I wrinkled my forehead and tried to imagine what it would be like if my mom and BamBam were the same age. That would not have worked in our house.

"Yup. It can get weird when the two of them geek out over the same generational stuff. Like they both saw the original *Star Wars* in theaters. Not together, obviously, but like they have the same memories about it. We sort of don't talk about my parents' age gap much," Ethan said, then added, "Okay, well, my grandma sometimes talks about it in a shady way when she's had two glasses of wine."

I snorted. "BamBam would do the same thing. She pretends to like my mom for my dad's sake, but I'm pretty sure she would like her to go to Antarctica for all eternity. At one point, after my grandpa died and she first moved in, she seized control of our kitchen and insisted on doing our hair before school. There is a reason my parents built her an apartment above the house rather than giving her a suite in it."

"The kitchen and the morning routine? That's diabolical."

"It really was. My mom is not the kind of woman to appreciate someone making her look like she doesn't know what she is doing. Although, in BamBam's defense, my mom really did not know what she was doing with our hair. My hair isn't as thick and my curls aren't as tight as my brother's and sister's, but none of us could withstand washing it every other day like my mom. BamBam staged a social intervention before we got teased off the playground." I shook my head as I remembered her coming into the room my sister and I shared with about a gallon of Pink Lotion, Blue Magic, and a wide-toothed comb, determined to get us together before we ended up "bald-headed."

"That's kind of what I like about having my grandma around." Ethan smiled as we weaved our way up the canyon. "Stuff that my parents don't get or freak out about, she usually has a different perspective on."

"Right!" I hadn't meant to get so excited, but this was a thing that my friends who didn't live with their grandparents couldn't understand. "It's like having an adult who can help you figure out your adults. I don't know what I'd do without BamBam. I'd probably already have given up. I'd wear sweater sets and be a junior accountant in training."

Ethan wrinkled his nose at me as if I'd grown a second head. "I really can't imagine you in a sweater set."

"Oh, you don't have to. Every year on picture day, my mom makes sure I'm in one. For last year's Christmas card, I'm even wearing pearls."

"No. You?" Ethan shook his head, like the mental image was as disturbing to him as it was to me in real life. "You don't really wear jewelry, do you? That feels wrong."

"It feels wrong because it is wrong." I laughed. The golden hour had officially begun, bathing the angles of his face in a gentle orange glow as we wound past rust-red canyons and scrub brush.

I tried to be stealthy as I started filming him driving, the scenery flashing by. Even if we didn't use this footage for anything, I wanted to remember this moment. Ethan in his element, singing along to music that was made for people decades older, in a car he loved. It felt like I was getting to see another side of him. Like I was seeing the Ethan that only close friends and family saw.

After a moment, he looked over at me and furrowed his brow. "Are you filming?"

"Yup. The lighting is perfect." I bit down on my bottom lip to keep myself from saying any other thoughts out loud. Like that this moment with him was perfect.

Ethan pushed his hair out of his eyes, then smiled at me. It was a big, goofy smile, meant to ruin the shot. I sighed, trying to sound irritated, but I couldn't make myself stop smiling back at him. At the beginning of the trip, him doing that would have made me nuts, but now, I found it—him, really—endearing. I stopped recording and put the phone down. Maybe I'd be able to get some more shots once we parked.

Ethan turned back to the road right as the song changed again, his eyes going wide as someone sang about how it might be nice to touch someone else's body. He cleared his throat and pressed a button. "Not George Michael right now."

"Wait." I tilted my head as a funny thought struck me. "Is your old-man mixtape a little sexy? Because now I'm curious about the song and—"

"Oh look. We're here," Ethan said in mock surprise as he changed the subject. The parking lot was small yet packed. Ethan slowed down to a creep. "Watch for a parking—aha!"

White reverse lights came on an SUV, and Ethan floored it to get to the spot before any of the other cars circling could figure out what was happening. Sliding into the spot at almost the same time that the SUV with Arizona plates pulled out, he grinned at me like he'd won us a prize at a fair. We were parked on the edge of the lot facing the overlook. If we wanted to, we could watch the sunset from the driver's-side window. Not that I wouldn't get out of the car. The view was simply too good to miss.

I was about to grab my gear, when Ethan held up a DJI Osmo. "Since it's crowded, maybe we just put my camera on the car and let it do the work. Then we can enjoy the sunset."

"Oh, alright." I felt strangely naked getting out of the car without my gear. Ethan's forehead wrinkled in concentration as he messed with the camera's positioning and the suction mount he was using to hold it to the car. Pink streaks started to trace the sky, gently highlighting his face. He was beautiful in this light.

Ethan must have felt me staring, because he said, "This will only take a second."

"Right."

Great. Now I was being a weirdo. I walked around to the front of the car and leaned on the hood with my hip, deciding to focus on the natural wonder we'd come to see. In front of us, the craggy painted rock faces were transforming—the strips of mountain that had been a rust color became a deep red, while the strips of white in the stone almost mirrored the darkening sky.

Behind me, I could hear the doors' hydraulics slowly shutting, meaning Ethan must have sorted out how to make the camera stay put. I figured he'd let me know when he was ready to walk over to the railing, so I kept my eyes on the sky as little wisps of clouds began to turn magenta. Below, the lights of Las Vegas started to sparkle.

"It's beautiful." Ethan appeared next to me. For a moment the two of us stood there, watching the sky. Then he asked, "Should we go over to the actual lookout?"

"I guess we should have the full experience." I smiled up at him, and we headed toward the railing.

Ethan took a sharp breath and then pulled out his phone. "I almost forgot. I took this just now."

I peeked at the phone. He'd taken a picture of the car at an angle that made it appear as if it were alone at the overlook, the sunset coming off in bright oranges and pinks against a deep-blue sky. I was technically in the photo, but because of the shadowing, you couldn't really tell it was me. Mostly, I was a sheet of hair and a pair of sneakers. It was a really good photo, like the kind a car company would pay big dollars to try to create.

"It's amazing. Professional-car-photoshoot vibes." I grinned.

"Would it be okay if I posted it? You can say no."

"Go for it."

"Really? I know you are choosey about what's on social media and all."

I waved a hand to signal that it was no big deal, even as Ethan's eyebrows crept up in surprise. "My mom is not following you, so I'm less concerned about it."

"Okay." Ethan shrugged, a lopsided smile working its way across his face as we started walking again.

By the time we'd reached the outlook railing, the fence was crowded with other sunset watchers. We managed to find a spot that probably would have fit one adult comfortably, but the two of us squeezed into it, our bodies pressed next to each other like we were standing at a concert. This wasn't the first time I'd stood this close to him, but that didn't stop my brain from noticing every detail, from the feel of his arm pressed into mine to the steady rhythm of his breathing, the smell of his soap mixing with the desert air.

A comfortable silence settled between us as we watched the horizon. Slowly, the sky changed again, the oranges and pinks replaced by blues and purples as the sun sank behind the mountains. I shivered and tucked myself a little closer to Ethan, hoping to siphon off a bit of his body heat. He pulled his attention away from the sunset to study me.

"Cold?" he asked.

"I should have brought BamBam's sweater from the back seat."

"Here." Ethan rotated slightly, wrapping an arm around me and pulling me to his side. I leaned my head against his shoulder, letting the warmth of him wash over me.

There are moments when the world seems too beautiful to be real. It's a feeling so intense that the joy of being alive becomes overwhelming. Where the best option is simply to breathe and soak in the idea that every single star had to align for this moment to happen. This place, with this sunset, felt like that. Like all the beauty in the world was wrapped into this sunset and tucked into my soul. I could carry the memory of it with me, but no camera could ever re-create it.

Ethan rested his head on top of mine, and it felt like we could have stayed with that sunset and been happy forever. In a way, I wished we could. I didn't want to go home in two days. This was a moment my parents would consider a diversion. I was off track, off task, and out in the middle of nowhere with a boy. Yet it was exactly the kind of imperfect that I wanted to last a lifetime.

Eventually, the sun disappeared entirely, and groups of people began to peel off and return to their cars. Ethan sighed, and my heart sank. I desperately did not want this night to end. "We should probably go. Don't want to be late."

"There's more?" I asked, lifting my head off his shoulder. Even though he'd said we should go, he hadn't let go of me yet, and I wasn't about to make him. I smiled up at him and tried not to notice how close we were. Close enough that I could reach up on my toes and kiss him if he'd let me.

"Can you stay out later?" Ethan asked, his hand sliding lightly down my arm to rest on my waist. The feel of his touch there sent my pulse racing and made my mind fuzzy.

"Uh-huh." I forced myself to keep my eyes fixed on him and my hands to myself, then held my breath, convinced he could feel the tension pulsing through me.

He bit down on his bottom lip and watched me for a moment, then nodded. "Good. You'll like this next place."

Ethan gently pressed on my hip, using his arm to guide us back to the car. My mind staggered even as my body started to move. If this was how the rest of the night went, I'd probably die from anticipation before he kissed me.

A little voice reminded me that while I couldn't have forever with Ethan, I could have right now. And if that was all I could have, then I should enjoy every second of it before the night was over.

CHAPTER SIXTEEN

THE REST OF THE SCENIC DRIVE PASSED IN A BLUR OF GRANDPA music that Ethan seemed to know every word of, and that I could begrudgingly accept were old-school bops. I even planned to add some of them to a playlist once we got back within cell range. Not that I was going to admit that to Ethan just yet. A girl had to have some pride.

"So, what about your family?" Ethan asked over a particularly catchy song about being just what someone needed.

"What about them?" I asked, feeling my shoulders tense up. Unlike Ethan, I wasn't about to hang out with my mom all day at her office or start listening to my dad's music while driving my dream car.

"I mean, what are they like?" Ethan peeked over at me for a split second before returning his eyes to the road. "Brothers, sisters? Are your parents accountants who wear leopard print like BamBam, or . . ."

"Absolutely not." I laughed. "They'd never admit it, but my parents care a lot about appearances and what other people think. I'm pretty sure they believe BamBam is a bad influence on me."

"Really?" Ethan's eyebrows crept toward his hairline.

"Yup. BamBam was the one who got me interested in film. They don't get her beauty 'hobby,' but it's helping put my sister through college, so they can't really comment." I put air quotes around the word *hobby* to be clear that it was their word for BamBam's business, not mine. "My dad even helps manage her bookkeeping, can see how successful she is, and he still doesn't take it seriously because the internet is not 'a real job.' He thinks it's a fad that will go away."

"Wow." Ethan's voice was low, like he was genuinely taken aback. "So, what do they think of you helping her?"

"They think it's fine for me to have a creative outlet as long as it doesn't interfere with school or embarrass them in any public way."

"How could you embarrass them?"

"You name it, I can do it." I took a deep breath and held up my hand to start listing. "Dressing sloppy in a photo—my mom hates that. Using the word *can* when I mean *may*—that will make my dad nuts. Generally, losing is frowned upon unless it is in a team setting, and it was clear you played well. A grade lower than a B plus, which is only acceptable if you told them you were struggling and worked with a tutor. Basically, if it's imperfect, silly, or open to interpretation, it's embarrassing."

I sucked in another gulp of air and realized my shoulders were scrunched up to my ears. Forcing myself to exhale, I dropped my shoulders, although I didn't really feel any less tense. Next to me, Ethan was silent as we slowed down for a red light. Panic laced its way through my veins.

What if he thought I was the one who was nuts? Really, was it so wrong to want your kid to use proper grammar and get good grades? Lots of people wanted that. And sure, it might be a little weird that my mom wanted me to look nice in every picture I'd ever taken, but she wasn't wrong about the internet being forever. It was basically an extension of my first impression for the rest of my life and—

"That's why you didn't want to put your face in the video. In case we don't win?" Ethan's voice was so soft, but it still felt like it might shatter me. I nodded, afraid that if I tried to speak, I might cry.

"And you don't use social media . . ."

"Because I don't want to risk documenting any imperfections." My voice was as small as I felt. I hadn't really tried to explain this to anyone before. Saying it out loud made it seem like an impossible way to live. "Plus, my mom would analyze my account relentlessly. She's probably looking for me in Cricket's stories right now, compiling suggestions for how I should wear my hair or avoid certain shades of green."

The light changed, and Ethan eased the car back into gear, his face serious as the Neon Museum came into view. Flipping on his blinker to turn into the museum parking lot, he sighed. "Have your parents met you?"

"What?" I laughed. "Of course they've met me."

"No, I'm serious." Ethan pulled the car into a parking space and shut it off, then looked at me, a scowl etched on his face. "Sure, you don't love getting dressed up and you have a high tolerance for glitter, but you are smart and funny and talented. What is a more perfect version of you supposed to act like?"

The question hung between us heavy as the air right before it rains. This whole trip, I'd been torn between being the me I wanted to be and feeling guilty over not being the version of me that my parents and BamBam expected. It never even occurred to me to question what that version of me would actually look like. I only knew that, to my parents, I wasn't enough. To Bam-Bam, I was more than enough as long as I followed her one rule. Of course, now I was lying to her face in order to spend time with Ethan, breaking her rule and risking her not supporting me, just like my parents.

"I . . ." My first instinct was to try to defend my parents, to offer the same excuse everyone from my siblings to our neighbors made for them. *They mean well.* But I couldn't bring myself to say that. At least not to Ethan. I cleared my throat, then tried out the truth, the words tasting bitter. "I'm not sure."

"Jamie, people mess up. They lose. That's life." Ethan ducked his head slightly to catch my eye. "The only way to avoid making mistakes is to not live at all."

"Or to live as someone else." I laughed, but the sound felt hollow. Thinking about the half-finished college application sitting on my computer, I shrugged. "My parents have a really good life planned for me." I started to list. "Business degree of some kind, join one of their firms after graduate school, then they'll help with a down payment on a house nearby, and Sunday dinners with them and my two point five kids. They might even let me get a dog someday if I'm responsible enough."

"You can't really be considering that life." Ethan blinked at me, incredulous. He reached for my hand. His fingers were callused from working with car parts. "Please tell me you understand that the pressure they put on you to be perfect is weird?"

"Intellectually, I know that." I ran my thumb over the back of his hand, then met his eye. "In practice, things are a little harder to navigate. My brother and sister handle the pressure better because they were already wired for it. They will both be doctors or accountants for sure, and happily so."

"I cannot imagine you as an accountant." Ethan laughed, then stilled. "Does your family know what you want to do?"

"I've tried telling them. My words never seem to sink in." My throat tightened, tears hovering behind my eyes. "BamBam knows. I think it's why she hasn't hired someone with more experience running a content business. She can't openly go against their parenting, but she is trying to help in her own way. It's why I love her so much. She's my lifeline."

"Maybe you should try telling your parents again. If Bam-Bam believes in you, they might see all the good things about you, too."

I knew my parents loved me and that they wanted what was best for me. I also knew that we had very different ideas about what was best for me. But Ethan was also right. The only way my definition of my future and theirs would ever align was if I risked making them upset. I couldn't stand at the crossroads much longer. College applications were due soon. My future was basically now.

I leaned my head back on the seat. "Showing them is so much harder than it sounds. Here, at the con, I'm surrounded by people who see a way to make a future where there isn't a clear path." I sighed. "My parents are different. They are the kind of people who need a well-maintained trail to follow at the very least—preferably a large highway with useful signage. I don't want to disappoint them."

"You won't. If anyone could figure out how to make this work, it is someone who is already making it work. They'll either adjust, or you'll be so rich and famous you won't care. You wouldn't be the first person to disappoint their parents." Ethan grinned and squeezed my hand.

"Who needs family when you can swim in piles of money?" I giggled, then dropped my chin to my chest as the weight of what we were joking about pressed down on me. "I hope they adjust."

"If they don't, you'll still be happy that you followed your dream." Ethan lightly grazed my arm. "Do you need a hug? You look like you need a hug."

"Yes." I laughed, the sound a little wobbly. "Telling people you are only human and your parents hate that is really hard."

Ethan released my hand. Reaching for the key in the center console, he said, "Come on, human being, let's get out of the car so I can give you a hug."

I waited for the door to open, then swung my legs out and was immediately reminded to grab BamBam's sweater. After pulling it on in one motion, I stopped to take my hair out of the sweater's neck before I caught Ethan's expression.

"What?"

"Nothing." He shrugged, a smile tugging at the corners of his mouth.

"I know that face. You've thought something is funny, and you won't be able to keep it to yourself for long, so you may as well tell me now."

"Okay." Ethan exhaled. "That sweater is the most spectacularly grandma sweater. I feel like you need a pair of giant glasses and a hair bow, then you could be one of Buzzy's fans."

I put my hand on my hip and shook my hair out. "I don't know what you are talking about. I borrowed this sweater from BamBam. And we both know that BamBam would never own a sweater that looks like Buzzy's."

Ethan cackled at my sarcasm as the car doors closed. Walking toward me, he pointed at his chest with both hands. "My bad. I forgot that our grandmothers are the most original people. Let's never tell them that their taste in sweaters is the same."

"I'll agree to those terms only if I receive the hug I was promised."

"You drive a hard bargain." Ethan spread his arms wide. I stepped into his embrace, burying my head against his chest and wrapping my arms around him. Ethan rested his chin on the top of my head, creating a protective shield for me to sink deeper into.

There are some hugs that feel like home, an embrace standing in for a lifetime of conversations that haven't happened yet but mean something just the same. Being here in a Las Vegas parking lot on a chilly evening with Ethan's arms encircling me was one of those hugs. Falling into the moment fully, I lost myself in the rhythm of his breathing, the way he smelled, and the way I felt in his arms. Not like I was being squeezed so hard I couldn't breathe or held so loosely that it seemed like a signal to let go. This felt like we fit.

Headlights shone in my face as another car pulled into the parking lot, reminding me that we were here for a reason. Reluctantly, I loosened my grip on Ethan and he slowly let go of me.

Taking a step back, we locked eyes, and he asked, "Feel better?"

"Yes, but— Oh, don't look so smug."

"I'm not smug, I promise."

"And yet, you still look smug." I shook my head and started walking out of the parking lot and up a little hill toward the museum.

"Never." I threw Ethan a sideways look as he jogged to catch up with me, smiling sheepishly. "Okay, it is less a smug thing and more pleased. You tried to be all aloof when I met you, and I have accurately predicted your emotional needs several times."

"Accurately predicted my emotional needs?" My eyebrows shot up. "You fed me chips and gave me a hug. That doesn't exactly make your emotional intelligence sky-high."

"And yet, something is telling me that if I asked if you wanted to hold my hand right now, the answer to that would be yes." My jaw dropped even as my heart started beating about a million times a minute. Ethan offered me that same smug smile and held out his hand. "Tell me if I'm wrong."

I glanced down at his hand for a moment, then back at him. The smile was still there, but underneath it was a hint of something else. Nerves, maybe? The thought that he was still worried I might say no made my insides melt.

"Alright, maybe you figured me out a little bit." I sighed and placed my hand in his. Ethan's smile spread, and all traces of apprehension washed away. Wrinkling my nose up at him, I added, "Don't go getting a big head or anything."

"Oh, of course not." Ethan shrugged one shoulder as we made our way to the museum lobby, the hum of neon lights already filling the air. "A couple lucky breaks. That's all."

The two of us walked in the kind of silence that doesn't need filling. The neck of a massive glowing guitar jutted up over a white fence into the night sky, letting us know that we were in the right place. The Neon Museum building was unlike anything I'd seen before. Like someone had taken seashells and placed them side by side on top of a brightly lit glass box.

"What time is your reservation?" a chipper employee asked as we reached the door.

"Eight-fifteen," Ethan told them.

The employee grinned and readjusted the hat on their head before waving us in. "Go ahead and wait in the lobby. The tour will get started in about seven minutes."

I did my best to smile, too, although that was partially my teeth chattering as the air continued to cool. In hindsight, I needed more cute outfits that involved pants.

The two of us walked through the doors and into the lobby. Inside, the bright-white shells resembled the vaults in a church ceiling. Behind a partially roped-off area, several people pointed at different display cases, speaking softly. I'd known this was a museum, and yet I wasn't prepared for how quiet it'd be, given all the bright lights around us. Stepping closer to Ethan, I squeezed his hand. He held on to my gaze. My heartbeat picked up all over again, and I wondered if I would ever get used to the way his eyes on mine made me feel.

"Welcome. I can scan your tickets here," said the employee behind a podium in the cordoned-off area.

Ethan let go of my hand, then reached into his pocket to get his phone. My palm tingled as cool air rushed into the place where his hand had been. I rubbed my fingers against the skin of my palm. At the start of the trip, I could've counted on one hand the number of times I'd thought about Ethan Wyatt—all of them tied to my grandma. Now I was officially the person who missed holding his hand. How had that snuck up on me so quickly?

"Jamie?"

The sound of Ethan saying my name pulled me out of my thoughts. The employee had finished putting a band around his wrist. I held my arm out and they snapped the wristband around mine, saying, "These are for the second part of the show. Have fun."

Ethan and I stepped into the waiting area and wandered toward a display case by the wall. Inside was an upside-down drawing of a building, a mirror staged over it so that the viewer could see the picture right side up as well.

"Oh," Ethan said next to me, sounding excited as he waved at the case. "I read about this."

"A drawing?"

"No. The building. The person who designed it is an extremely famous Black architect. He learned to draw upside down because white clients didn't want to sit next to him, which is weird because he was building their homes," Ethan digressed, his forehead wrinkling as he tried to process the cognitive dissonance, then, accepting that he couldn't, shook his head to get himself back on track. "He designed celebrity houses and stuff. What's his name?" Ethan pushed his hair off his forehead as he tried to remember.

"Paul Revere Williams?"

"Yes! Did you already know this, and I just explained this to you for no reason?"

"Architect is on my parents' list of acceptable careers, so they reread his picture book biography to me often as a kid." Ethan bit down on his lip sheepishly. I pointed to the wall. "Okay that, and the sign."

"Well, that is one way to know his name."

"I still appreciate the enthusiasm." I nudged him with my hip. "Oh, and thanks for earlier."

Ethan quirked an eyebrow.

"When you called me smart and funny and talented."

"Oh." His cheeks reddened. "Well, I wouldn't thank me just yet. I did leave a quality off the list."

"Is it my stunning fashion sense?" I smiled, spreading my arms wide to model my giant sweater again. "Because I think we thoroughly covered that already."

"No." Ethan laughed and shook his head. Looking directly in my eyes, he said, "I forgot to add that you're beautiful, too."

Now my face was hot. I opened my mouth, then closed it again, willing my brain to think of something clever or cute to say.

"Everyone here for the eight-fifteen tour?" A voice rocketed around the lobby, causing both of us to jump and saving me from myself. Next to me, Ethan's hand flew to his chest. It was an extremely dainty gesture for someone who I could have used a lot of adjectives to describe—enthusiastic, hot, thoughtful, hot (again)—but definitely not dainty.

Ethan threw a look at me as the people around us nodded at the tour guide. "What?"

"You clutched your pearls like Buzzy," I said, trying to get my laughter under control.

"Someone dressed like their grandma shouldn't throw stones," Ethan said in mock offense, a smile creeping into the corners of his mouth as he let his hand fall away.

After a few half-hearted mumbles, the guide grinned. "Alright, then let's get started. We are standing in the lobby of the old La Concha Motel, designed by Paul Revere Williams . . ."

"Shoot," I whispered to Ethan, trying to keep my voice down even as regret snaked its way through me. "I left my gear in the car."

"Oops." Ethan shrugged as if I hadn't spoiled his whole plan.

"I can try—"

"Don't worry about it." Ethan gently bumped his shoulder against mine, his voice low in my ear. "We've got our phones if we want them. If not, we'll just enjoy ourselves."

I watched his face for a sign that he was upset, but if anything, he seemed almost happy about it. As if taking a night off from the internet and filming had been his plan all along . . .

If that was his plan, then this was most definitely a date. I grinned up at him.

"Ready?" Ethan asked as the people around us started moving, confusion lacing its way into his expression.

Great. Now I was staring at him with emoji heart eyes like that would compel him to kiss me. Not weird at all.

"Yup." I nodded with too much enthusiasm and tried to wipe the absurdly big smile off my face. "Let's go see some lights."

"Okay." Ethan eyed me like my sudden burst of enthusiasm was making him suspicious, then followed the crowd out the door.

"Wow." I exhaled. "This is gorgeous."

"Right," Ethan whispered back, his face tinged with the same wonder I felt.

Outside was like stepping into another world. On The Strip, all the neon lights were overwhelming. Like my attention span was being torn into fifty-eleven different pieces. But here, in the quiet of the night outside the city's main hustle, the neon was magical. Like someone had cast a spell over us.

As the guide started to explain all the vintage signs, from the Moulin Rouge, the first desegregated casino on The Strip, to the Red Barn, one of the first gay bars in Las Vegas, my perspective on the city shifted. Sure, it was still chaotic, but there was a heartbeat here. Like a hundred other cities, Las Vegas, beneath all the glitter, was deeply human.

At different points, Ethan and I stopped to take pictures of each other with the signs. Half of them were blurry because we were rushing, and at least a third of them had Ethan making silly faces at me, but it didn't really matter. Tonight, under the glow of the lights, every picture felt perfect.

"Wait, hold still." I pulled out my phone to take another picture of Ethan, the pinkish glow from a flashing WEDDING INFORMATION sign highlighting his cheekbones and giving his normally sandy-blond hair a reddish tint. He looked at the sign, then back at me, then did an exaggerated wink at the camera.

"Switch." Ethan waved at me to come stand where he was standing, even as the tour group started to move to the next sign. I blew a kiss at him. Ethan took the picture, then pretended to grab the kiss and smash it to his cheek.

"You're extremely cheesy." I laughed as we tried to catch up with the group.

"Sure, I'm cheesy. But you have to admit, I'm pretty gr-ate." Ethan snorted as I groaned. "Get it? Because cheese is grated and—"

"Oh, I understood the pun. It was just really bad."

"I make no apologies."

"But you should." I cackled. "That joke was beneath you, Grandpa."

"My car music should have been your first clue. Proud grandpa right here." He beamed at me and tapped his chest.

"Thank you all for joining us here. For those of you who are seeing the show, hang around for fifteen minutes, and we'll call your group," the guide said, interrupting our giggles long enough for the two of us to pull it together. "Until then, feel free to take pictures or visit the gift shop."

"Come on. We have to take another picture." Ethan nodded toward the La Concha Motel sign.

"Maybe someone from the group will—" I eyed the yard for

a group that wasn't already occupied with their own glittering neon photos, then turned back to him and shrugged.

"I have long arms." Ethan held his arms out to demonstrate his reach. "And it doesn't have to be perfect."

"Alright, but when it's blurry and we have to find someone to retake it, don't say I didn't tell you so." I laughed as I walked over to his side. Ethan threw his free arm around me, and I tucked myself underneath it, snuggling against him, then smiled up at the camera.

"Three, two, one." I felt his countdown vibrate through his chest as Ethan prepared to take the picture. After a series of screen blinks, he let his arms fall and repositioned himself slightly so we could both see the pictures. I tried to ignore the fact that my side felt cold with his absence and watched as he scrolled through a series of off-kilter photos.

"Okay, well, they're definitely not perfect," I said. The two of us were in frame, but the sign was crooked and half of it was missing.

"What do you mean? Everything that matters is in the picture."

"Sure. If by 'everything that matters' you mean half a neon sign, then you are correct."

Ethan stared down at the photo and then back at me, half smiling. "You're the part that's important to me."

The gentle hum of neon bulbs buzzed between us as I processed exactly what he'd said.

"Ethan, I . . ."

I paused midsentence and tried to collect my thoughts. I couldn't pretend that I didn't care anymore or that we were nothing more than friends. And it was obvious he wanted something from me. I wasn't a rebound or just some girl to make his ex jealous. If he'd gone to this much trouble to arrange tonight, it was safe to say Ethan cared about me just as much as I liked him.

In my mind, telling him how I felt was easy. But now that I was trying to do it, none of my words seemed quite right. The feel of his hand in mine came back to me. I wanted my words to feel like that memory, warm and reassuring. I reached for one of his hands, holding his fingers loosely in mine as I studied our skin. My mind whirled through a thousand phrases.

I like you.

No.

I really like you.

Still not enough.

You get me.

Bland.

Please don't let me go.

Desperate . . . and a little unhinged sounding.

"Yes?" Ethan gently prompted me, and I peered up at him. The same honey-brown eyes that had caught my attention on the plane searched my face, reminding me of a thousand small moments with him. Time spent together that I didn't know would matter now seemed like everything to me.

Ethan mattered to me.

That was it. That was the phrase I wanted to say. Taking a deep breath, I pulled my shoulders back.

"If you are here for the nine-fifteen display, please follow me."

Not for the first time, a museum employee's voice made both of us jump. I tried not to resent them for ruining my perfect moment a second time. Ethan's face appeared stunned, as if someone had thrown a football directly at his head and barely missed.

"Thanks for arranging this." I sighed, feeling the courage I'd managed to scrounge up disappear under the expectant gaze of the museum employee. Why was I such a wimp? People put themselves out there and got rejected all the time. Instead, I seemed doomed to miss the moment forever.

"Oh, of course," Ethan said. Gently, he rearranged our hands so they were properly clasped, then looked down at me, checking to see if this was still okay. I smiled up at him, praying that it would convey all my unarticulated feelings. The ones I understood and the ones I didn't, all of which added up to the idea that Ethan felt like my person.

Even though, according to my parents, I was too young to have a person. And according to BamBam, this particular "young person" was meant to be in my no-person zone. But I'd worry about all that after I was brave enough to tell Ethan everything.

"We should go." Ethan nodded in the direction of the employee who was now walking out of the park. We wandered back across the street as the guide walked us through a series of murals focusing on the unsung heroes of Las Vegas.

"You could totally make a movie about this," Ethan whispered as we moved to the next mural. "Old Las Vegas."

I eyed him to see if he was serious. When he didn't laugh,

I leaned into him playfully. "I feel like it can't be a heist movie, though. That's been done. Maybe I'll make a love story."

"*A Las Vegas Love Story.*" Ethan moved his hand in an arc as if seeing a title on a marquee. "Has a nice ring to it. I'd see it."

"At this point, it is clear to me that you will sit through anything," I joked.

"Only if you make it."

My heart seemed to beat twice as fast as he smiled down at me.

Our guide stopped at the entrance to another outdoor park, pulling my attention away from Ethan as they said, "And this is where we keep the signs we can't repair. It's also where our show starts. It's set to music that is gonna make you want to shake what you got. We'll leave everything lit up after the show, so don't worry about taking pictures now. Just enjoy the experience."

Ethan and I exchanged glances, then tried to swallow our giggles. The employee looked like the kind of person who would shake what the good Lord gave them any day of the week to any song, including a polka if it came on. Part of me hoped they would play some of Ethan's old-man music to see if he could resist the urge to dance along with the show.

As the employee went over the rules about filming (don't do it), Ethan whispered, "This is what I wanted you to see. I watched that video you did where you colorized all those old photos of BamBam. I bet you could do something like this with that skill."

I felt my eyebrows creep up my forehead. That video of

BamBam was a couple years old, back when I was experimenting with different photo-treatment techniques to see what people would click on. I'd loved it, but it hadn't been popular, so I'd stopped doing it. Apparently, Ethan not only went that far back in my creative history; he remembered it.

"What—" I wanted to ask him what he saw in those videos, when the lights dropped and we were plunged into darkness.

Moments later, a projector reincarnated the long-dead signs, as an old jazz standard about love and Las Vegas played. The lights displayed on the signs weren't neon, but in some ways, they seemed more magical, like someone had colorized an old photo and placed us in it. Suddenly, we were back in time, the reanimated neon transporting us to the early days of the city with all the glamour and mystery that entailed. With the lights swirling around us, it felt like I was on a dance floor waiting to be swept up in Ethan's arms.

I'm not sure that either of us made the conscious decision to stand closer to one another. All I know is that by the time another slow jazz standard came on, Ethan's arms were around me. I leaned my head back to rest on his chest. The rhythm of his breathing and the warmth of his body against mine was soothing. Like it was just us two living in the illusion the old signs cast.

Eventually the music faded, and we were left with the sparkle of projected lights. Other guests started to take pictures, but Ethan and I didn't move—unwilling to let go of the last little bit of magic. Nestled against him, I let my mind drift back to the museum and the words I'd been trying to find. I could still say them now. Even if he never kissed me, Ethan deserved to hear the truth. Closing my eyes, I took one deep breath, before reaching up to take hold of Ethan's hand again. Exhaling, I leaned away from him, slowly unwinding our bodies so that I could face him.

Ethan swung our hands back and forth, then smiled at me. "Are you ready to leave?"

"Not yet. I want to tell you something. Or, I don't know . . . talk about something." I shook my head, my eyebrows drawing together in concentration as Ethan's smile faltered slightly. Taking a deep breath to slow myself down, I tried again. "I mean, I want to talk about you. Us. I want to talk about us."

"Uh-huh." Ethan's brow furrowed even as he tried to keep his surprise out of his tone. "Okay. What about?"

The little piece of me that wasn't freaking out about opening up wanted to laugh at how nervous he sounded. The rest of me was pretty sure that even though it was cold out, I might anxiety-sweat through BamBam's sweater.

After taking a careful, slow breath, I said, "When we were talking at Red Rock, you mentioned that you were interested in someone new and I—"

"Oh." Ethan's entire body relaxed. Stepping a few inches closer to me, he said, "To be clear, the someone new is you. I'm interested in you."

I tilted my head back and grinned. "Yeah. I figured that part out."

"Okay, because I didn't think I was being subtle, but you didn't say anything so then I resigned myself to potentially dying in the friend zone of an unrequited crush."

A gentle laugh rolled through Ethan's body, then he bit down on his lower lip to keep himself from saying more. We were close enough now that I could see the fine lines of his cheekbones highlighted in the shimmer of the neon signs. I wanted to reach out with my free hand and trace the reflection on his skin. Instead, I reached down and took his other hand.

"You were not subtle." I stepped an inch closer to him. "I just hadn't figured out the perfect words to say that I felt the same. Maybe I still haven't, but I really like you, Ethan Wyatt. You matter to me."

For a moment, Ethan was still, and I started to wonder if I'd actually said anything out loud, or if this entire thing was a dream. Then a slow, quiet smile made its way across his face. Ethan glanced to the left and then the right as if he were waiting for someone to tell him this wasn't real. When that person didn't appear, he looked back at me.

"I thought you knew?" Ethan took a small step closer to me. We were close enough that I had to tilt my head back slightly to be able to see that smile. "You don't need to be perfect with me. I want you exactly as you are, Jamie Webb."

My heart was beating wildly. Ethan licked his lips, and my breathing became shallow as desire coursed through me. I leaned into him, closing the gap between us. Searching his eyes, I whispered, "So then, is there no perfect way to ask if I can kiss you?"

Ethan laughed quietly, then dipped his head so our lips were almost touching as he said, "That is the perfect way."

His lips brushed mine. The kiss was shy at first, soft and gentle, like he was testing to see if I was really there. I untwined our fingers, sliding one of my hands up the plane of his chest, enjoying the feel of him, solid beneath my hand. My touch seemed to free something inside of him, and Ethan deepened the kiss, releasing my other hand and wrapping his arms around me, pulling me closer to him so our bodies were aligned.

My mind shut everything that wasn't him out. The press of his hand on the small of my back. His hair between my fingers. The smell of him. His taste. Like mint and something untamed and sweet. Whatever it was, I wanted more of it.

Slowly, Ethan relaxed his hold on me, and I held on tighter to him, still dizzy from the kiss. "What . . ."

Ethan leaned his forehead against mine and whispered, "The lights are on."

My mind cleared enough to realize that he was right: They had turned on the bright park floodlights again, taking the magic of the re-created neon with them. I sighed, letting my hand fall away from the back of his neck. "I'd rather stay here with you."

"Kissing me is not location dependent. I'll always be where you are."

DAY 5: LUCK OF THE DRAW

CHAPTER SEVENTEEN

"TIME TO GET UP, KIDDO." BAMBAM SHOOK ME AWAKE WITH EN-tirely too much enthusiasm. "We got to move."

"I . . ." I pushed up my bonnet, which had slipped down my forehead, and tried to get my bearings. What was she talking about, and why was she talking to me about it before dawn? I'd gotten back from my actual-real-not-a-sneaky date with Ethan a sliver before eleven, which meant that I was getting less than eight hours of sleep. Not that BamBam knew why I was so tired.

"Picking up the rental car in T-minus twenty minutes. Bam-Bam is not sitting in Los Angeles traffic," BamBam said, looming over me as vague bits and pieces of a college-tour plan came back to me.

"What . . . time—"

"Chop-chop." BamBam clapped, the sound echoing against our sparse hotel walls. "LA waits for no one. Your USC campus tour starts at eleven a.m."

That rattled my sleep-deprived brain into gear. The only reason my parents had let BamBam pull me out of school was because she had promised them a full day of college tours. It just so happened that the schools with the best business programs on the West Coast also happened to have good film programs. Sure, I'd be busy pretending I was interested in business all day, but at least I'd be seeing my potential future. As it stood, my plan was to get into one of these schools, then quietly change majors. Obviously, my parents much preferred SISU and were not exactly enthusiastic about paying out-of-state or private-school tuition, but I was counting on Bam-Bam's powers of persuasion to get me across that bridge when the time came.

". . . not to mention UCLA at two p.m. I might have us drive around Pepperdine and Loyola if I can pull it off with the traffic. I told your parents we'd try. Let's go!" BamBam barked at me, even though I was sitting up. Looking over at the clock on the bedside table, she said, "I'm calling the car now. If you aren't out of those pajamas by the time it comes, then I guess that's how you'll be meeting your future classmates."

With that, she picked up her phone, and I ran to the bathroom. I wasn't sure that I'd ever gotten dressed that fast, but within fifteen minutes, I was in the cab while BamBam happily chatted with our driver about the best slice of German chocolate cake he had ever had. Of course, BamBam got the recipe.

I continued to slowly wake up my brain as BamBam schmoozed with the rental-car-counter person until she'd managed to get us an upgrade to a convertible, because as BamBam put it, we weren't going to LA out of style.

Before the sun truly came up, we were fully on the road, nursing regular coffees because BamBam refused to wait around for them to make me my specialty drink. Instead, she told me to chuck an extra sugar in my coffee, before she pulled away from the curb going somewhere between 75 and 87 miles per hour, because, "Baby, the only people in LA going the speed limit are tourists."

I considered arguing that we were, in fact, tourists, but she'd already put on her Donna Summer and was howling along way too loud for me to argue. So I prayed that Mom wasn't awake and watching my phone hurtle toward Los Angeles at light speed.

Three hours and fifty minutes later, we were clearing the University of Southern California's security gates. Turning toward me, BamBam said, "We need to hurry."

"We're over an hour early."

"Not if you want to make an appointment with the film school admissions people, we aren't." A slow smile crept across BamBam's face as she winked at me. "Surprise!"

"I—" My brain stalled as I processed what was happening. BamBam had mentioned that she'd made an appointment with an admissions officer to talk about the school. I'd assumed she meant USC generally or maybe the economics department or something. "How?"

"I filled out the form like everyone else. I may be internet famous, but I'm not famous enough to get you special treatment."

She laughed and reached over to smooth a hand over my hair, tucking it behind my ear as she gave me a once-over—likely searching for ways to make my rush job palatable to the adults I'd be speaking to shortly.

"Why?" I blinked at her, trying to understand why she would risk upsetting my parents.

"Honey." BamBam arched an eyebrow at me. "You've been moping all trip about having to spend another summer working in an office and avoiding that SISU application. I'd have to be the most oblivious human on the face of the planet not to figure out you're creative like your grandma."

Excitement and nerves twined themselves together and began racing their way through my bloodstream as I got out of the car. I was here at possibly the best film school. And I was going to talk to someone about attending. "Mom and Dad missed my creativity."

"Parents are a different thing. They think their kids are excellent at everything. Mostly." BamBam frowned a little as she pushed herself out of the driver side. Brushing the thought away, she added, "Plus, I wanted to give you a special surprise to thank you for all your hard work. You've done so much for me. I wouldn't be traveling, making a little pocket money, and being fabulous without you."

I shut the car door and tried to swallow the lump in my throat as the memory of me and Ethan together last night threatened to drown me in guilt. While I'd been out sneaking around, she'd been working on making my dreams come true. "I very much doubt that you wouldn't have been fabulous."

"Well, yes. But only locally fabulous. Now I'm globally fabulous, and haters like Buzzy can stay mad." BamBam cackled and came to stand beside me. "Now let's go. You and me aren't gonna miss this one."

With that, BamBam took off, leaving me to catch up as I tried to contend with the fact that I really didn't deserve my grandma's trust and effort right now. Worse, I'd never been more grateful to have her by my side.

"So, here's the thing." BamBam paused to take a sip of her cocktail and adjusted her sunglasses. "Sterling suggested, and I'm inclined to agree with him, that we had such great chemistry during the master class that we should do a series of videos together. As luck would have it, he used to do a regular segment similar to Cookies and Tea with someone y'all's age, but that's not working out right now."

"Oh. Really?" I tried to keep my voice neutral even as images of Emmie swam to the front of my mind. Apparently, both BamBam and I were benefiting from her bad judgment now.

"It's that little blond girl that had that eyeshadow palette in Beauty BB's last year. What's her name . . . ?" BamBam snapped her fingers, trying to force a name I knew all too well to come to her. My heart sank. If Ethan was right, Emmie's business was about to take a serious hit after Beauty BB's stopped carrying her palette. That meant people would be watching her downfall for longer than I'd anticipated, with Ethan as collateral damage, making it much harder for us to sneak around once we got back to Chicago. Not that we'd talked about what to do about dating when the convention ended yet.

"Gosh, what is her name? You know, she has that book thing—"

"Emmie Kristoff."

"That's her!" BamBam shouted, and pointed at me.

I looked around to make sure no one overheard us talking. We were on the rooftop patio of a restaurant in Santa Monica that, according to BamBam, was known for its celebrity sightings. While I was too desperately underdressed and uncool to ever be considered a celebrity, BamBam was absolutely not. We kept getting looks as people tried to place her from somewhere while doing the time-honored LA ritual of wondering if they'd seen a person famous enough to tell their friends about later. It made me nervous, but BamBam was loving it.

In another life, she easily would have fit in at any one of the content houses in LA. In fact, part of me wondered why she hadn't moved here already.

Maybe she didn't want to move away from our family . . .

Or maybe she knew we weren't ready for her to leave us.

The thought that the reason she hadn't left Chicago might be, at least in part, me, gnawed at my already guilt-ridden insides. The constant school pickups, the rides to debate team competitions, not to mention the cookie baking and homework help she'd given me and my siblings. Wasn't retirement supposed to be fun? I always imagined watching *Dateline* with my parents was fun for her. But from this angle, I was starting to think it was the other way around.

"Anyway, then I'm thinking, if people like our videos, you and I can approach some of his sponsors for a lipstick series or something." BamBam grinned with satisfaction as she got to the root of her plan.

"Hmm." I nodded along as the memory of me and Ethan at the museum came back to me. The way it felt to be wrapped in his arms. Snuggled against him. I really didn't want to let him go. However, if I wanted to keep him, I'd have to be super careful around BamBam. The balancing act today alone was stressing me out. Just to be safe, I'd changed his name to Go Kart in my phone and was literally waiting until she was in the bathroom to answer his texts. One wrong move and the woman who was giving up so much for me would find out how I was repaying her kindness.

"It'd be a good way to tag onto his work without cutting into his glitter empire. That way everyone continues to play nice."

"It sounds like you've really thought this out." I swallowed my betrayal and forced a smile onto my face.

"Well, you know how much your grandma loves a goal and a plan." BamBam squeezed my hand. "We came here with a plan to reach a younger audience, and look at us getting it done. Maybe you and Sterling will want to work together, too? He is moving to LA soon, and it might be time for you to learn how to work with someone other than me."

BamBam laughed, and my heart sank further into my chest. I was already learning that skill, and I couldn't even tell her. Keeping this secret from BamBam was getting less fun even as spending time with Ethan was becoming more wonderful.

"Speaking of a goal." BamBam checked her watch. "We've got options. I know you liked USC and UCLA, but we could try and drive by those other schools like I promised your parents. Or we could blow it off, go to Venice Beach and dip our toes in the Pacific. What do you want to do?"

"I've never been to the Pacific before." I pushed my intrusive thoughts away as visions of muscle-packed people lifting weights on a beach as others Rollerbladed by in spandex like in *Barbie*, *Roller Dreams*, and every other movie about California scrolled through my mind.

"Well, in that case, let me get the check." BamBam waved at a waiter, then added, "If your mama and daddy ask, we couldn't get to those campuses in time with all this LA traffic."

BamBam winked at me, then I reassured myself that just because I couldn't tell her about Ethan yet didn't mean I wouldn't ever mention him.

Eventually, she would find out about our video when I won the prize money. Although, it'd probably be better to wait to tell her I was still seeing Ethan until after she got a product deal from working with Sterling. By then, she'd be so focused on her new deal and so excited for me that she wouldn't even dwell on us dating.

That timeline could work out. In fact, it had to if I wanted to keep both of them in my life. Watching BamBam tap her phone against a portable credit card reader, I put my concerns about lying to my grandma to bed. I had a plan. This would work out. Until it was time to tell the truth, I'd just have to enjoy a day at the beach. And that, at least, I knew I could do.

DAY 6: THROWING
THE GAME

CHAPTER EIGHTEEN

"FOCUS, JAMIE," I CHIDED MYSELF AS SOON AS I REALIZED I WAS staring off into space again. I had told BamBam that I needed to skip breakfast to finally work on my college application essay for SISU. In reality, I was sorting through all the new footage Ethan had sent me last night, as well as everything I'd collected, so that we could start picking out the shots we liked best.

Only, I couldn't focus. I'd fantasized about kissing Ethan more than I cared to admit. All the daydreams paled in comparison to what it actually felt like to kiss him. Now I basically couldn't think about anything other than him. His hair, the color of his eyes, his lips . . .

I'm doing it again! Shaking my head, I put my fingers back on my keyboard and tapped the space bar to play a clip. Of course, it was another one of Ethan waving at me. I laughed and then dragged the clip into a file titled Ethan Waves. Maybe I'd make a joke video and send it to him . . .

The buzz of a text message pulled me out of my daydream. Picking up my phone, I felt a hum of excitement hit as Ethan's nickname came up.

Go Kart: No breakfast?

My heart fluttered. He wondered where I was. Thought about me. I typed back.

> Nope. Trying to sort our footage before this afternoon

Go Kart: So dedicated

> Want me to bring you coffee?

I was halfway through typing YES PLEASE when I remembered BamBam. She was currently at breakfast, but for how long? Ethan had brought me coffee before, and we didn't get caught. Then again, there was the other time when Buzzy *had* caught us. Even if I managed to sneak around my parents' rules, our grandmothers were a different story. As much as I wished it, just because we'd kissed didn't mean the situation with our grandmothers had changed—they were still enemies. I frowned and tried to push the problem out of my mind. There was no clear solution to that mess, and I had too much else to think about right now.

> BamBam will be back soon

As soon as I sent it, my heart sank. I imagined Ethan reading the message and the disappointment on his face. Quickly, I double texted.

246

> See you this afternoon?
> Coffee on me

I went back and forth about adding a little heart or a coffee emoji, then decided I was overthinking everything and hit Send. If Ethan couldn't figure out that there was a heart somewhere in that text, then BamBam might have been right about the whole family being dense.

The phone dinged again with another text from him.

I looked down and laughed.

Go Kart:

No need to abandon him yet. Soon, we'd graduate and maybe he'd want to move to California from Chicago with me after graduation. Could we keep this a secret until then? It was kind of an impressive mental leap to go from one kiss to living together in Los Angeles without us even talking about college plans, but at the start of the trip, I would have said it was impossible to go from being inactive participants in a family blood feud to a kiss, so who knew what the future had in store?

A little voice poked at the back of my mind, offering the idea that not having our families find out about us for ten months was basically impossible. I frowned at my reflection in the mirror above the desk as I thought about trying to sneak around BamBam and my parents for that long. I'd have to tell all of them, eventually, if being with Ethan in LA was my dream.

Eventually being the key word. That was Future Jamie's problem. Right now, I'd enjoy the moment. Ethan and I could figure out the rest later. After we won this prize, everything would fall into place. My parents would see that I could be successful and BamBam would forgive me. Maybe. I hoped.

I turned my attention back to my computer. Something about this footage was off to me. Like we'd missed an important part of the TrendCon story, but I couldn't figure out what. I rubbed a hand over my face and tried to think. Whatever was missing, I needed to identify it ASAP, or this video would feel like every other commercial for Las Vegas.

Glancing at the clock in the right-hand corner of my screen, I sighed. Pretty soon, BamBam would be back, and I'd have to work on my actual application. Unless I didn't.

Ethan was right. I'd have to tell my parents that I didn't want their future sooner or later. Maybe it would be better if I told them now. I could enlist BamBam's help. She could warn them, maybe soften my parents up before we got back and I told them directly. That would give them more time to get over the fact that I wasn't going to be the perfect daughter. Plus, Ethan and I could then spend some of the summer together. I'd have graduated by then, so we wouldn't even be breaking my parents' no-dating-until-graduation rule. My phone buzzed again.

I picked it up, expecting to see Ethan, but it wasn't him. I opened the text, then turned to the room door.

> **Nittha:** We're here to save you.
> Open the door.

I was about to laugh at the joke, when someone banged on the door, accompanied by Gabby's voice, shouting, "We know you are in there. Open up."

"Coming," I yelled back, trying to keep my curiosity in check as I shuffled to the door. I was supposed to see them later tonight at the farewell pool party. I'd told them that I'd give them all the details about my adventure with Ethan then. Maybe they'd come to gossip early?

I pulled the door open, and Nittha's anxious face greeted me. She was clutching Cricket so close to her chest that I would have been worried for the little dog's ability to breathe if she weren't so busy licking Nittha's face.

"Oh, thank god," Nittha sighed as soon as she saw me.

Next to her, Gabby was furiously chewing on her lip. Checking left, then right down the hallway, she pushed a cup of plain coffee from the breakfast buffet into my hand. "This is for you. I know it's not the good stuff, but we wanted to get here as fast as we could. We're so sorry. We swear, we didn't think this would happen. Are you okay?"

Before I could ask why they were sorry, both of them hustled past me and into the room, concern radiating off them. I checked the hallway for whoever Gabby was worried about, then closed the door to face them. Their anxiety was making me nervous. Eyeing the plain coffee suspiciously, I said, "I'm fine. Should I not be?"

Gabby's eyes went wide as Nittha winced. The two exchanged glances, silently negotiating something. Nittha gave her head an infinitesimal shake, causing Gabby to glare at her and tilt her head to the side. After a moment, Nittha let out a heavy sigh.

"So, Emmie posted a video." Nittha paused to rock Cricket back and forth. After taking a deep breath, she added, "About how Ethan has moved on."

"Oh." My mouth went dry.

"It's not that bad. She was trying to tell her fans to move on, too, because both of them were letting go. I don't think she meant it to be a big thing." Gabby jumped in where Nittha had left off. She sounded like she was trying hard to make everything seem like no big deal. "She didn't name you. But since Sterling and I all posted videos of you and Ethan at go-karts, BamBam and Buzzy had those big fights, and Ethan posted a photo of a girl and a car, people kind of . . ."

Gabby's voice trailed off as she moved her hand in a circle, like if she didn't say the words they wouldn't feel so bad.

Nittha eyed Gabby, hoping our friend would finish the story. When she didn't, Nittha blurted out the rest. "People figured out that you and Ethan are a thing. Most of the comments are nice, though, and—"

"Comments?" I asked, my face hot as my brain shuddered under the weight of trying to connect the dots. Why should I care if people said things in Emmie's comments?

"We're so sorry." Gabby jumped back in, apprehension running across her face. "If we'd known Emmie was going to do that, obviously we wouldn't have posted anything. I think it'll blow over fast and—"

"I don't get it. Emmie is super popular." I shook my head, trying to make my friends make sense. "She gets comments all the time."

Gabby's shoulders slumped, an expression of utter defeat crossing her face. "They aren't commenting on Emmie's videos."

"Like on Ethan's?"

Nittha nodded, a deep crease forming on either side of her mouth. "And BamBam's."

"Oh." A panicked laugh bubbled up from somewhere inside of me. People were saying things about me. On the internet. Where my parents could see them. Or, worse, BamBam.

A million terrifying scenarios ran through my mind. At any moment, BamBam could decide to check her accounts and see that I'd been lying to her. About not only who I'd been with but where I'd been and what I'd been doing. Mom or Dad could be reading them right now. They'd be furious. Mom would probably call me tacky for sneaking around, and Dad would say this was a sign that I needed to get my act together. Then the business internship at Mom's office would be off the table, and I'd probably end up at military camp like my sister that summer she got caught drinking at a house party in ninth grade.

The visual of me in a uniform, crawling around on the ground or trying to do a pull-up, was too much. My chest squeezed, and I felt like I couldn't catch my breath. I handed Gabby my coffee, then doubled over, putting my hands on my knees and trying to block out the buzzing in my brain.

"I think you should sit down," Gabby said from somewhere over my right shoulder. I saw Nittha's pink manicure grab onto one of my forearms. Gabby's black one grabbed my other. Somehow, they managed to pull me over to the bed.

"Here. Take Cricket," Nittha said in an unusually calm voice as she shoved the dog into my lap. Sitting down next to me, she began rubbing my back. "She'll help, I swear."

As if on cue, Cricket stood up on her hind legs and put her

paws on my chest, then started trying to lick my face. I scooped her into my arms, holding her close to me and letting her warm, fluffy little body anchor me in the room. Objectively, I could tell I was panicking. I just couldn't figure out how to calm down. Closing my eyes, I tried to think about breathing in through my nose.

"I'm gonna get you some water, and a cold towel for the back of your neck. That always helps me," Gabby said, already on her way to the bathroom.

A moment later, she was back with a damp towel that she placed around my neck. Between Cricket and the cold, I was starting to relax. Opening my eyes, I looked from Gabby to Nittha. "Did BamBam seem upset?"

"I don't think she knows yet," Nittha said, still rubbing my back.

"Good." I nodded and handed Cricket back to her. "I can make sure she doesn't find out."

I stood up and walked over to the table where my laptop was waiting, then started logging in to every one of BamBam's accounts and her content-management platforms. If I worked fast, I could get rid of the comments. Taking the towel from my neck, I turned around to face Gabby and Nittha, who were watching me like I'd officially broken from reality.

"I'm gonna delete everything so BamBam and my parents don't find out."

Gabby grimaced, her voice gentle as she said, "Jamie, there are a lot of them. And you like Ethan, so maybe it would be better to tell the truth—"

"Absolutely not." I shook my head. If I was going to tell Bam-Bam, it couldn't be like this. She was my only cheerleader. I wasn't willing to lose her and then go home to face whatever disappointment my parents felt without her support. If I ever told BamBam about this, it wouldn't be because the internet was about to tell her first.

"Jamie, maybe we should talk about—" Nittha started.

"You two should go." I cut her off. "I'm not mad, but I have a lot to do."

Facing the screen again, I could feel their eyes on me; probably debating whether they should really go. I didn't have time to worry about that now. I forced myself to sound light as I said, "Really. I promise I'm not mad. I'll check in with you later."

"Are you sure?" Gabby asked, her voice uncharacteristically soft, as if she thought I might break if she pushed too hard.

"One hundred percent." I started clicking through Bam-Bam's YouTube notifications.

"Okay, well," Gabby said slowly over the sound of the bed sighing as she stood up. "We're here if you need us."

"And you're still coming to the pool later?" Nittha asked, Cricket's collar jangling as she got up from the bed.

"Maybe. I'm supposed to meet Ethan, too." My hands froze on the keyboard at the thought of him. In my panic, I'd forgotten that he was likely going through some version of this downstairs. My heart squeezed just thinking about him being alone. Exiled from Emmie's friend group and unable to hang out with me and my friends because I wanted to avoid bringing more attention to us. Hopefully, his car friends were at the breakfast, and he could hide with them. Sure, they were mostly middle-aged-parent types or rich exotic-car drivers, but at least he'd have people. I shrugged, pushing him out of my mind. I couldn't worry about Ethan right now either. I didn't have much time to fix this.

I glanced over my shoulder to find Nittha and Gabby still hovering in the doorway. "I'll text you."

"Okay," Nittha said, her voice flooded with apprehension.

"Call if you need us before then?" Gabby asked, sounding less like the brash Florida girl that she typically was.

"Promise." I nodded, then turned back toward the screen, waiting until I heard the door close behind them before I started reading the comments.

Gabby wasn't wrong. There were a lot of comments, and the problem was, they were all mixed in with BamBam's most recent GRWM videos, so I had to go through each one individually unless I wanted to risk deleting actual thoughts from Ms. Mini followers. Taking a deep breath, I started scanning for anything that seemed to stick out.

Your granddaughter is ruining people's relationships.

I deleted the comment and tried to ignore the fact that this person was clearly living in some strange dream world where Emmie and Ethan were on a break and not in the very real world where they'd broken up.

Your granddaughter could use some makeup tips. Woof.

Ouch. I wrinkled my nose as I hit Delete. Not everyone was going to like my face, and that was fine.

Like grandmother like granddaughter. This whole family can't dress for shit. I'd be embarrassed to leave the house like y'all.

If I didn't know better, I would have sworn my mom wrote that one. But she would never say the word *shit* on the internet. I deleted the comment and tried not to think about how much it stung to have something my parents thought about me repeated by people who didn't know me.

After a while, I got pretty fast at spotting the problematic comments. As Nittha had promised, not all the comments were mean. Some people were there to be nice to BamBam and me.

Y'all need to grow up. This is Ms. Mini's video. Her granddaughter aint even online

You have too much time if you are really out here commenting to someone's grandma about their relationship

Get a life and your own boyfriend, trolls!

I appreciated these people, even if I had to hide their comments, too.

I was nearing the end of the comment section on her longer videos when one caught my eye.

She can't even make a decent video for her own grandma.

My breath got stuck in my throat. The comment was posted under the video with the colorized old photos. This was a video I was proud of. I'd even uploaded it with my name in the credits.

And someone thought it was garbage. Worse, hundreds of people had liked the comment.

My finger hovered over the touchpad as a little voice said that maybe this person had a point. My heart sank as my parents' words came back to me. Just because I liked doing something didn't mean I was good at it. Maybe I did need a backup plan?

That couldn't be true if Ethan had liked it, right? But what did him liking the video actually mean? He'd already admitted he didn't mind my experiments, since they were mine. He could have been lying. My parents could be keeping me honest. Maybe people liked BamBam enough to ignore my attempts at creativity? Was I embarrassing myself with this? Maybe it'd be better for her to hire a professional team now, since I was leaving for college soon. She made enough money to.

Nope. I shook my head forcefully, trying to shake the thought away. These people were here to be mean. I hit Delete and reminded myself that the whole point of these comments was to get in my head and cause a rift between me and Ethan. I'd delete all the comments and see him later, and everything would be fine. Hopefully.

CHAPTER NINETEEN

IN HINDSIGHT, I SHOULD NOT HAVE PICKED THIS TABLE. IT WAS IN the corner of Beginners Luck, out of the line of sight of most passersby. But that also meant I couldn't see Ethan coming unless I leaned way into the aisle, thereby defeating the purpose of the table in the first place. Maybe this whole meeting was a bad idea. I should've asked Nittha or Gabby to borrow one of their rooms. That would have given us more privacy. Okay, more privacy from strangers and way less privacy from my friends.

Logically, I knew the comments on BamBam's videos had very little to do with reality. But that didn't stop me from feeling paranoid. I adjusted the hood on my sweatshirt so that it was closer to my neck, pulled the brim of my hat down, then focused on sorting through more clips. I'd hoped I'd be further along in my video outline by now, but it was what it was. With any luck, Ethan would trust that I had a real plan if I just sort of waved my hands around and spoke with enthusiasm.

"Hey." Ethan's voice pulled at my focus. I looked up to see him walking toward me, a smile on his face. He had circles under his eyes, like he'd been up half the night but was putting all his remaining energy into sounding like he'd slept more. Even exhausted and in his sweats, he was still cute. I wondered if he'd been up thinking about me, or if he'd seen the video last night. Surely he would have texted me if he'd known sooner.

"Sorry I'm late. My grandma needed help getting repacked and moving one of the heavier suitcases. Of course, they are all heavy because she overpacked." Ethan laughed as he came directly to my side of the table and leaned down to kiss my cheek as if a whole subsection of the internet weren't currently freaking out about us. My back tensed, and I held my breath, like becoming a human plank would somehow prevent anyone from seeing us.

Dropping into the chair across from me, Ethan furrowed his brow as his eyes scanned my face. "What's wrong?"

"Nothing."

"Jamie." Ethan tilted his head to one side as he leaned forward and put his elbows on the table. "Your facial expressions are about as subtle as a leaf blower. Please tell me."

I laughed, the movement shaking loose a little bit of the tension in my chest. "Emmie posted about us."

"Oh, that." Ethan's lip curled.

"I think she meant well," I added hastily.

"She probably thought she was ripping the Band-Aid off so everyone could move on." Ethan sighed and slumped back in his chair. "It's not so bad, I guess."

"Except that y'all's shippers posted on BamBam's videos."

"They posted on your grandma's videos?" Ethan's eyebrows disappeared under his mop of messy hair.

"It's okay. I deleted all the comments I could find, so we're good there. I think. I'll keep an eye on it for the next few days." I studied the fraying cuff of my sweatshirt, running my fingers across the edge as if the texture would help me feel calm again.

"I'm so sorry."

"How do you live like this? With people constantly judging you?"

"I swear this is not my life. Three hundred and sixty-four days of the year I can go to the grocery store and no one knows who I am."

Ethan slid a hand across the table, palm up, waiting for my hand to join it. I hesitated, my mind flickering between want and fear. A fleeting look of hurt washed over Ethan's face and was gone as fast when our eyes met. I didn't want him to feel bad, but with so many people watching for us, I also had to think about not crushing BamBam.

"It's probably already blown over, and BamBam will never be any wiser." I tried to sound like it would all be okay soon, even as a fresh wave of anxiety coursed through me.

Ethan's eyes searched mine. "I'm sorry about this. Truly."

"I know this isn't your fault. I'll be okay, really. It's just not how I want BamBam to find out about us." I sighed and tried my best to paste on a smile that we both knew wasn't real. Giving my shoulders a shake, I added, "Enough about Emmie's video. Let's talk about our soon-to-be prize-winning work."

"Yes, please." Ethan brightened and shifted, taking his hand off the table as I pushed my computer between us so we could both see the screen. "Show me what you got."

"So, I didn't quite get as far on the rough cut as I wanted to this morning, but I still think it'll give you some sense of where I was going. Imagine fun music and some bright overlays either for lower thirds or some other transition."

Holding my breath, I pressed Play, and a series of jagged jump cuts moved us from landmarks to Ethan smiling as he showed off the ridiculous singing car and then footage of people enjoying product demos at the con. I even managed to slip in a quick clip of BamBam and Buzzy's panel before things took a murderous turn. With each cut, my nerves picked up. It occurred to me that outside of my family, no one had ever seen a rough draft of anything I'd done. What if he hated it? Or worse, thought it was boring?

"It's super rough, I know. But if we move between clips using neon shapes so everything will have a kind of bubbly, bright feel. Maybe use a filter in the same shade as the shapes so everything pulls together." My words came out in a nervous jumble as the video stopped playing. Ethan watched me, his expression focused and unreadable. My heart started to pound. I sucked in a breath, then added, "Of course, this is all up for discussion. If you hate it, we can start over or—"

"I don't hate it," Ethan cut in, shaking his head. "I like it. I'm just thinking about the transitions. What if, instead of neon, we used the con's color scheme as the filter? It would be more blues and reds, which might feel a little like an ad for the American flag—"

"But not if we do it right," I said, a grin stretching across my face as my mind started to work through the different ways that we could use a filter to help the transitions. "We could use less saturated shades. And if we keep boxy shapes to a minimum—"

"Exactly," Ethan said, his voice bouncing off the wall behind me as he leaned in. "And maybe we pick music that is upbeat or playful."

"Wait, you don't want your dad's music in this? Because I feel like the whole world should know about your dad-like behavior."

I started giggling as Ethan blinked at me, then threw a hand over his heart, rolling his shoulders forward in mock pain. "Ouch, Webb. You wound me every time you hate on my dad-like music taste."

"My bad. Grandpa-like."

He smirked. "Much better."

We exchanged glances then started cracking up, the sound ricocheting around the crowded coffee shop. Ethan dropped his head onto his forearm to stifle his laughter as I threw my hand over my mouth and focused on a random chip in the table varnish to try to pull myself together. When I finally managed to stop giggling, I glanced up again and felt like the wind had been knocked out of me. About six feet behind Ethan was a person around our age holding up their phone. We were being filmed.

Whatever joy I'd managed to recover in the last ten minutes disappeared in an instant. Ethan lifted his head up, his smile fading as soon as he caught sight of my face. Following my deer-in-the-headlights expression, he peered over his shoulder and then quickly turned back to me.

"Ignore it." Ethan's voice was low, trying to get my attention as I shrank farther into our booth. He seemed like he was in physical pain watching me try to disappear.

I flicked my gaze back to where the video creeper had been. They'd dropped their phone and were pretending to be very interested in the tile on the coffee bar counter. Somehow that made everything feel worse. They'd invaded our privacy, and now all of us were supposed to pretend they hadn't? It was so strange and violating. Later, they'd probably post it, destroy my home life, and have no idea what they'd caused.

My mouth felt dry. If other people's videos kept going up, there was no way I could reasonably hide any of this from Bam-Bam or my parents.

"Jamie?"

Ethan's voice sounded like it was coming to me from underwater, pulling me up from underneath my clouded thoughts and drawing me to the surface.

Suddenly, everything was very clear.

There was no world where anonymity and Ethan coexisted. If I stayed with him, BamBam would find out. If I chose him, I would lose her just as soon as my parents finished taking away my phone and grounding me until I went off to college. I wasn't ready to let the relationship I had with BamBam go. At least, not while I still lived at home. Maybe never. BamBam had always been in my corner. A life without her hugs and reassuring words, even her outrageous antics, seemed like a colorless existence. Like choosing to be without the sun.

It was stupid of me to think that a video contest would somehow make my parents see me as more than the flawed daughter they'd failed to fix. Even if Ethan and I won, I wasn't going to have it all. My parents would find out I'd broken their no-dating rule, and I wasn't going to have much of anything other than a way to pay for part of college, if I was lucky. If we didn't win . . . it wasn't like I could just move into the dorms with my siblings and pretend I was supposed to be there. I'd be on my own.

"Jamie, are you okay?" Ethan asked, ducking his head slightly to try to catch my attention, his voice tinged with nerves.

I shook my head, ignoring the pinpricks at the back of my eyes warning me that tears weren't far off. In a weird way, that intrusive-video person had saved me from myself. What happened in Las Vegas was going to leave Las Vegas if I didn't stop this now. The thought tore a bitter laugh out of me.

"Is this a bad idea?" My words sounded hoarse. I would have taken a sip of my drink if the thought didn't turn my stomach.

"The shapes in the video?" Ethan's voice was uncertain.

"No." I sucked a breath in through my teeth and shut my eyes. I couldn't see his face and do this, or I would lose my nerve. "Us."

"Why are you saying that?"

I slowly opened my eyes to see Ethan's jaw muscles tightening as if he was resisting the urge to say or do something while he waited for an explanation.

"There is no way this can stay a secret, and we both know it. Our grandmas could find out about us at any time. Every minute we sit here is a risk."

"Then let them find out." Ethan didn't even try to deny that we were being silly. If anything, he sounded like he'd made peace with the idea that we were going to get caught. "They'll get over it."

"Will they, though?"

"Of course they will." Ethan's mouth dropped open, as if I'd asked an outrageous question. "I could see my grandma having a problem if you were an axe murderer or one of those people who try to force religious literature on her outside of a grocery store, but you're not."

"Maybe your grandmother would. But mine? BamBam is still actively mad at someone who said her outfit was tasteless in 1973."

"I mean, that is rude."

I started to laugh, then caught myself. "The point is, Bam-Bam would not."

Ethan's face fell. When he spoke, all traces of humor were gone. "You can't possibly be breaking up with me over our grandmas' stupid feud? You know how ridiculous that sounds."

My heart pounded in my chest, my face getting hot as resentment coursed through me. I wanted the kind of loving family Ethan had. The kind people in movies had. And on paper, I did. Two parents with good jobs who wanted the best for me. But in real life, that couldn't be further from the truth. Their love came with a million strings attached, and their idea of what was best for me was so narrow I couldn't even wear the wrong-colored socks without criticism.

"When you say it like that, sure, it sounds ridiculous. But I can't risk not having BamBam. I care if she hates someone I like." I took a deep breath, pulling my shoulders back and forcing myself to look at him. "I'm not like you. I don't have a dad who wants to play goofy old-school music while the whole family hangs out together. I have a dad who thinks that my creativity is his future financial burden and a mom who thinks I could be pretty if I'd only try. BamBam is all I've got."

"You don't have to give her up to date me." Ethan shook his head, his voice taking on a desperate edge. The air between us felt heavy as the café's espresso machine whirled and scratched as it made drinks. "We can come up with a plan. We'll figure it out. Please . . . don't do this. Don't start hiding again."

"I'm not hiding." That word snagged on my mind, irritating me like a grain of sand in my eye.

"Yes, you are." Ethan's voice had a hard edge as his eyebrows knitted together.

"No, I'm not." I shook my head, the tone of my voice matching his. "I just want to get along with my family. You wouldn't understand."

Ethan snorted. "Your family is different than mine, but that doesn't mean mine doesn't argue. We're just brave enough to talk through it."

"So now I'm ridiculous and a coward?" My words sounded sharper than I'd meant them to.

"I didn't mean it like that." Ethan held his hands up as if the gesture alone would slow down the conversation. "What I meant was that my family can disagree and still work it out."

"That explanation didn't make it better." I closed my laptop and glared at Ethan, daring him to say anything other than that he was wrong.

He took a long, slow breath and then another. After what

felt like forever, he said, "Being who you are takes courage. But who you are is better and more loveable than the person you're showing your family. You have a choice, Jamie."

"I . . ." The words halted in my throat. It felt like he'd dumped cold water on my anger. I wanted to stay mad. Mad was easier. But I didn't have a response to what he'd said. Tears pricked at my eyes, and my gaze fell to the table. I did not want to cry. I wanted this to be over. He wasn't wrong about me protecting the parts of me that my parents wouldn't love. But the problem wasn't simple. If my parents' unconditional love and support were as easy as wishing for it, I'd have had those things by now. I didn't know what the answer was. I only knew that I wasn't willing to lose the love my grandma offered in order to find it.

I bit down on my lower lip to try to stop it from trembling, then took a shuddering breath. "I wanted to choose you."

"That's the part that hurts." Ethan's shoulders sagged even as his jaw set. He stood up and took a deep breath. "You don't have to choose me. Or anyone, really. Just choose you. You have too much to offer to waste your time chasing someone else's idea of who you should be."

Then he turned and walked away, my heart splintering with every step. As soon as he rounded the corner, tears started to roll down my face. I'd told myself this was for the best. And it was. But right now, it just really, really hurt.

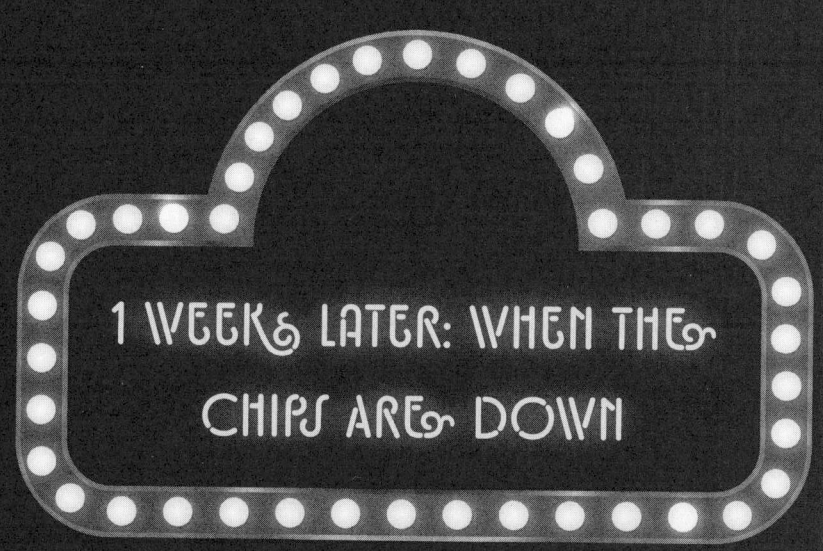

1 WEEK LATER: WHEN THE CHIPS ARE DOWN

CHAPTER TWENTY

I PUSHED THE HOOD OF MY BROTHER'S OVERSIZED SWEATSHIRT off my head and walked into Dalia's Dry Cleaning, hoping it would make me look less pathetic. I'd spent the week since I got back to Chicago wallowing in self-pity. Mostly, I'd managed to keep from crying in front of my family and at school, but all bets were off when I was alone, making the drive to and from places, being in the shower, or being in my room potential cry-fest hot spots.

"Remind me again of the phone number, sweetheart," Dalia said, her fingers hovering above the black keyboard. She hadn't asked me anything unusual. I literally gave Mom's phone number every time I picked up her and Dad's starched shirts, but something about the question made me feel like the floor was going to fall out from under me.

"Seven, seven, three—" I stopped as my throat tightened. It wasn't that long ago that Ethan had asked me for my phone number—

Nope. I shook my head. I wasn't going to think about him in public. Swallowing the lump in my throat, I started again. "Eight, six, seven—"

Unsummoned, tears started leaking out of my eyes. Of all the things that could have made me start to cry in public, this was the one that broke me? A phone number?

"Are you okay, Jamie?" Dalia looked alarmed as I sucked in a shuddering breath.

"I'm f-f-fine," I stammered as my vision clouded over. The bell above the door dinged to indicate another customer had walked in, and I peered over my shoulder to see who else was about to see me surprise-cry. An older person in a bright purple jacket and very crisply creased pants was waiting behind me in line, staring at me like I might be contagious. *Great. I'm scaring people on top of being miserable.* Taking another deep breath, I tried to start again, feeling the weight of the person's eyes on my back. "Five—"

Another big tear rolled down my cheek, and something that felt suspiciously like a hiccup-sob forced its way out of my chest. Swiping at the tear, I turned to my left and saw the small alterations booth in the corner. Dalia nodded encouragingly, but I couldn't get the next number out. I missed Ethan. And no amount of running stupid errands for my parents on a Saturday was going to change that. Glancing back at Dalia, I choked out, "I need a minute."

Dashing into the booth, I managed to draw the light-blue velvet curtain behind me before dropping onto the little wooden bench to sob. I tried to focus on my breathing and push the thoughts of Ethan out of my mind. I'd broken things off for a good reason. It was just really hard to feel okay about it right now.

"I'm okay. I'm okay. I'm o—"

"Want me to call someone?" Dalia said, her voice delicate from the other side of the curtain as the customer bell rang again.

"No, th-th-thank y-y-you," I blubbered. Although, calling someone did feel like a good idea. I fished around my giant front pocket trying to find my phone so I could video call Nittha and Gabby, since they were the only ones who even knew about Ethan in the first place. Pressing the Call button, I sniffled. Almost immediately, they both came up on-screen.

"Hey, friends!" Nittha bounced, the pink walls of her bedroom flashing at me like silent, happy little trolls.

"Hey. Hey." Gabby grinned at us. She was sitting outside in the sunshine, one of those typical skinny Florida-subdivision palm trees waving at me from the background as if daring me to keep it together.

"I can't pull it together." I wheezed as thoughts of Ethan threatened to send me to the next level of crying-mess, aka the puddle stage. If I hit that, there'd be no calming down anytime soon.

"Oh my god, what's wrong?" Gabby asked. "Are you sick?"

At the same time Nittha said, "Do we need to cancel next weekend?"

I exhaled, my entire body collapsing as me and my oversized hoodie became one with the little wooden bench. Part of me wished I had texted them the truth. But after everything that happened last week, I'd been too busy trying not to snot-cry in front of BamBam to do much of anything other than message them with an excuse that I wasn't feeling well and therefore wasn't going to be at the pool party. I left out the part where I'd waited for BamBam to leave so I could look for breakup playlists to sob to in the shower instead of wrapping up TrendCon with my friends. In retrospect, admitting that Ethan and I were done, and that I wasn't going to enter the contest, so there was no reason for them to come all the way to the Chicago area regional event to see my big directorial debut, would have been the less chaotic thing to do.

"Jamie, this long silence is making me nervous," Gabby said, lifting her sunglasses up and leaning closer to her screen. "And where are you?"

"Wait, don't say whatever it is yet. I need Cricket." Nittha dove off of her bed.

"You are really gonna make us wait longer." Gabby glared at Nittha's empty square.

"Unlike me, Cricket is very good with emotionally difficult situations," Nittha hollered from somewhere off camera. "Okay, we're back. Go ahead, Jamie." Nittha waved Cricket, who was wearing a pink polka-dot bow and matching collar, at us. "Please tell us you aren't in Point Nemo or something."

"Where is Point Nemo?" I sniffed.

"Middle of nowhere. It's basically inaccessible. We're learning about it in school," Gabby said. I was glad they went to the same online school so she could decipher Nittha's particular brand of random. "Tell us what's going on. You look like you were attacked by a wild pack of sloths."

"Do sloths come in packs?" I wrinkled my nose. Nittha giggled, but Gabby wasn't having it. "Okay, okay. I'm at the dry cleaner's. In the alterations booth."

"What?" Gabby asked, looking deeply disturbed.

"Why are you there?' Nittha's forehead creased with confusion. "And why are you crying?"

I took a deep breath and stared up at the noise-absorbing tiled ceiling trying to decide where to start. In the background, the shop's bell dinged with the entry of another customer who Dalia whispered a greeting to, presumably so as not to disrupt my recovery during a stage-three public meltdown. That was kind of her.

Turning back to the phone, I let the whole story come out, at first in measured, deep breaths and then, as I got closer to actually breaking things off with Ethan, in another round of pathetic, messy sobs. For maybe the first time in years of friendship, Nittha and Gabby didn't interrupt me to ask questions. Instead, they let me blabber with only an occasional break for me to wipe my nose with the sleeve of my sweatshirt.

"So, yeah. There is no video and no Ethan. But that's okay." I tried to end the story on a happy note, although my voice sounded like I was dangerously close to wailing again.

Gabby blinked at me for a second, while Nittha rocked Cricket back and forth like a baby, both of them waiting to see if I was done sob-talking or if I was going to break into actual howls now.

"Low-key feels like maybe you could have told us immediately after this happened and not like a week later when you had a breakdown at the dry cleaner's, so you didn't have to be sad by yourself." Gabby nodded; after a beat, she added, "But I'm glad you're telling us now."

"Me too." I sniffed. Telling them hadn't exactly made me feel better. I did, however, feel like a human ball of emotions crammed into a dirty sweatshirt, so there was that.

"We're not mad," Nittha added, more as a warning to Gabby to ease off unless she wanted another Jamie-shaped tear puddle to appear. "Jamie, do you want to talk-talk about this or cry-talk about it? Like, where is your headspace?"

"Good question." Gabby leaned back in her chair. "Are we all shaking our fists at the sky and saying we hate Ethan? Or are we exploring the root cause of our feelings? Both are valid."

"I don't know? Both?" I said, feeling like maybe I wasn't as done crying as I thought I was. "Like, I want a hug, for Ethan to be miserable without me, and for everything to be okay."

"Got it." Nittha nodded and waved Cricket at the screen. "Virtual hug."

"Yup, big puppy snuggles," Gabby said flatly. Pushing her sunglasses back over her eyes, she added, "Are you okay with me asking a hard question now?"

"That wasn't a very long virtual hug," Nittha chided, laying Cricket down next to her.

"Shh, it's Jamie's turn." Gabby waved playfully. "Jamie, don't take this the wrong way, but don't you think a lot of assumptions were baked into this breakup?"

"Okay, yes." Nittha nodded in agreement. "I thought so, too."

My nerves tensed up, and I played with the cuff of my sweat-shirt, waiting for Gabby to wait for Nittha to finish so the former could ask her question. "I'm not asking this to be mean, but like, how do you know your parents wouldn't support your career aspirations or that BamBam would hate you?"

I paused, forcing a gulp of air into my lungs as my throat tight-ened. My vision blurred as a fresh round of tears threatened to start up again. "My parents are constantly on me. The only time they aren't telling me to be better is when I'm asleep, or at mock trial, because parents aren't allowed to speak in the courtroom."

"Do you need a Kleenex?" someone who was decidedly not Dalia called from the other side of the blue curtain, causing my friends and me to jump.

"Shhhh," Dalia hissed at the customer. "Boy trouble. She's gonna work it out with her friends."

"No, thank you." My voice sounded strained as I answered the customer.

"Been there. Let us know if you need one," the nosy yet thoughtful customer said.

"I will." I swiped at my eyes, then turned back to my friends. "Sorry."

"Anyway." Nittha shook her head, as if trying to remember her thought after such an interruption was a wearying task. "When was the last time you actually said to their faces that you want them to stop? Or that you want to do literally anything other than math for a living?" Nittha asked, her voice gentle even as her words stung.

I opened my mouth to respond, then paused as the ground started to fall out from under me. Had I ever actually told my parents what I wanted? Or had I simply assumed they knew? My mind wandered over every conversation we'd had about the SATs, college visits, and summer programs, searching for any moment when I'd spoken up. Car rides with Mom, Dad talking over TV commercials, even my sister prodding me about applying to live in the math-focused dorm at SISU with her . . .

Not once did I actually say no and stand my ground. I'd start saying no, then waffle as soon as someone questioned me. At the time, it seemed like everyone was badgering me, but what if they weren't? What if they were trying to figure out what I wanted as much as I was? I'd been so busy protecting my dream that I'd never stopped to ask if I actually needed BamBam to guard it or if I just needed to have a conversation. I took a shuddering breath, trying to get control over another wave of tears as the realization that I had a role in my own unhappiness threatened to send me back into the puddle stage of crying.

"Jamie?" Nittha's voice pulled my attention back to the screen. "My parents have all kinds of unsolicited opinions. They almost had a heart attack when I told them I wanted to go to school online and manage Cricket full-time, but after a couple of months, they came around."

"I don't think anyone's parents are super excited about them not becoming the person they planned for. I mean, my grandma wanted my dad to be a doctor. He imports luxury olive oil." Gabby frowned slightly. "Honestly, it's probably better to tell them now than after they spend money on a degree you don't use. My grandma doesn't care about what my dad does now. She is still real mad about the cost of med school, though."

"See," Nittha said, waving her hand at the phone. "Besides,

BamBam is not going to let anyone put you out of the house over being a film major or having a boyfriend a couple of months early. That's not her style."

"You might have a point." I sniffed. The image of my parents putting my stuff on the curb and BamBam helping me move it right back into the house worked its way through my mind, making the corners of my mouth twitch up slightly.

"I know we have a point." Nittha laughed.

A weak smile crossed my face. Now that I thought about it, it was a little funny that I'd ever thought my parents would blow up over this. If nothing else, they cared too much about what other people thought to publicly exile their youngest daughter. The worst-case scenario was they didn't help with college. But Mom and BamBam had worked their way through school and been fine. Their support would be nice to have, but I'd figure it out if I didn't have it.

"Speaking of BamBam . . ." Nittha said.

"Oh no." I shook my head so hard that strands from my braid came loose.

"Oh yes. You didn't think we could skip that giant waving red flag of a made-up judgment, did you?" Gabby giggled, then took a deep breath and set her face in a neutral expression. "How do you know she'd cut you off over Ethan?"

"Okay, you have to admit that I have good reason to believe that," I said, holding up one finger. "You have personally seen umpteen GrannieGate meltdowns."

"We don't have to admit any such thing." Gabby pushed her curls over her shoulder like she was brushing away my reasoning. "Her beef is with Buzzy, not Ethan."

"BamBam blusters a lot, but has she ever actually gotten truly mad at you?" Nittha added, her brow wrinkling as she tried to think through my and BamBam's history. "As soon as she realized you hated math camp and liked movies, she came up with a creative outlet for you. That doesn't sound like a lady who cuts her grandkid off."

"BamBam did do an entire video series on reasons she will fight someone for her grandkids." Gabby snickered as the new-customer bell went off again.

"It was technically reasons any grandma will go off on a stranger," I mumbled, not quite ready to process what my friends were saying. (We'd re-created outfits from *Tekken* and shot her rocking back and forth on her heels. It was funny.)

"Okay, but the scenarios were all extremely specific and clearly about her grandkids, so . . ." Nittha shrugged as she dragged out the *o* in the word *so*.

"True." I sighed and swiped at my eyes with the back of my hand. At this point, my sweatshirt was getting too gross to keep using as a tissue.

I'd started crying the second I saw Buzzy and Ethan get on our plane to go home. BamBam hadn't said anything, just gave them a dirty look and threw her arm around me. She hadn't even asked why I was upset. Just kept me sheltered until I fell asleep. It was the same thing she'd done for me as a little kid. We'd always been close like that. She didn't need words to feel that I was hurt. She could always predict when I needed a hug, a joke, or a talking-to. I'd gotten used to BamBam reading my mind. But I was older now. This wasn't the same as a skinned knee or a bad grade. This was me wanting to grow up, and like with my parents, that version of me was a little different from what she expected. Again, maybe this time, I did need to use my words.

Dropping my chin to my chest, I shut my friends out for a fraction of a second longer as everything clicked into place. Ethan was right. I didn't need to hide to be happy. Winning some prize wasn't going to make the truth easier. I needed to be a little braver and a lot more honest. Both were risky in their own way, but at least if I said something, there was a chance I could be happy by my own definition.

I lifted my head up to catch Nittha and Gabby making wide eyes at one another's squares like they were worried they'd finally broken me. Pulling myself up straighter on the bench, I sighed. "I messed up with Ethan, didn't I?"

"Yes," Nittha said. "Big-time."

"Oh, absolutely," Gabby said simultaneously.

"Ugh, why aren't time machines real?" I moaned as both of my friends nodded like bobbleheads. "Maybe he'll develop amnesia and forget about the entire thing?"

"Or the what-happens-in-Vegas rule. It'll be like the fight never happened," Nittha added with too much perk to sound like she believed it.

I could almost feel Gabby's side-eye through the screen as she said, "The entire relationship happened in Vegas, so for Jamie's sake, let's hope it doesn't work like that."

The three of us burst into a round of silly giggles, the kind that are less about the joke than the people you are joking with.

Finally, Nittha straightened up and sighed. "So what are you gonna do about Ethan and the video?"

"I feel like there are a couple things I need to fix before I can even think about that video or Ethan."

"Well, don't wait too long to figure it out. We've already got plane tickets." Gabby grinned. "And know that if you decide not to do anything to fix this, we still love you, but we'll expect you to come up with a better, more fun plan than going to that screening party."

"Which we will fully post all over social media." Nittha added, "With your permission of course."

"Post away." I waved my hand to dismiss the concern as a true smile stretched across my face for what felt like the first time in forever. "I don't know what I'm gonna do, but I know it's not going to be hiding from anyone on social media or anywhere else."

And I meant it. I just needed to tell my family first.

"That's our girl," Nittha said, sounding like someone's motivational coach. "And look at it this way, at least you got to cry with the fresh laundry smell."

"Yeah, I should go. People probably want to use this booth to try on their clothes or something." I giggled, pushing my flyaway hairs out of my face. "Thank you, friends."

"Feel better. We'll be there soon." Nittha smiled, waving Cricket's paw at us. "Love you."

"Please call and tell us stuff before you start crying in public next time." Gabby laughed, then added, "And I love you, too."

"I love you both." I waved, then touched the End Call button, my heart feeling lighter.

Sighing, I forced myself to stand up and pushed the curtain open. Stepping out of the alterations booth, I came face to face with Dalia and a man with thinning hair. Both were staring at me as if they had been listening to every word uttered between my snotty sobs. Behind the man was a woman with very dark hair and a distinct jawline, standing next to someone who looked like her brother. They were also watching me. My face got hot as I started to think about how long I might have had an audience for my lowest moment in public.

"Just one minute," Dalia said, holding up a hand to the man, who stepped aside and began conspicuously staring at anything other than me. Reaching for a group of shirts on a rod, she handed them to me, then held out a credit card reader so I could tap my mom's card to pay. Pulling the reader back toward her as it began to print out a receipt, Dalia smiled up at me as she tore the piece of paper off. "You are all set."

"Thank you." I smiled weakly, hoping that I could convince my dad to pick up his own dry-cleaning from now on so that I would never have to see anyone in this room again. "And thank you for letting me use the, uh . . ." I gestured over at the little curtained box and shrugged before turning back to Dalia and finishing with, "alterations room."

"Oh, don't mention it." Dalia smiled at me as if I weren't a puffy-eyed, tear-splotchy mess. "And tell your grandma I say hi, and that she better be ready to lose a hand or two at pai gow next week."

"Of course," I said, mentally making a note to literally never mention this moment to my grandmother or anyone ever if I could help it, then waved as I walked toward the door. "Have a good day."

"You too, sweetheart. And good luck with that boy," Dalia called as I walked out the door, the bell dinging. It was a good thing I'd made up my mind to talk to my family about Ethan already, since Dalia sounded like she would be asking BamBam and any neighbor she could find for an update on me and my business soon. I guessed it was only fair for her to gossip in exchange for my unauthorized use of the alterations room.

CHAPTER TWENTY-ONE

I WALKED INTO MY HOUSE, FEELING THE WEIGHT OF MY CHOICES start to sink into my chest as I hung the dry-cleaning in the hallway closet. Talking to Gabby and Nittha made everything feel simple. But now that I was staring the whole tell-your-family-to-back-off plan in the face, execution seemed much harder.

I closed my eyes and imagined what my life would be like if I didn't do this. Since I'd gotten home, Mom and Dad had been asking about my college applications nonstop. Dad had also arranged an extra math tutoring session so that I might not miss a point or two on the SATs when I retook them in a few weeks. I could still hear his voice reminding me that I had to get that math score up for an economics degree. Meanwhile, Mom had examined every blurry photo of me that BamBam had taken and declared that I needed to go shopping for summer clothes so I wouldn't have to borrow any more of Gabby's "Florida wardrobe," whatever that meant.

Nope, I couldn't do the rest of my life avoiding Florida clothes and obsessing over math. This might be hard, but the alternative was decidedly worse. Slipping my shoes off, I caught sight of myself in the closet mirror and paused. This would probably go over better with my parents if I weren't wearing a pair of my brother's oversized sweats . . .

Also, nope. I wasn't going to do a complete wardrobe change for this conversation. I trudged toward the family room, where my parents were sitting on opposite ends of a cream-colored couch working on their devices. Our family room had an East-Coast-beach-house vibe to it that I was pretty sure my mom had ordered entirely from a Pottery Barn catalog, including seashells on stands. Mom's friends envied the room, which I guess made up for the fact that my family had never been anywhere near Cape Cod.

Neither of my parents looked up when I came in, so I tried walking around to stand in front of the perfect sea-blue ottoman that rested between the couch and the TV. Unable to bear the pressure any longer, I cleared my throat. "Mom? Dad?"

My dad glanced up from his tablet, then blinked. Mom finished typing something on her laptop, smirking as she tapped her touchpad, then took off her reading glasses and flinched. Maybe I should have changed clothes.

"Yes, Jamie?" Dad prompted, eyeing his tablet.

"I have to tell you something." I shuffled my feet on the rug, trying to figure out where to start. My stomach twisted and untwisted itself in knots as the muscles in my neck tensed. I thought about yelling *Just kidding* and running back to my room before I could pass out from the stress, but then changed my mind. I took a deep breath, then said, "I do not want a business degree."

"That's fine. What do you want to do? Study architecture?" Dad waved his hand as if this wasn't worth the dramatic announcement, then picked up his device. Turning to Mom, he said, "I didn't think she liked that summer program last year."

"No, I don't want to be an architect or an economist." I cut in before my dad could digress any further. After exhaling slowly, I forced the words out of my mouth. ". . . I want to study film."

For a brief moment both of my parents were silent, shock running across Dad's face while Mom went pale.

"Oh, thank god. After that long pause, I thought you were going to say you were pregnant or something." Mom sighed, the color rushing back into her face as she reached up to touch the delicate necklace she wore every day. It had five stones on it, one for each member of the family.

"What? Why would you think that?" The panic I'd felt moments ago dissipated as I tried to process how weird my mom's mind was when she wasn't trying to convince everyone that she was normal.

"Your sweatshirt is three sizes too big. And you've been sulking and crying in your room all week." She looked from me to Dad like this was obvious.

"Teenagers sulk, June. That's a thing they do." Dad frowned slightly as he set down his tablet again. "They don't need to be pregnant to do it."

"Your phone had you driving around all over Vegas, and you

weren't with BamBam. So I checked Nittha's and Gabby's social media, but you weren't with them." Mom gestured at me. "You can see where I would think that."

"Not really. I barely even go to parties unless BamBam invites me," I said, getting sucked into my parent's digression before I could stop myself. "It's kind of a stretch to go from ill-fitting sweatshirt to *She's pregnant*."

"You may have a point." Mom shrugged, a sign that this was the biggest concession she was willing to offer at this stage.

"She's basically a nun." Dad sniffed. "And when you think about the timeline for that—"

"Actually, can we focus on the thing I said?" I glared at my parents, willing them via my death stare to never bring up my dating life again. "I don't want to go to business school, and I cannot stress this enough, I desperately don't want to be an accountant." My dad leaned back, surprised by the force of my words, while my mom's eyebrows shot toward her hairline in offense. I tried to backtrack. "Sorry. It is a great way for you all to provide for the family. It isn't for me, though."

It felt like my parents were silent for a full minute while they processed what I was saying. Finally, my mom sighed and pointed to the ottoman. "Why don't you sit down?"

I stood still, adrenaline coursing its way through my veins. The part of me that had spent years being angry wanted to refuse to sit in order to preserve the option of stomping out of the room to drive my point home. The rest of me recognized that having to run away to avoid my parents' pressure was unlikely, given how tired my mom sounded. Plus, stomping or throwing a fit had never once gotten me anything but grounded. Exhaling my shaky anger, I lowered myself down onto the cushy ottoman, crossing my legs with my feet under me, even though I knew it would get on my parents' nerves.

"Honey, I'm surprised." Mom's voice was softer than I was used to. Typically, when I disappointed her, these conversations felt like an accusation. Like I was the one who was wrong for wanting something different. "Why are you only telling us this now?"

"Did you just figure this out?" Dad asked, giving me an out if Mom's question was too overwhelming, which also felt all wrong. Dad was a man who got me up early on the weekend so that I wouldn't effectively jet lag myself by sleeping in. My dad did not believe in outs.

I took a deep breath and shook my head. "I've known for a while."

"How long is a while?" Mom asked.

"Pretty much since I went to that first SISU business administration camp in the seventh grade." I winced, thinking about all the money and time they'd spent hauling me to junior entrepreneur events, math camps, and architecture club. "Nothing has ever made me less happy than spreadsheet macros."

"But you are so good at coming up with new ideas for Bam-Bam's business. She mentioned the potential makeup marketing expansion you came up with," Dad said, appearing genuinely confused.

"I came up with that as a way to challenge my production skills. I wanted to film in a mirrored hall." I paused as I thought about it more. From my parents' angle, every time I tried a new style of video, they thought I was developing new ways for Bam-Bam's hobby to bring in revenue. We were all seeing the same thing from our different lenses on the world. I shook my head and smirked. "I also wanted to see if I could edit footage I didn't shoot."

"So when BamBam said that making videos was just your creative outlet . . ." Dad's voice trailed off.

"It was, at first." I nodded. I might have kept the truth from them, but I wasn't about to throw BamBam under the bus with her own son.

"This whole time, we've been encouraging you to do something you don't want to do." Mom's forehead wrinkled as she said this. It was a statement mostly for herself. "Jamie, I guess I'm not understanding. Why not tell us sooner if you felt this strongly?"

"You and Dad were so adamant about me being an accountant, or banker, or something practical, like my future was a done deal before I was born. We even had a picture book about the first Black governor of the Federal Reserve. If that doesn't scream *Become a banker*, I don't know what does." I bit down on my bottom lip, trying to force myself to be honest. "And I tried to mention maybe not working at your office this summer to you, Mom, but you told me to worry about my grades instead. Plus, you all put so much time and money into all these activities. I . . ." I shrugged and ran a finger against the weave of the ottoman's fabric, searching for the right words. "I didn't know how to make it stop. And I didn't want to disappoint you any more than I already have."

"You don't disappoint us." Dad said this so fast and with so much force it almost knocked me over. "Why do you think we are disappointed in you?"

"You've literally called me Messy since I was a toddler." I raised an eyebrow at Dad as if daring him to challenge me.

"That's a nickname," Dad said, sounding defensive. "You were always covered in something sticky when you were little."

"I'm not two anymore, and you're still using it," I said, glancing down at my sweatshirt cuff and hoping that I wouldn't have to use it as a tissue again. "Plus, you talk about my videos like the time I spend on them might kill you."

Dad appeared crestfallen. In my mind, he was being judgmental, but watching him now, I wasn't so sure that he meant to be. I turned my focus to Mom, mostly so I didn't have to see my dad looking so sad.

"And, Mom, at least three times a week you make me change my clothes for some random fashion violation. You literally watch my friends' social media and critique my clothing choices. Does that sound like someone who is going to be open to hearing *I hate your life plan for me*?"

"I don't do that." Mom shook her head.

"You criticized my sweatshirt this morning, then asked if I planned to put on 'a little makeup' before going to the store to buy Oreos." I used quote fingers around *a little makeup* in case it wasn't clear that I was imitating her.

Mom tilted her head from side to side as if trying to find a way to claim that she hadn't done those things. Unlike Dad, she didn't seem crushed, or even totally convinced that I was right, but I could tell that I'd gotten her to think about the possibility that she could be wrong, which might be as close as I was going to get today.

She exchanged glances with Dad, the two of them communicating silently in the way that people who have been married for more than twenty years can. Finally, she sighed. "Jamie, I think I can speak for both your father and myself when we say that we are sorry. Our goal was never to make you feel trapped or like the odd one out."

"We wanted to support you and your siblings' passions. Your BamBam did that for me. She was hard on me, but sacrificed to make sure I had everything to chase my dreams, pushed me to be my best even when I didn't think I could be. We wanted to do that for you, too. You were good at math, so we followed that, the same way that we encouraged your brother in science and your sister in, well . . ." Dad frowned, then admitted, "More math. Sometimes, when the only tool you have is a hammer, everything becomes a nail. Your mother and I had numbers, and evidently it became our hammer with you and your future."

I laughed at the bizarre way he managed to stretch the metaphor, even as my throat started to tighten.

"And we cannot tell you how sorry we are that we've made you feel like a disappointment. It's no excuse, but I grew up with a tremendous amount of pressure to be put together. My family didn't have much money. My parents tried to make up for that by maintaining appearances." Mom sniffed as she sorted through her own painful memories. "It was a different era. I didn't want to pass that on to you kids, but clearly, I didn't do as good of a job as I'd hoped."

"I'm sure the nickname didn't help," Dad said, scooting over and wrapping an arm around Mom, pulling her into him until she leaned on his shoulder. "The point is, we have reasons why we did the things we did, but none of those reasons was ever intended to hurt you."

It wasn't that I didn't know all this about my mom or dad. BamBam had said as much in Las Vegas, but I'd never heard them say it before. All their rules and plans had always seemed arbitrary. Like they'd made decisions about my life without me. It turns out, they thought they were making them with me this whole time.

In a way, it wasn't that different from what I'd done to Ethan. Only, when he asked me to make the decision with him, I didn't listen.

"I think I knew that." A big soggy tear rolled down my face, and I swiped at it.

"I wish this were the kind of thing that you didn't have to think you knew. Love and support are the kinds of things you want your kid to know unconditionally." Mom's voice wobbled. Unlike me, she did not use the edge of her clothing to wipe away tears, instead opting to pat under her eyes with her index finger in order to keep her makeup in place.

Dad squeezed Mom's shoulder. Running his free hand over his face, he said, "Jamie, it would be a lie to say that your mom and I can change overnight. But what I can promise you is that we are willing to work on easing the pressure off you if you are willing to give us a chance. Can you give us a chance?"

"Yes." My voice sounded small, and I made sure to nod as

big as possible to make up for it. Relief flooded Mom's face as Dad exhaled slowly, his expression still pained. The three of us stared at each other and then laughed. Objectively, we all had puffy eyes and sounded a little pathetic, but we'd made it through the hard part. Sort of.

"Since we are making some changes . . ." I hedged, just to see how they'd respond. I didn't need to have all my hard conversations with them today. I just needed to open the door to the idea of another one soon. "About the no-dating rule—"

"We'll talk about that specific restriction later. Give us time to adjust to this one first." Dad grinned big and leaned forward to tap my knee as he said, "Can I politely suggest a hug? No pressure."

I snorted. "Yes. You can have a hug." I unfolded my legs so I could stand up, then immediately flopped down onto the couch between the two of them. Wrapping one arm around each of them, I added, "But only because you asked nicely."

My parents piled on top of me then, all three of us laugh-crying. Finally, Dad freed himself, while Mom continued to hug me, stroking my hair like she had when I was little. Then Dad said, "May I make one more polite suggestion?"

"If it is asking me to minor in math so I have a backup plan, then no," I ribbed him. Next to me, I could feel Mom shaking with laughter.

"That wasn't my suggestion, though it's a good one," Dad said, then immediately held his hands up when Mom and I groaned. "Kidding."

"What's your suggestion, Leon? Tread carefully." Mom used her warning voice.

"Jamie, I know your mother and I aren't telling you what to wear anymore, but that sweat suit is about ready to get up and walk away on its own."

"You borrowed this from your brother's room, and I don't think it was clean." Mom scrunched her nose. "We can wash it, and you can put it back on if you want. Or we can get you your own sweat suit. Then you'll never have to worry about smelling like your brother again."

"I think I'm done with wallowing clothes for now," I said, giving the sweatshirt a sniff. "I'm gonna go get in the shower."

"That's my girl." Dad smiled at me.

"Before I go, I have one more request."

"And that is?" Mom asked.

"Can I have one more hug?"

"I think we can do that," Dad said.

CHAPTER TWENTY-TWO

I REACHED FOR THE DOORKNOB TO BAMBAM'S APARTMENT, then hesitated. In the shower, still all warm and fuzzy over the conversation with my parents, the thought of telling BamBam about Ethan had seemed like a small hill to climb. But now that I was standing at her doorstep, about to admit to lying, sneaking around, and general deceitfulness in the arms of her nemesis's grandson, I felt like I was standing at the base of Mount Everest without enough oxygen to make it to the top.

But as much as I wanted to go find my brother's sweats and hide again, I couldn't. And not because Mom immediately took those sweats out of the laundry and was likely digging a hole in the backyard to bury them in. I couldn't because it didn't feel right anymore. Somewhere between being smothered by hugs from my parents and Gabby and Nittha's encouragement, I'd changed. If I wasn't going to hide the good stuff from my parents, I couldn't hide stuff from BamBam either. She'd always been on my side of the happiness equation. Leaving her out because I was scared felt wrong.

Biting down on my lip, I twisted the doorknob at the same time as I knocked. Poking my head around the door, I called, "BamBam, can I come in?"

"In here," she answered from the living room. Holding my breath, I stepped into the apartment and closed the door. The first thing anyone saw when they walked into BamBam's place was her bright, friendly kitchen, up in yellows and gingham. Once I rounded the corner into her living room, I'd find her tucked into her usual corner of the sofa. She might not want me to come back here for a while. The thought of not seeing her or this place again caused tears I didn't know I had left to prickle at the back of my eyes.

Exhaling, I pulled at the sleeves of my lavender-colored long-sleeved shirt, then slipped off my shoes and shuffled into the living room. BamBam was sitting exactly where I expected, clutching a physical copy of our neighborhood newspaper. As she glanced up over the paper, BamBam's smile faded as soon as she saw me. "Hey, baby, what's going on?"

"Nothing much." I did my best to sound casual even as the pit of my stomach plummeted. BamBam raised an eyebrow at me in a way that said she 100 percent did not believe me, and what little calm I'd managed to muster evaporated. "I need to tell you something."

"Okay, have a seat." BamBam set the paper on the arm of the sofa and patted the space next to her. Fixing me with an impassive stare as soon as I sat down, she asked, "What's going on?"

"I lied to you, and I'm not proud of it. I'm sorry." I said the words in a quick and messy tumble, forcing myself to look her in the eye as I apologized.

"Lied about what?" BamBam said, her voice as even and patient as it had been when I was six.

"I lied about where I was and who I was with in Las Vegas." I grimaced. From her end of the couch, BamBam watched me, her lips pursed to the side as she waited for more details. It was clear from her expression that she wasn't pleased, and she was not about to make this easy on me.

"Remember when I asked if you wanted to enter the contest for the TrendCon vid?" I paused and BamBam nodded, crossing her arms. I directed my gaze toward the fabric of the couch so I wouldn't lose my nerve, then continued. "Well, when you said no, I went to Nittha and then Gabby, and they were busy, so eventually, I got desperate, and Ethan Wyatt offered to help me." My armpits were starting to sweat, and the corner of my mind that was not consumed by freaking out noted that I should've waited to shower until after I'd had this conversation.

I glanced up to find that BamBam's expression had not relaxed even a fraction of a centimeter. Taking one hand off her elbow, she gestured at me. "Go on."

My pulse spiked, and I wondered if BamBam could hear my heart thudding. It felt so loud to me that I was pretty sure half of Chicago could hear it. Attempting a calming breath in through my nose, I then exhaled the words in a rush. "Anyway, we started working on a video, and I got hungry, and he bought me my favorite chips, and we went to the Bellagio fountain and snuck out to a couple other places—and, actually, Las Vegas is underrated in the romance department, so then we kissed. I really liked Ethan, but then I didn't want to keep lying to you, so I broke things off, which is why I was crying on the plane. I didn't mean for this to happen. It just did. And I'm so, so sorry. I know you hate all things Buzzy Timmons."

I took a deep breath, my entire body feeling like I'd run a mile. BamBam's eyes had gotten bigger with each hurried word. Now that I was done confessing, she narrowed them at me. My molars were clenched so hard that my jaw hurt, and I didn't dare breathe. I hadn't been exaggerating when I'd told Ethan that BamBam was my lifeline. Even with my parents agreeing to back off, the thought of BamBam being truly angry with me was unbearable.

I'd spent nearly every afternoon of my life with her for as long as I could remember. The memory of her hands, strong and sure, picking me up when I'd stepped on a nettle when I was four. The taste of her cream-cheese brownies—she always made two pans, one for me and my sister, who liked nuts, and one for my brother, who didn't. The way she'd walked into my room after I'd had a meltdown over not testing into trigonometry and asked if I could help her film a video about hemming choir uniforms for her church's women's club. That video had changed both of our lives, and I wasn't sure I could bear it if my video with Ethan changed them again for the worse.

BamBam shifted the cross of her arms and yawned, as if I hadn't confessed to betraying every ounce of her trust and our friendship. "I knew about most of that."

"What?" I blinked at her. It felt like my brain and my body had been disconnected and neither was entirely sure what to do with this new piece of information.

"You are a terrible liar. But I'm glad you finally told me." BamBam frowned at me, deep creases forming in her brow as she narrowed her eyes. "I do not like being lied to."

"I don't understand . . ."

"Honey, I may be old, but I'm not stupid. I lived through the seventies. There is nothing that you can do that I haven't already done. In fact, I feel sorry for kids now." BamBam cackled, and I was torn between feeling relief and wanting to know what she had gotten up to in the seventies. Shaking her head at a memory she was not going to share, she added, "I saw the way that boy was looking at you on the plane ride over to Vegas, and I said to myself, *That boy thinks she's cute.* Then the way he was hanging around even after I embarrassed you both at the panel. Plus, people were mentioning you all over my comments—yes, I saw those. You ain't slick. Out here deleting comments, thinking Grandma doesn't know how to use the internet."

"I—"

BamBam held up a finger at me, using the international sign for *be quiet.* "Then I saw the way you were crying on the plane home, and I thought, *I sure hope I don't have to whoop that boy's ass for making my baby cry.*"

"Kinda did the crying part to myself . . ." I mumbled.

"You sure did." BamBam raised an eyebrow and crossed her arms again, then leaned back on the couch to wait for my explanation. "What made you think I would ever put a petty grudge above you?"

I sat up straighter, filled my lungs with air, then paused. In all my panic over the last week, it never really occurred to me to interrogate why I thought BamBam would turn her back on me. When I started speaking again, the words were slow and halting. "I guess I wasn't sure where you'd land. I mean, Dad is your son. And I know the rules. I wasn't supposed to date anyone, so I didn't want to put you in that position. Plus, I wanted to be loyal. You despise Buzzy."

BamBam's face relaxed as she listened. "Part of the trick of being a grandma is that you are raising both an adult and a grandchild. With your dad, I can coach him, but I can no longer make decisions for him. And the things I wasn't proud of as a parent, I get to do over with my grandbabies. I pushed your dad a little too hard, so with you and your siblings, I wanted to give you space to explore. Your parents were in charge of discipline, so you got to have fun and feel safe with me."

"And I did feel safe—still do." I corrected myself. "You gave me a creative outlet, but you never told Mom and Dad to back off. You're not one to hold your tongue, so when all this stuff happened with Ethan, I was worried it would push you away. That you wouldn't be on my team anymore."

"Oh." BamBam uncrossed her arms as her eyes searched my face. "It's funny. I never thought of it as needing to pick a side. To me, being a grandma isn't being a referee. I think of it as cheerleading. As long as you or your parents aren't going to hurt you or themselves, I keep my focus on supporting the whole family, not moderating relationships. I figured you had a strong enough will that you'd tell your parents about your future when you were ready. Just like you'd tell me the truth about Ethan when you felt like you needed, too."

"Technically, I did do that," I said, my voice coming out in a shaky laugh.

"I know. Which means I was right. As I frequently am." Bam-Bam smiled and shook her head. "But it doesn't feel like much of a win knowing how bad you felt. I'm sorry you thought you had to go it alone and hide things."

"It's okay," I said. That was the most classic BamBam response, pointing out that she wasn't wrong even as she admitted she could've acted differently.

BamBam studied me for a second, as if she was deciding whether or not I actually thought it was okay. She sighed and said, "Even if you and your parents are at odds, I'm still in your corner. I'm just in their corner, too. I want all my babies to thrive. When you have this much life experience, your job is to help everyone figure out how to love and respect each other, not to decide the winners and losers. Does that make sense?"

"Kind of," I admitted after a beat of silence. "I mean, I understand all of the words but—"

"You haven't lived long enough yet." BamBam finished the thought for me. "That's okay. Keep it in the back of your mind for when you get to be my age."

"I can do that." I grinned at BamBam as relief flooded my nervous system. She wasn't mad at me, and she didn't want me to be anyone other than me. My heart squeezed as I thought about the last few hours. I might have cried more than I'd ever cried in my life. But I also hadn't felt as at home and free as I did right now.

Bouncing across the couch, I threw my arms around Bam-Bam, catching her off guard so that my weight put us sideways. As soon as she managed to right us, BamBam wrapped her arms around me. The scent of her lotion, lavender and honey, washed over me as I snuggled against her. "I'm sorry I lied to you, BamBam."

"I'm glad you came around to being honest. That's what matters," BamBam said into my hair, giving me an extra squeeze before releasing me. Holding me at arm's length she asked, "So what are you gonna do about the video?"

"I don't know." I sighed, letting my shoulder sink and my head drop to my chest. "Honestly, I don't know if I can make it without Ethan. I certainly can't submit it."

"Tell me more," BamBam commanded, releasing my shoulders.

"Well, for one, why would Ethan ever talk to me again? And second, because the video idea, while technically good, is a little boring."

"Let's deal with the technical stuff first," BamBam said, going into her Ms. Mini Business Mode. "Why is it boring?"

"It was meant to be a love letter to Las Vegas, but it feels like a standard commercial for Las Vegas with a convention cut into it."

"So there's no love story in your love letter?" BamBam said this like a question, but we both knew it was rhetorical, so I nodded and waited for her to finish her thought. Tilting her head at me, she added, "It sounds like you aren't telling the story about Las Vegas you were meant to tell. Maybe if you solve that problem, the first one with Ethan will solve itself."

BamBam's words seemed to suck the air out of my lungs. Memories flooded in of all the goofy footage of Ethan waving at me. Him driving flashy cars. The random video he took of me setting up my gear at the Silver Influencers panel. Us, sweaty and lost while trying to find a sidewalk on the way to the aquarium. Ethan talking me through go-karts, or singing his old-man songs. Images of a sunset spent with one another. Neon kisses captured on camera. While I was trying to convince people to fall in love with Las Vegas, he was trying to convince me to fall in love with him.

All this time, I'd been telling the wrong love story.

"But it's your video." BamBam shrugged. "You do what you want."

"BamBam, you are a genius." My mind started to spin as a new story unfolded.

"I know." BamBam smirked, then rocked forward, using the couch's armrest to help herself stand up. "Now you go get your computer, and I'll get us some cookies. You got some work to do, and I need to call Buzzy if you two are gonna be an item. I deserve a cookie for that."

I grinned and got off the couch without so much as a word. It was time to let myself be the main character in the story. I only hoped it was a story that Ethan still wanted to tell with me.

2 WEEKS LATER:

ALL BETS ARE OFF

CHAPTER TWENTY-THREE

I STOOD IN THE PARKING LOT OUTSIDE THE VENUE FOR THE watch party, my nerves shooting little bursts of anxiety to every part of my body as yet another pair of headlights turned into Odell's, one of Chicago's most popular family-friendly sports bars and restaurants. After all the conversations we'd had about cars, I didn't actually know what kind of car Ethan drove, so I was forced to squint at each driver, keeping an eye out for his shaggy hair. This car was a blue minivan, so I didn't bother. There was no way, even with two little sisters, that Ethan was driving a minivan. That was not a mechanic's car.

My palms were sweaty from clutching my phone, despite the fact that it was chilly tonight. According to it, I had about eleven minutes until the event began. A corner of my brain started to panic. What if Ethan didn't come? My whole plan would be ruined. Then again, what if he came and refused to speak to me? My plan would be equally ruined, and I'd probably be a pathetic, snot-crying mess . . . again.

Nope. I pushed the thought away. If it didn't work out, then Gabby and Nittha were waiting for me inside. I'd go stand by my car and text them an SOS, and they'd take me home.

Holding my breath as another pair of headlights flashed in the windows, I squinted at an older-model white Volvo. My heart, which had been panic beating nanoseconds before, seemed to stop cold. That was Ethan.

My mind started working in overdrive as I watched Ethan park. First debating if I was standing in a good spot—didn't want to jump out of the shadows and terrify him. Then worrying that maybe the outfit I'd picked out with Gabby and Nittha was too plain—blue jeans and a rounded-necklined white T-shirt that was made of a supersoft fabric Ethan wouldn't actually get to touch because I was basically drowning in a cropped pink puffy jacket. I had nearly convinced myself to shed the jacket and wait for him in the restaurant, when he got out of the car.

Slowly, Ethan moved toward me. With each step a piece of my heart chipped off. I missed his walk and the lopsided smile that often came with it. The smile wasn't here now.

"Hey, Jamie." Ethan stopped a few feet away from me, far enough that I couldn't reach out and touch him. The distance made my heart ache.

"Hey." My voice sounded smaller than I wanted it to. I'd practiced what I wanted to say to him a hundred times over the last few days. But now, with him standing here, my carefully planned speech seemed to fall out of my mind. "I didn't know if you'd show up."

He shrugged. "Grammy was adamant that I come. So here I am."

Ethan pressed his lips together, glancing from me to the ground. Sighing, he gestured to the door and said, "I'm meeting Sterling, so see you in there?"

Without waiting for an answer, he walked past me toward the door.

"Wait, Ethan." Something about watching him walk away for a second time jogged my mind. Ethan froze, his shoulders tense. Turning on his heel, he crossed his arms and then faced me. Doing my best to swallow the nerves that were threatening to silence me, I said, "Can we talk?"

"We already are." Ethan shrugged, his tone flat.

"I mean, about us."

"What is there left to say? You made your choice."

I winced. Even though his words were true, they still stung.

"That's what I want to talk about." A muscle in Ethan's jaw twitched as if he was biting down on something he wanted to say. The motion was almost imperceptible, but he might as well have started running, given what it did to my nerves. Taking a steadying breath, I forced myself to look at him. "I owe you an apology."

Ethan's eyes went wide with surprise as he rocked back on his heels. A small smile crossed my face as a peek at the warm, open Ethan that I'd gotten used to in Las Vegas shined through the mess I'd made. Catching sight of my expression, he attempted to recover his nonchalance, pressing his lips into a flat line and putting his hands in his pockets.

"Jamie Webb is admitting she made a mistake. That's shocking." Ethan shook his head. "Guess you couldn't find anyone else to help you with your video?"

The little spark of hope that had flared up in my chest sputtered. Did he really think so little of me?

I toed the gravel beneath my feet and sucked in a cool breath of air. "I didn't try to find anyone else."

"Oh." All the anger seemed to rush out of Ethan, and he stared at the same gravel I'd recently found so interesting. He appeared as lost as I felt. I took a step toward him, pausing when he picked his head up, and said, "Sorry. That was mean."

"It's okay." I laughed, feeling some of the heartache between us ease. "After all, I was pretty mean to you."

"Still. It's sort of hard to maintain the moral high ground if you're being an asshole." Ethan gave a halfhearted laugh.

"I promise, if you still want to be mean after I'm done, you'll have ample opportunity." I exhaled with a nervous smile and took another small step toward him, holding my hands up in an I-come-in-peace gesture. "Over the past week, I've reviewed what happened in my head more times than I can count. It wasn't fair of me to get upset with you over what Emmie did, unless I was going to get upset with my grandma, Nittha, Gabby, and literally everyone else at that con—except for Cricket."

"Obviously." Ethan smiled, then let his expression grow serious again.

"I meant what I said. I couldn't figure out how to manage the risk of losing BamBam. It turns out, losing you hurt like hell, too. Please don't." Ethan shook his head like he didn't believe me. I took another small step toward him, my chest aching as I watched frown lines appear on his face. "After I got home, I tried to forget everything you'd said, but I couldn't."

"Because I was right? Or because your grandma's channels are being spammed by angry fans?" Ethan tilted his head to one side, watching me as if we were at the part in a scary movie where something unexpected jumped out and tried to murder the main character. His face was not reassuring.

"Okay, let me get this out before I lose my nerve." I reached out to touch his arm, my hand stopping in midair as he watched me. I dropped my hand and moved a step closer. "You were right. I was hiding. At a certain point, I got so desperate for a sense of privacy that I just stopped being visible in public at all. It stung to hear, but once I thought about it, you weren't wrong. And I couldn't go back to pretending I didn't know I wasn't an active participant in my own life."

Ethan took a deep breath, preparing to say something. I shook my head, willing myself through the hard part.

"I talked to my parents." Unlocking my phone, I plowed on before he could interject. "I also told BamBam about you. Then I thought about our video. What we did was fine, but after everything we'd been through and everything you'd said, I started to think that maybe I'd been approaching the story wrong. Take out your phone."

"What?" Ethan's face was incredulous even as he reached into his pocket.

"Trust me." I turned on Airdrop, then waited for Ethan's phone to appear. Tapping my phone to his, I said, "There are two versions of the video. The one we planned and one that's more . . ." I wavered for a moment, searching for the right word, then said, ". . . personal to us."

"I don't understand what is happen—"

I reached over and tapped the Accept button for Ethan. "Watch them, and it'll make sense. You can decide what you want to do. You can submit one or none. It's up to you."

Putting my phone away, I watched as he squinted, trying to connect the dots. My heart hammered around inside my chest. "Whatever you choose, I understand. And I'm sorry."

Giving Ethan a small smile, I ducked my head and walked toward the restaurant door. Everything that I could say, I'd said. The parts that I couldn't find words for were in that video. If Ethan played it, and he still couldn't forgive me . . . I didn't want to think about that.

As soon as I walked into the restaurant, I spotted Nittha and Gabby, who were leaning left in their chairs, trying to see out the window where Ethan and I had been standing. Odell's had a bajillion TVs all over the place. Tonight, they'd agreed to show the TrendCon entries on one of their big screens toward the back of the restaurant, mostly because it was a rare Saturday in the fall when none of the major sports had anything going on. I started weaving my way toward the high table my friends had picked out at the back of the restaurant, desperately trying not to make eye contact with the knot of Midwestern creators who'd all gathered here. Sterling waved at me, and I smiled back, hoping it was polite enough that it didn't seem like I was avoiding him. I still hadn't completely gotten over his role in the whole glitter debacle. Plus, I wasn't about to risk him following me back to our table to I-told-you-so my potential heartbreak.

Spotting me, Gabby started waving, too, but like she was signaling a plane from a desert island. Nittha, who'd left Cricket in the care of BamBam, since Odell's didn't allow dogs, turned all the way around in her chair, her eyes wide, as if blinking at me in Morse code. People could accuse our friend group of a lot of things. Subtlety would never be one of them.

"So . . ." Gabby said as soon as I got within earshot.

I shrugged and tried to keep my face neutral. "It's up to him now."

"Okay, but how did he seem?" Nittha said, leaning on the table with both of her elbows as I sat down.

"I . . ." My voice trailed off as I watched Ethan come through the door. Unlike me, he moved through the room easily. Nodding and waving back at people as if he wasn't also holding my entire heart in his hands.

"Hello. Jamie, are you with us?" Gabby waved in my face, then stopped when she realized where my attention was directed. "Okay, be chill. If the night ends and he didn't submit your video, Nittha and I will be your bodyguards. We'll leave right away."

"After we let the air out of his tires. You do know which car is his, right?" Nittha asked. She sounded like her usual light, bubbly self, but there was enough of an edge to it that I wasn't entirely sure she was joking.

"No one is committing any misdemeanors." Gabby made a face at Nittha that suggested she was worried about her judgment sometimes. "We'll go to the drugstore, buy some ice cream, go home, cry a little, and watch junk TV while talking shit about Ethan's bad haircut."

"I don't think it's a bad haircut." I wrinkled my nose at Gabby.

"You wouldn't." She rolled her eyes.

"It's more like a lack of haircut than—" Nittha's voice was drowned out by too-loud hype music blaring from the speakers while a massive Kelly Sparkles appeared on-screen, looking like he'd stuck his finger in an electrical socket. "Hey, hey, party people. Welcome to the first-ever TrendCon Regional VidCast."

My palms started to sweat as Sparkles went over how the entries would be played, how people could vote, and what the prizes were for third-, second-, and first-place videos. I tried to keep my eyes on the screen instead of following Ethan's every movement as he leaned over and said something to Sterling. Chills ran through me, and I wondered if I was going to be sick. I wanted to blame my nerves on the idea that tonight I could win $150,000, but in reality, I was mostly anxious about what that video would say about my future, if any, with Ethan.

The thought alone made my stomach turn. I needed to splash cold water on my face or something. Anything to help me calm down. As the first video started playing, I mouthed *Bathroom* to my friends and slid off my bar stool. Trying to ignore the cold sweat running down my back, I edged along the railing that separated the bar from the restaurant so I could get to the bathroom. I made it exactly two feet from our table before I knocked into someone.

"Sorry," I mumbled, then stopped.

"Are you okay?" Ethan asked, concern on his face.

"Nerves."

"You did set up a kind of high-stakes situation for yourself." He half smiled, and my heart felt like it was tearing in two. The next video started playing, casting a bluish light across his face and taking my mind back to that afternoon at the pool when all this started. Ethan leaned his back against the railing. "What do you think so far?"

"Think? About what?" I searched his face for any hint of what he was feeling as my mind tried not to pull itself apart. I'd said I wouldn't ask him about the video. I told him he didn't even have to speak to me. The fact that he was standing here had to be a good sign, right?

"About our odds of winning." Ethan nodded toward the screen as if it were the most obvious question in the world.

"I think it depends on which video you chose." The part of me that wasn't on my best behavior wanted to reach out and shake him. My mind was as far away from the competition as Chicago was from Cape Town. "It seems like the first vid they played has roughly the same idea as our general tourist video."

"Hmm," Ethan hedged. "And the second one?"

"You tell me."

"I don't know." Ethan's eyes studied my face, and it took everything in me not to bolt from the room. "I didn't watch it."

It felt like gravity had increased its pull around my heart. At any minute, it was going to fall out of my chest and shatter on the floor. He hadn't watched the second video. He wasn't here to make up. He was here to let me down gently. How could four words hurt so badly? Tears started to prickle at the corners of my eyes, and I took a long, deep breath.

"Okay." I exhaled slowly, wondering how long I would need to stand near him before I could turn around and give Gabby and Nittha the signal for us to get out of this place. Deciding that the approximately three seconds I'd already waited was long enough, I said, "I accept this, but I'm gonna go."

Ethan opened his mouth to say something, then paused as the screen behind me caught his eye. A smile worked its way across his lips as the next video started playing. Light washed over his face, and all my escape plans froze. I knew that light. I'd watched it about a million times this week. Turning in time, I caught a clip of Ethan waving at me from behind a camera, and then a mirror clip of me waving back at him.

Our sixty-second love story. Everything I'd wanted to say to Ethan working its way across the screen. Only, he hadn't seen it.

"Please don't go." Ethan reached out and caught my hand as if he could sense that I was getting ready to bolt. He took a step closer to me. "I didn't want to watch this without you."

Everything but him and the screen seemed to slip away as we stood together, watching as BamBam and Buzzy chided us during the panel. From my camera's angle at the back of the room, it's clear from the way Ethan was looking at me that Bam-Bam really did notice his feelings long before I did. Somewhere in the back of my mind, I could tell people were laughing before the next image came through: the two of us standing close as we tried to figure out how to film the fountain. Him putting on my helmet at go-karts. Holding hands over a sunset. Blowing him a kiss at the Neon Museum. Then the title card: *Las Vegas: Sometimes what happens here stays with you.*

The screen faded into the next video, and I could feel Ethan watching me. "So that's how you really feel?"

I tried to read his face. Whatever future there might be for us hung in the balance, and I wanted to choose my words carefully. "You asked me to trust you. Trust that everything would work out if I chose you, but I was too afraid. You weren't responsible for what happened because of Emmie's videos, or my family's behavior, but I pushed you away like you'd had a role in everything all the same. I'm so sorry."

"Yeah, you leaving hurt. A lot, actually." Smiling half-heartedly, Ethan shook his head. "Like I cried. More than once."

"If it helps, so did I." I rested my free hand on his arm. The piece of me that wasn't feeling awful for hurting him was comforted when he didn't pull away. "Really, I'm sorry. I should have chosen you right then and had some faith that it would work out. If you'll let me, I'm choosing you now."

Ethan laughed, then glanced down. He was still holding my other hand. He'd had every chance to let go, and he hadn't. It wasn't forgiveness yet, but relief began to course through my system anyway. I missed holding his hand.

"For someone who doesn't do social media, you killed your first serious attempt." This time, his grin was genuine as he leaned toward me.

"Someone wise said I have to put myself out there." Threading my fingers through his, I stepped a few inches closer to him. I was near enough that I could see the flecks of gold in his eyes.

"If I forgive you, can you promise to not freak out about what the internet says about us?" Ethan asked, his gaze tracing my face with an intensity that surprised me.

"Yes." I nodded and stepped another inch closer to him so

there was only a sliver of space between our bodies. "I promise I will not have that level of freak-out ever again."

"Then I forgive you." Ethan's lips tugged into the slow, sweet smile I'd gotten used to. Dropping his voice so only the two of us could hear it, he said, "And it's good that you won't freak out because I am going to kiss you now, and I'm pretty sure we have an audience for it."

"Audience or not, I choose you."

"That's all I wanted." Ethan let go of my hand and wrapped his arms around me. Pulling me toward him, he closed the last bit of distance between us. The sounds of the world and our past mistakes melted away as our lips met.

His kiss tasted like a smile and felt like neon lights. It was a kiss made up of sunsets, old-school music, and embarrassing cars. It was sealed with bags of chips and complex coffee orders. It held promises of movie nights and days by the pool. More than shared secrets and inside jokes, this kiss was real. It held a future with a thousand kisses like it. The kind of kiss that meant wherever the future took us, we'd choose to have that adventure together.

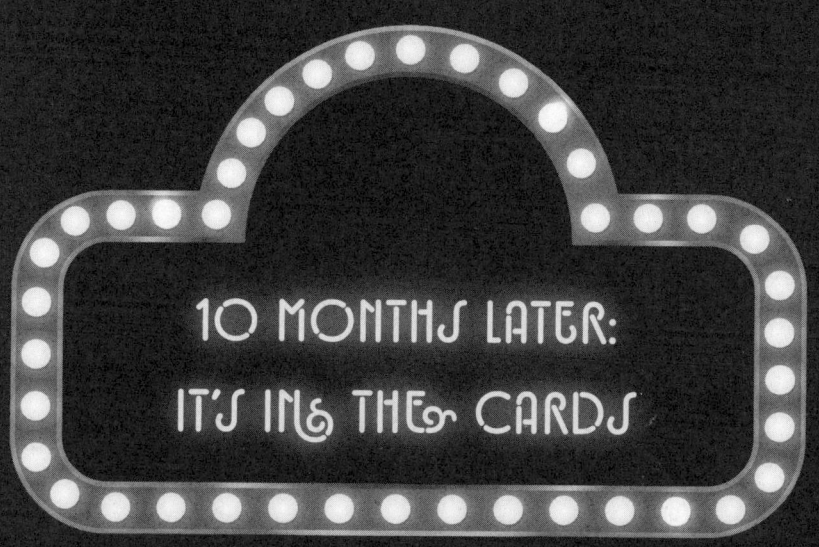

10 MONTHS LATER:
IT'S IN THE CARDS

EPILOGUE

"DO WE NEED THAT?" ETHAN POINTED TO MY HARD-SHELLED portable lighting-rig case, then turned back to the trunk of his car.

"Of course we do. How am I supposed to film without my lighting rig?"

"You could rent one, like everybody else in Los Angeles." Ethan chuckled, running a hand over his freshly cut hair. "Or borrow Nittha's lights. I'm sure Cricket has some."

"Maybe we don't bring all your winter coats?" I wrinkled my nose at him. "You will need exactly none of those at any time in the next six months."

"Or I could ship the lights to you if you really need them," BamBam said, waltzing out of the front door, holding a plate of brownies. Buzzy followed behind her at a careful distance.

"That's a perfect solution." Ethan grinned and walked over to BamBam. Taking the brownies from her, he said, "Thank you,

Ms. Mini. These brownies are one of the things I'm gonna miss most about the Webb house."

"Well, baby, I'll text you the recipe." BamBam winked.

"I'll text you mine as well. And the recipe for that pot roast you love so much," Buzzy added, edging past BamBam with her cane dangerously close to my grandma's shins. Both of them wore expressions that implied they were on their best behavior for our sakes . . . and they hated it. A lot.

"I'm sure we'll make good on any and all recipes the two of you send," Ethan said diplomatically, before heading out to the car to set the brownies with my jalapeño chips.

Ethan and I had taken third in the contest, which meant we got $35,000 to split on behalf of the city of Las Vegas and lifetime bragging rights as the original TrendCon love story. For me, that meant some new gear, a week spent at SISU's *cinema* summer program, and enough money to make a small dent in my first-semester tuition at USC, which was good, because that private-school bill almost sent my parents into cardiac arrest.

For Ethan, the prize meant fixing up the old convertible SUV we were about to drive away in, stepping back from content creation, and ensuring a cushion to get himself settled at LA City College while he figured out what was next for him. Had I encouraged him to follow me to LA? Yes. Did I have any regrets? Absolutely not.

And of course, we'd both set aside money for the cross-country adventure we were about to take.

"You have to promise to post videos and pictures." Mom held up a hand as soon as I opened my mouth to protest. "I don't care what you wear in them. I only want to follow along and make sure you're safe."

"She can do that with phone calls and texts, June." Dad smiled and spread his arms wide to give me a hug. Pulling me close to him, he added, "But I'd be okay if you posted, too. And you know your BamBam would love it. She never misses a chance to brag about you."

After the TrendCon contest, I'd decided to set up my own accounts to feature my work. Mostly, they featured sketches or shorts I'd convinced Nittha and Gabby—whose team had won the TrendCon contest—to star in, plus a few of my favorite videos with BamBam, including a sponsored video from a new Black-owned makeup brand wanting to break into the seasoned-women's market.

"I'm contractually obligated to do both, I think." I laughed as Dad released me directly into Mom's embrace. "You two are my parents, so of course I'm calling you. And the parks department is paying me . . . kind of."

Between those videos I'd started sharing and the TrendCon win, I'd been able to convince a few state parks and local governments to partner with me and Ethan on our drive out. It wasn't exactly a big movie deal, but a few free camping sites and diner meals wasn't a bad place to start.

"Alright. I think that's everything," Ethan said, slamming the heavy SUV trunk door. Just behind my parents, Ethan's mom, dad, and four sisters were here to see him off, all of them clutching tissues and pressing their mouths into the same flat line like that would stop any of them from being sentimental. It worked for exactly three seconds, until Izzie started crying, at which point the entire family dissolved into a messy pile of hugs and sniffles, Ethan included.

My sister and brother had come home from SISU to see me off, and I gave them a big joint hug, the three of us trying not to laugh at how unemotional we were compared to Ethan's family.

"Time to say goodbye so you two can get on the road. Come here and give me a hug." My grandmother's voice came from over my shoulder right as my siblings released me.

BamBam's eyes were watery even as a big smile bloomed on her face. My throat tightened as I stepped toward her outstretched arms. As excited as I was to go to California, I was not excited about leaving BamBam behind. Not that she was home much anymore. In an unexpected twist, while the video series I came up with for BamBam in Las Vegas hadn't drawn much interest from big makeup brands or Sterling's partners, it had gotten the attention of tourism boards that wanted to recruit vibrant retirees to their towns. Thus, BamBam had spent the last nine months honing her own filming skills everywhere from Palm Springs to the Florida Keys and even Tuscany. She was officially a globe-trotting Grannie now. Not that she wouldn't show up in a Sterling James video from time to time just to keep Buzzy on her toes.

"I'm so proud of you, baby." BamBam wrapped her arms around me, squeezing and rocking me back and forth like she had always done. Speaking low so only I could hear her, she said, "You know your grandma doesn't have favorites, but I sure am gonna miss you."

"I'm not really ready to say goodbye," I said into her shoulder, holding on to her tighter.

"I know. But it's time." Gently releasing me, she said, "You've grown into who Grandma raised you to be. It'd be wrong of me to keep you here when the whole world is out there waiting for you."

"I'll miss you." I sniffed and swiped at my tears with both hands.

"I'm only a phone call away, no matter the time zone." Bam-Bam reached out and ran a hand down my arm as she laughed. Turning to Ethan, she put on her best stern-grandma voice and said, "You take good care of my baby, you understand me, young person?"

"Yes, ma'am." Ethan smiled, throwing an arm around my shoulder and pulling me to him, then giving me a kiss on my temple.

"Well alright, then, enough goodbyes," BamBam pronounced, stealthily running a hand under her glistening eyes. "You two get on the road. And have fun."

"We will. Love you." I waved at my family as I walked to the passenger's side door, a chorus of don't-forget-to-texts and see-you-soons following us into the car. After buckling my seat belt, I pulled my sunglasses out of my bag and popped them on. Meanwhile, Ethan adjusted different mirrors to see around all the stuff we'd crammed into the car.

"Ready?" he asked, glancing at me.

"Almost." I grabbed the cable that connected the SUV's old stereo to my phone and pulled up the Old Man Driving playlist we'd spent months creating together. I hit Play, and a song about life being a highway started. Grinning wildly at him, I said, "Now I'm ready."

Putting the car in drive, Ethan eased us away from the house, the two of us waving out the open sunroof and watching our families shrink in the mirrors. Once they disappeared, both of us grew quiet, the weight of change settling in. Stopping at a light, Ethan reached for my hand. Lifting it to his lips, he kissed my knuckles gently. "I'm glad your grandma didn't scare me off that day on the plane. I wouldn't have wanted to miss this moment."

"She tried, trust me." I giggled. Running my thumb along the edge of his hand, I thought back on our relationship, and my chest squeezed. "If I had to do it over, I'd still choose you."

"That's all I needed to hear." Ethan's lips tilted into a smile as he turned his attention back to the road. Twining his fingers between mine as the light changed to green, we turned onto the highway to begin our next adventure.

It seemed like yesterday that we'd boarded the same plane, his shaggy hair and freckles catching my eye. In so many ways, Ethan and I were different people than who we'd been that day, both of us braver and more honest for having each other. But in as many ways, we were the same. He was still the person I was excited to drink my impractical coffees with, who wanted me to know car facts and old songs. My arms were still comforting to him on a bad day, and his hands were still the ones I wanted to hold.

As we headed toward the horizon, I realized that even if I'd written the script, I couldn't have imagined a better ending to our Las Vegas love story. Or a better beginning to our sequel.

ACKNOWLEDGMENTS

No book is entirely the product of the author. People inspire ideas that attach themselves to an author's heart. Those ideas, given time, become books. Then more people come along and shape that book. Sometimes the product is the book the author imagined; other times the book takes on a life of its own. *Reel Love* is one of the latter, and the people who shaped it deserve all the credit for it. If you enjoyed it, thank them! (And if you didn't, don't be like Emmie's fans and tag them in your reviews on social media. That's not cool!)

The first thanks is due to my editors: Wendy Loggia, for acquiring this book; Bria Ragin, for reimagining the story; and Makena Cioni, for keeping the trains moving. Another round of thank-yous to Sandra Chiu for my lovely cover, Angela Carlino for the wonderful cover design work, and Cathy Bobak for the text design. Additional thanks go to Tracy Heydweiller for managing the production of this book. And of course, a thank you to Liz Byer, Caroline Kirk, Cindy Durand, Jamie Johnson, and Colleen Fellingham for the keen eyes and copy edits.

As always, I want to thank my agent, Nalini Akolekar, and the team at Spencerhill Associates for their tremendous work managing this book as it came into the world, and me and my books generally.

I would never be able to finish any book without my family and friends. Thank you for listening to and supporting me. I am deeply grateful for you all. Similarly, to my readers, thank you. Whenever I thought I was done, one of you would come along and ask just the right question to keep me motivated. You all are the best!

Finally, to my grandmothers and the elders who helped raise me: This isn't the book I thought I would write for you, but as with every one of my books, your grace, style, and humor continue to influence me. I am who I am because of you all. Thank you and I love you, always.

ABOUT THE AUTHOR

Born and raised outside Seattle, Addie Woolridge is a classi-
cally trained opera singer with a degree in music from the University of Southern California, and she holds a master's degree
in public administration from Indiana University. Woolridge
lives in Northern California. She is the author of *The Home-
coming War*.

addiewoolridge.com

X 𝗼